"What's Not to Love?"* About the Novels of Cathryn Fox

"Sizzling, irresistible, wonderful." —*New York Times* bestselling author Lori Foster

"Will be sure to steam up even the coldest winter night, and warm the hearts of readers in every climate." —Wild on Books

"Each and every love scene explodes into fiery sensuality that will melt your heart. Tastefully written . . . blazing hot!" —Joyfully Reviewed

"Scorchingly erotic, some of the hottest sex I've read. . . . The three heroes are mind-blowingly fabulous; the heroines are intelligent and likable." —*TwoLips Reviews

"Wonderfully written. . . . The sensuality level was off the charts!" —The Romance Studio (5 Heart Sweetheart Award)

"Steamy stories sure to bring your blood to a boil on a cold winter's night . . . always satisfying." —Romance Junkies

"Supersexually charged erotic romance . . . hot-and-heavy tales. . . . Hearts will race and brows will rise" —*Romantic Times*

"Humor, sex, science, relationships, and sex . . . a pleasing, prolonged pleasure read." —*Midwest Book Review*

"Fun, sexy, and sassy—a Cathryn Fox book is a must-read great escape!" —Sylvia Day, author of *Pride and Passion*

"[A] wonderful blend of passionate sex and witty intelligence." —Fresh Fiction

"Hot, enthralling, and simply delicious . . . a must read!" —Romance Reviews Today

Also by Cathryn Fox

The Hot Line

Sun Stroked

Eternal Pleasure Novels

Instinctive

Impulsive

Impulsive

An Eternal Pleasure Novel

CATHRYN FOX

HEAT

HEAT

Published by New American Library, a division of
Penguin Group (USA) Inc., 375 Hudson Street,
New York, New York 10014, USA
Penguin Group (Canada), 90 Eglinton Avenue East, Suite 700, Toronto,
Ontario M4P 2Y3, Canada (a division of Pearson Penguin Canada Inc.)
Penguin Books Ltd., 80 Strand, London WC2R 0RL, England
Penguin Ireland, 25 St. Stephen's Green, Dublin 2,
Ireland (a division of Penguin Books Ltd.)
Penguin Group (Australia), 250 Camberwell Road, Camberwell, Victoria 3124,
Australia (a division of Pearson Australia Group Pty. Ltd.)
Penguin Books India Pvt. Ltd., 11 Community Centre, Panchsheel Park,
New Delhi - 110 017, India
Penguin Group (NZ), 67 Apollo Drive, Rosedale, North Shore 0632,
New Zealand (a division of Pearson New Zealand Ltd.)
Penguin Books (South Africa) (Pty.) Ltd., 24 Sturdee Avenue,
Rosebank, Johannesburg 2196, South Africa

Penguin Books Ltd., Registered Offices:
80 Strand, London WC2R 0RL, England

First published by Heat, an imprint of New American Library,
a division of Penguin Group (USA) Inc.

First Printing, May 2010
10 9 8 7 6 5 4 3 2 1

Copyright © Cathryn Fox, 2010
All rights reserved

HEAT is a trademark of Penguin Group (USA) Inc.

LIBRARY OF CONGRESS CATALOGING-IN-PUBLICATION DATA:

Fox, Cathryn.
Impulsive : an eternal pleasure novel / Cathryn Fox.
p. cm.
ISBN 978-0-451-22996-0
I. Title.
PR9199.4.F69166 2010
813'.6—dc22   2009040825

Set in Centaur MT
Designed by Alissa Amell

Printed in the United States of America

To Paula, who reads everything I write and always makes it better. We began this journey together, the exact same day in fact, and look how far we've come. We're quite the team, you and I.

Impulsive

Chapter One

Hurried steps carried Ray Bartlett across town; his dark clothes and the black sky masked his foolhardy presence. As he approached the train tracks, the silhouette of the old abandoned building on the other side of the railroad came into view, prompting him to reach into his pocket and pull out the heavy tin can he always brought with him—a familiar beacon in a dark, eerie night.

"Here, kitty, kitty," he called out as he gently shook the scratched and dented container of sardines, letting the thick oil inside slosh about in an effort to herald his approach. He pitched his voice low, knowing the sound would carry in the breeze and alert the lone occupant of the building to his presence, and signal her to free the latch. His glance darted around, and he hoped like hell he'd gone undetected by any resident gangs, should they be lurking about. After all, he was a far cry from his elite Gold Coast neighborhood and was now stepping foot into Chicago's seedy south side—a testament to his foolhardiness, for sure.

As he took note of his shaking fingers, he slid the can back into his breeches and stuffed his hands into his coat pockets to still his rather unusual jitters. His discomposure was partly because he'd snuck out of his dorm (and should he get caught, the consequences doled out by the headmaster would be most severe), and partly due to his excitement at seeing the girl waiting for him on the side of town he had no business frequenting—the side of town the folks in his social circle avoided like a diseased wharf rat. But, unlike him, they didn't have Sunni Matthews waiting for them.

Sunni . . .

God, his heart raced and his body grew needy just thinking about her. She had a certain energy: a light in the darkness that filled him with a deep warmth and unearthed things he'd never felt before.

Everything from the way her golden hair framed her porcelain skin and the way her beautiful blue eyes sparkled with love and laughter to the way she trusted him completely and thoroughly with her body, heart, and soul rattled his emotions and rendered him practically senseless. Ribbons of want—no, *need*—worked their way through his veins because he knew he was only minutes from gathering her into his arms, pressing his mouth to hers and paying homage to her lush body until the early hours of the morning.

As he took in the shape of the slumbering structure tucked just inside the woods, a mixture of joy and sadness invaded his thoughts. He was thrilled to spend a few stolen moments with Sunni—he ached to embrace her, to feel her naked body against his skin—but it pained him to know that he'd wake up tomorrow between a set of starched white sheets, and she in a dusty cot. His heart twisted and his stomach clenched. He halted his forward momentum and fought down the feeling of helplessness, as well as the pang of loneliness that ate at his guts like a thousand hungry cockroaches.

Soon, he reminded himself. Soon they'd be together forever, and he'd make things better for her. It was a promise he'd made to her a long time ago, and a promise he intended to keep.

Off in the distance, the whistle of an approaching train pulled him back to reality. The high-pitched whine broke through the unnatural silence as he carefully counted the wooden sleepers and made his way over the tracks—tracks he knew better than to cross. Yes, it was dangerous, maybe even downright suicidal, for him to venture into this part of town, but it was a damn strange thing how love affected one's ability to make rational decisions.

He ducked into the woods and glanced around, camouflaging himself among the towering maple trees and densely packed foliage. As he stepped onto the overgrown walking path, he once again took note of the unusual quiet surrounding him. Not even the cacophony of the bullfrogs from the swamp just beyond the tracks could be heard. It was as if someone or something had scared them silent. That thought aroused the fine hairs along his nape as the long, unkempt weeds and gangly blades of grass climbed up his breeches and pawed at his ankles.

He blinked to adjust to the dim light and took two measured steps forward. Because there had just been a week of heavy rain, the heels of his patent leather shoes sank in the wet, moss-laden ground. Ray turned up the collar of his wool sack coat against the cool autumn breeze and carefully picked his way forward, his heart pounding harder and harder with each footstep.

Overhead, the tightly knitted clouds peeled back to reveal a full moon. The bright beams broke through the canopy of high leaves and provided sufficient light for him to see the dark metal latch on the door, still a few feet out of reach. His lips turned up in a smile, and he shook the can again to let Sunni and the menagerie of tomcats seeking warmth and shelter inside know that it was he who approached, not some gang member sneaking up on them.

A low noise—not unlike the growl of a wild wounded animal—came from behind, taking him by surprise. Survival instincts kicked in, and he glanced over his shoulder in time to spot a shadow moving in the distance, weaving in and out of the trees in a drunken circular pattern and keeping a wide berth.

Ray narrowed his eyes and peered into the darkness. The shadow sat low, crouched on all fours. He took it to be some sort of dog, but bigger than any canine he'd ever encountered. Ray was not by any means a small man, but to take on a rabid dog without weaponry would certainly make him a dense one.

As his pulse pounded, his skin prickled in warning and

propelled him forward. Moving swiftly, his long legs ate up the short distance to the building. Before he could reach the latch, a low noise serrated the air and stopped him dead in his tracks. His blood ran cold and he swallowed hard. The strangled sound carried in the wind as he slowly turned in the direction of the growl. He took great care not to make any sudden movements while he tracked the shadow as it closed in on him. A moment later, a large canine stepped into the clearing and two pewter orbs flashed beneath the full moon.

What the hell kind of animal has pewter eyes?

A burst of adrenaline pushed Ray on, and he yanked open the door with much more force than was necessary and charged inside. With his breath coming in quick, unsteady gasps, he slammed the door behind him and collapsed against it, using his body weight to seal it shut.

The light from the candle flickered as Sunni approached. Her palm closed over his cheek and the warmth of her hand drove back the cold of the night. "Ray, what is it?" she asked.

With concern in her eyes, she looked past his shoulder at the secured door. "Were you followed?"

He shook his head and let the tension drain from his body as he took pleasure in the alluring sight of Sunni and the seductive way the soft candlelight fell like a halo over her petite frame. As he drew in her distinctive floral scent, his heart swelled and his cock thickened, forcing him to struggle to find his words.

He widened his hands to show the animal's excessive size.

"Wild dog," was all he managed to get out as his blood raced south.

She frowned. "I thought I heard the same dog earlier when I snuck in here." Just then, one of the many tomcats hissed at the door before it turned its attention to more pressing matters, like the food in Ray's breeches. The cat brushed up against Ray's leg and pawed at his pocket—and the can of sardines he knew would be inside. As a few other cats moved closer and joined in the chorus, Ray pulled out their food.

Sunni carefully positioned the candle on the ledge next to them, away from the boarded windows, and went to work on feeding the hungry felines. After opening the can and placing it on the floor, she turned back to Ray and furrowed her brow. "What should we do?"

"Let's wait it out." Every instinct he possessed warned him of danger, causing a foreboding shiver to prowl through him. It took effort to keep his voice even as he added, "With any luck, it will just lose interest and wander off."

Her fingers stroked his hair. In an obvious attempt to lighten the mood, she went up on her tiptoes and whispered, "I'm not afraid of any wild dog attacking me when I've got a protector like you, Ray."

Ray slid his hands around her back to anchor her to him. His edgy laugh churned with passion. "Maybe it's *me* you have to worry about attacking, Sunni." His erection pressed insistently against her stomach, and he diligently fought down the urge to tear her clothes from her body and ravish her like an animal in heat. A torrent of emotions washed over him, but he knew he'd never act purely on primal impulses—not with her, not with his Sunni, because it was never just about sex with her. She deserved so much more than that from him.

Her blue eyes gleamed with mischief and she caught her bottom lip between her teeth. "Speaking of attacking, what on earth shall we do to occupy ourselves while we wait for the mongrel to lose interest?"

She looked at him with pure desire, and his body responded with a shudder. God, he loved her openness, her sense of adventure. He'd never had the inclination to divulge—let alone indulge—his secret fetishes to the girls in his social circuit. Sunni had never looked at him like he was a circus sideshow for wanting to tie her up and have her at his mercy. He wasn't sure where that deep-seated need to dominate her had come from, only that it was strong and was not to be denied. Ray could just imagine how the women in his neighborhood would react to his unusual desires. Nevertheless, Ray only ever wanted to share those intimacies with Sunni.

His mind raced back to her playful question and considered the invitation in her voice. "Do you have something in mind?" he asked.

She palmed his thigh muscles, then slipped a hand between his legs to cup his aching cock. She gave a breathy, intimate laugh and playfully responded, "Maybe not something in mind, but definitely something in . . . *hand*."

As desire jolted through him, they exchanged a long, lingering look, and any fears he had about the rabid dog abated. His fingers tightened around her waist, and he pulled her impossibly closer, crushing her small body to his.

"Sunni," he murmured as he captured her mouth in a slow, simmering kiss, "you do have a way with words."

Eager hands slipped under his coat to massage his shoulders, and her throaty purr resonated through his body. "And here I'd rather you had your way with me."

A low moan rose from the depths of Sunni's throat with the tantalizing sweep of Ray's tongue inside her mouth. He tasted like sweet ginger candy, and she momentarily wondered if he'd eaten any on his long trek to visit her. But then her thoughts fragmented when he spun her around and pressed her back to the door. Chocolate eyes latched on hers, and a lock of dark hair fell over his forehead as he pinned her with a smoldering glance. Erotic heat pulsed through her, and the air around them grew charged with sexual energy. Sunni sucked in a tight, anticipatory breath, her body aching to join with his.

Knowing exactly how she liked it, Ray moved with agility, taking control of her pleasure. With deft fingers he gripped both of her hands and restrained them above her head. His other hand began a leisurely journey up her dress. Pressure brewed inside her, cyclonic heat spiraling outward, spreading, building strength, and obliterating her last vestige of composure as the agonizing slowness of his seduction nearly undid her.

"Ray . . ." She tossed her head to the side and swayed slightly. God, it had been so long since his last visit. Too long. "Please."

Her quivering thighs absorbed the warmth of his exploring fingers and she gave a little whimper of need. He pushed against her, and the length of his hard cock had her mouth watering, yearning for a taste of his salty cream. She bucked against him, her sex growing damp as his fingers came perilously close to her nether lips. Strong muscles bunched as he teased her with the soft pad of his thumb, his fingers circling but never quite touching the spot that needed it the most.

Sunni gave a sexually frustrated moan, then drew in his familiar aroma of man, spice, and pool water. As a varsity swimmer, the scent had long ago penetrated his flesh, but it was a scent she'd grown quite fond of. Her hands trailed over his skin and she began burning up, frantic with need. As she hungered for him, her chest rose and fell rapidly and her distended nipples bore into his pectorals, alerting him to the urgency of her arousal.

She shifted in an attempt to force his fingers to her sex. "Touch me, please . . ." she whispered into his mouth.

He trailed kisses over her jaw. "Oh, I will, baby." He licked along her earlobe, and a warm shiver traveled all the way to her toes. She remained still, absorbing and hanging on to his every word as he went on to give a detailed itinerary of what he planned to do to her. "I'm going to touch every inch of you with my fingers, my mouth, and my cock. You have my word on that. But first I want you at my mercy; then I'm going to make you wild with want." With that, he reached around her back to toy with the laces binding her dress.

As his warm breath wafted across her cheek, she decided it was time for feeling, not talking. Submitting herself to him completely, she murmured, "Take me, Ray. You are my master, and I'm yours to do with as you please."

She shut her eyes and listened to the soft rustle of her clothes being removed; the seductive sound brushed over her skin like a lover's kiss and elicited a shudder from deep within. As Ray stripped her naked, the tangy scent of her arousal saturated the old building, and the sound of his indrawn breath told her he'd picked up on her heady scent. When he cleared his throat, seemingly rattled by her feminine aroma, it brought a smile to her face. She loved the effect she had on him, loved knowing that she had the ability to unnerve such a powerful guy.

His voice came out a little gruffer than usual when he murmured, "Sunni . . ." The way he said her name, so intimately, so possessively, spoke volumes and told her that she belonged to him and him alone.

Her lids fluttered. "Mmm?"

He pressed against her and buried his mouth in the crook of her neck. "You know it's never just about sex with you, right?"

The vulnerability she heard in his tone touched her deeply. Her heart skipped a beat and she reached out to him. "Yes, Ray. I know . . ." she assured him.

And she did know. Everything in the way he touched her and how he talked to her made her feel special, cherished, the way no other man had ever made her feel before. Ray was different. Far different from the other rich boys who paraded up and down the streets in their affluent neighborhood. She trusted Ray with her body in a way she'd never trusted another, and despite what her mother claimed, he was not merely slumming or using her for sex. Sure, her mother had her daughter's best interests at heart, but she didn't know Ray like Sunni knew Ray. Nor did she understand the level of trust and intimacy between them.

Even when she handed control over to him, giving him the power to do with her as he wished, he still took painstaking care of her body and her needs, touching her with the utmost devotion and ensuring he made it especially good for her. But their unions weren't just about sharing bodies and exchanging intimacies. They talked about their pasts and their future, sharing their hopes, dreams, and even their fears.

"Look at me," he demanded in a soft tone.

Her lids fluttered open in time to see him step back and make quick work of his own clothes. Her gaze panned over his hewn athletic muscles and settled on his magnificent erection, and it suddenly occurred to her that she wanted him so much, she felt dizzy.

Her legs swayed and he gripped her waist to support her, his strong arms encircling her in a protective manner. She'd come to learn that inside the bedroom, Ray Bartlett was a dominant by nature. And, in turn, he'd shown her the exquisite pleasure to be had in the role of a submissive, a role she'd happily take on for him and him alone.

Coaxing him to spread her body on the prepared blankets and take her, she slid her tongue over her bottom lip, and the slow, sweeping action drew his gaze.

His nostrils flared and he gestured toward the makeshift bed on the floor. Lust exploded inside her as she followed his gaze. "Lie down and spread your legs for me."

She almost whimpered in delight.

Obliging, Sunni moved across the room. After positioning herself on the cushiony blankets—which were strategically placed between two posts—she proceeded to widen her legs. As her body beckoned to his, Ray took a long moment to just watch her, and she could practically feel his raw ache of lust as it reached out to her.

She crooked her finger, impatient for his touch. Ray grabbed the candle and stalked closer. How she loved the way he moved, with such confidence, such determination. He dropped down next to her and placed the candle beside them. As the flames created warmth and coziness inside the cabin, his urgent hands raced over her skin. Shifting, he leaned into her and pressed a kiss to her mouth and neck, going lower until he reached her aching breasts. She sensed his restraint, his fight for control, when he swiped his tongue across her sensitized nipples. His erection throbbed against her leg and she writhed in ecstasy. In no time at all, their bodies began melding as one. When Ray drew one rigid bud into his mouth and sucked so hard she could feel little tremors deep in her core, she had no idea where his body ended and hers began.

"Mmm." The curls between her legs dampened, and she grabbed a fistful of his hair in a silent plea for more.

Ray tilted his head back. His eyes were full of urgent need as he gripped her hands and drew them over her head. He had that look on his face again, the one that spoke of his needs and hidden desires—desires that he'd only ever shared with her. He exhaled a low, slow breath, and when his glance went to the silk ties beside her, her heart pounded harder and her body pulsed in sweet agony.

He grabbed one binding and trailed it over her skin. Little goose bumps broke out on her flesh. Need churned inside her when she met his eyes and read his intent. As he fueled her desires, moisture pooled on her sex and dripped languidly to her anus, lubricating her every passage.

Ray drew a candle closer and held it over her. Her pussy lips glistened beneath the light. "You're very wet, Sunni."

A whimper of excitement caught in her throat. "I've missed you," she rasped.

His gaze moved over her face in a long, leisurely inspection. "Do you ache as much as I ache when we're not together?"

Her chest tightened, and since a reply was beyond her, she simply nodded in response.

"Do you touch yourself when I'm not here, Sunni? To take the ache away?"

The gleam in his eyes turned wicked. Sunni swallowed, and the sound of her throat working cut through the silence. "Yes . . ." she managed to get out.

His nostrils flared and he gripped her thighs. With a quick tug, he pulled them farther apart, and proceeded to wrap one binding around her ankle.

His mouth curved. "Show me."

Desperate to ease the ache inside her, Sunni slipped a hand between her legs and stroked her pulsing clit. Ray's eyes lit with dark desire. As she continued to pleasure herself, Ray tied her leg to the post and went to work on securing the other. Once her feet were sufficiently restrained, he stood and walked around her.

At the sight of his hard, naked body, she greedily worked her fingers over her clit until small spasms began to take shape deep inside her womb. Moments before she became unhinged and succumbed to her orgasm, Ray pulled her hands away from her sex and secured them over her head.

"No . . ." she cried out, but that soft cry segued to a heated moan when Ray returned to his original position and tucked himself between her spread legs, making a slow pass over her sex with his tongue. "Yesss . . ." she hissed, and shivered in delight with that first sweet touch of his tongue.

As she shuddered in surrender, he buried his face deeper and ravaged her sex, his mouth sucking and nibbling, his tongue licking and probing. As she watched him feast on her, she couldn't quite put into words how much she loved being at his mercy. He dominated her in the bedroom, controlling her every pleasure and her every pain. Never would she ever grant any other man such latitude.

His thumb circled her clit and it swelled in response to the stimuli. The furtive brush nearly pushed her over the precipice. She gave an erotic whimper and arched into his touch.

He pushed one thick finger inside her and she cried out with pleasure. White-hot desire claimed her, and her sex muscles clenched and held him tight.

The pleasure in his voice excited her. "Sunni, Christ . . ." He glanced up at her, and the warmth in his eyes revealed an intimacy between them that went well beyond sex.

She shifted beneath him, the silk bindings tightening on her limbs and raising her passion to new heights. As she lay there, held hostage to Ray's touch, he turned his attention back to her throbbing clit. His tongue glided over her engorged nub while he slipped another finger inside for a deliciously snug fit. Blood flowed thick and heavy through her veins as volcanic pressure built inside her.

He pumped his fingers in and out, his tongue working her clit into a heated frenzy. Desire and other emotions twisted inside her, and her body trembled almost uncontrollably. God, he touched her in places so deep she'd thought she'd died and gone to heaven.

As his fingers burrowed, controlling the depth, rhythm, and pace, her sex muscles gripped him hard. "Ray, I need . . ."

He drew in a sharp breath and tenderness stole over him. "I know, Sunni. I know." He began pumping harder, faster, and in the span of a second, her whole world closed in on her. Nothing existed but this man and this moment. Perspiration broke out on her skin, and she felt herself falling deeper and deeper into the euphoric abyss.

"That's my girl," he whispered. His voice dropped an octave as he added, "Let yourself go, kitten."

Just hearing the intimacy in his tone when he called her kitten was all that was needed to take her over the edge. As a surge of love tightened her heart, her body flushed hotly. A heartbeat later, she found herself tumbling into an orgasm. Her sex throbbed, and she closed her eyes to concentrate on the erotic sensations. Her pulse racing, she rode out every delicious wave as a melee of emotions tore through her, warming her right down to the tips of her bound feet. She gave a whimper of relief and undulated her hips as her liquid heat drenched his mouth.

Like a cat lapping its cream, Ray worked his tongue over her until he'd devoured every last drop of her silken desire. Once he had her completely clean, he leaned back on his heels. He licked the moisture from his mouth, and his nostrils flared as he watched her. Sunni eyed his erection and swiped her tongue over her bottom lip. His cock pulsed beneath her gaze, and all she could think about was taking it into her mouth and pleasuring him the way he'd pleasured her.

When her gaze traveled back to his face, he angled his head and asked, "Do you want to suck me, Sunni?"

Without bothering to mask her enthusiasm, she nibbled her bottom lip and nodded. Eagerly.

He went to work on removing the bindings from her feet

and hands, then tugged her up. "On your knees, and put your hands behind your back."

Her entire body quivered at the authority in his command. Ray remained on his knees and circled his arms around her waist. His erection jutted forward and rubbed against her stomach. Rivulets of hot cream pearled on the head of his penis and dripped onto her abdomen. Ray drew one palm back and slapped her ass. A wheeze escaped her lips, but it was a sound of pleasure, not pain. She pulled in a fortifying breath and waited anxiously for another.

When none came, she whispered, "More."

"Shhh," he responded. "I'll give you more when you're ready for more. Now be a good little kitten and suck my cock." Oh, God, she loved his commanding attitude. "Open your mouth and get ready for me."

Ray climbed to his feet, and Sunni poised her mouth like she was told. His cock brushed over her cheek before coming level with her lips. Sunni opened her mouth wider to accommodate his thickness and drew him in. She worked the tip with her tongue, swirling and tasting, her head bobbing back and forth in a slow, steady pattern.

He growled and ran his fingers through her hair. "Jesus . . ." Ray rocked on his feet and moved her curls away from her face, enabling him to watch the action. His cock thickened, and she could feel the blood rushing through his veins; he was so very close to losing control. She sucked harder, then lowered her head to lap at his balls.

With that, Ray growled and said, "Sunni, promise me you'll never be with another man this way, that you will never submit yourself to anyone else."

She glanced up from his cock to see the agonized and vulnerable expression on his face. She drew him deeper into her mouth, her actions answering his concerns, but that wasn't good enough for him. He inched back, placed his finger under her chin, and tipped her head until their eyes met.

Possessiveness flashed in his eyes. "Tell me," he commanded.

"I'll only ever submit myself to you, Ray. I promise. Only you will ever be my master."

Ray dropped to his knees and pressed his lips to hers. His kiss was so gentle and emotional, it weakened her entire body.

"Sunni . . ." he whispered into her mouth, and eased her back down onto the blankets. "I need to be inside you. Now."

She wrapped her legs around his waist, and in one fluid movement he sank into her damp heat. "Oh, God." She clawed at his back as pleasure forked through her.

As basic elemental need took hold, his breathing turned choppy, labored. He drove into her, harder, faster, drawing out her pleasure despite his desperate need for release.

He levered himself up on one arm to keep the bulk of his weight off her and slipped a thumb between their bodies to caress her clit. Her nails bit into his skin, and she gave a broken gasp. Sensations pulled her under, and without warning another climax ripped the world out from beneath her. Her pussy rippled with pleasure and her liquid heat dripped over Ray's cock.

When her muscles tightened around him, he stilled his movements, pushed her hair from her forehead, and pressed his mouth to hers. "I love you, kitten," he whispered as he released high inside her.

They remained in that same position for a long time, neither one wanting to break the comforting contact or sever the tremendous connection between them. God, sex with Ray was perfect, so damn perfect. In fact, *everything* with Ray was perfect.

When Ray finally rolled beside her, Sunni gave a long contented sigh, pulled a blanket over them both, and snuggled closer to enjoy the easy intimacy between them.

"Hey," he whispered.

Sunni chuckled. Ray never was much of a talker after sex. Or moments before sex, for that matter. Not enough blood left in his brain, she supposed. "Hey, yourself."

She stifled a yawn and took note of the wax pooling at the base of the candle, knowing that their time together was almost over. She fought down the pang of sadness, determined not to mull over that worry and enjoy every moment they had left.

The wind outside seemed to pick up, rattling a few loose boards. What sounded like a tree branch or an animal claw scratched against the door. A strange sense of uneasiness closed in on her as her mind revisited the lurking dog.

Unnerved by that thought, she lifted her chin, bringing Ray and herself face-to-face. She regarded him with wide eyes and questioned in a shaky voice, "Ray?"

"I hear it." He tapped her backside, and sifted his hand over the floor in search of their clothes. "We'd better get dressed." Even though he'd worked to sound casual, she could hear the underlying concern in his voice.

The sound grew louder, and the cats inside the building began hissing, spitting, and circling, their hackles rising in both fear and warning. Sunni's heart raced, and as a burst of anxiety constricted her chest, she glanced around for a weapon.

"Do you think it—?"

Ray pressed his finger to her lips to hush her. He pitched his voice low. "Pull your clothes on. Quickly." With the tips of his fingers, he snuffed out the candle. They stood there draped in darkness, save for the long column of moonlight that sliced through the thick cracks in the decaying rooftop.

As Sunni hurried into her dress, Ray threw on his own clothes and stepped to the door, the floorboards groaning beneath his weight and pinpointing his location. He pressed his ear against the wooden slats and listened.

As her tension increased, it took effort to draw in air. They stood there in silence, waiting, listening. After a long while, the threatening sounds dissipated, even the wind seemed to die down, and Sunni almost drew a premature breath of relief.

Ray sank to the ground to peer out of the two-inch gap between the doorframe and the floorboards, but when a big, furry paw with razor-sharp claws grabbed for him, he cursed and jumped to his feet.

Sunni clutched her chest with one hand and took a step back. "Oh, God, Ray," she cried out, and reached for him with her other hand.

Taking them by surprise, the animal smashed against the door, bowing the wood and sending Ray backward. He landed with a thud, but quickly climbed to his feet and positioned Sunni behind him to shield her from an attack. She could feel his heart pounding in his chest, and the coldness in his hands as they held her back.

A loud howl sliced through the air and curdled her blood. It was a sound unlike anything she'd ever heard before—dark, menacing, and downright scary.

"What the hell?" Ray murmured, and picked up a long, pointed piece of lumber. By this time, the cats were hissing and spitting louder, the majority of them jumping to the roof trusses. Under attack, the old wooden door moaned and groaned, the rusty hinges threatening to let go.

Sunni watched, transfixed, as a few slats of wood smashed to the ground, leaving a big gaping hole in the door, large enough for the animal—or, rather, beast—to stick its head through. Silver eyes pierced the night and sized up the prey inside. At first glimpse, Sunni knew the stick Ray was wielding like a weapon was equivalent to stepping up to home base with a matchstick. They were in serious trouble here, and she could think of only one way out.

Coldness penetrated her bones, and her knees practically buckled beneath her. She tapped Ray on the shoulder and pointed upward. "We need to get high."

He nodded, but before either of them had a chance to move, the night creature went up on its haunches and threw its hefty body against the door. The hinges didn't stand a chance against the weighty assault, and the door splintered and collapsed to the floor before them. Moonlight came filtering in, and lit up the animal's large, dark-haired frame as it stepped inside. Bigger than any dog she'd ever come across before, the beast stood before them, its bearlike claws pinning the door beneath it. Saliva pooled on its muzzle, and it bared a pair of pointy incisors.

Sunni's thoughts came to a screeching halt, and her legs wouldn't budge as she met its steely gaze. For one long moment, shocked silence lingered. Her pulse leapt in her throat, and she wrapped her shaky hands around Ray's waist.

He pried her fingers free. His tone rose in warning: "Sunni, move. Slowly." The panic in his voice snapped her out of her trance and prompted her into action.

She fought down her rising hysteria and began to back up toward the crates near the back wall. If she could stack them, she and Ray could climb to the rafters, to safety.

Walking backward, she moved with caution, taking care not to make any sudden shifts. A movement out of the corner of her eyes caught her attention, and before she realized what was happening, one of the cats jumped into her arms. That must have been what provoked the wild animal.

It lunged forward, moving with a speed no normal canine possessed, and landed on Ray with a resounding thud.

"No," Sunni cried out, but it was too little, too late. Sharp teeth tore at Ray's flesh, then gripped him by the neck and tossed him around like he was nothing more than a rag doll. As Sunni watched in mute terror, she couldn't breathe. She couldn't even think.

She stumbled backward, and her jerky actions drew the animal's attention. With its lips peeled back, it left Ray and stalked closer to her. Terror stole the scream from her lungs, and she knew there was no escaping the creature's jaws.

One pounce had her falling to the floor. Pain exploded inside her as the animal ripped into her shoulder. The pungent scent of wet dog and coppery blood filled her senses and churned her stomach. She struggled and tried to get out from under its death grip, but the animal was too big and strong.

Then, suddenly, the attack stopped and the beast climbed off her. She remained motionless, not daring to make a sound.

The frothing animal nudged her with its nose and began to circle her, crimson blood painting its muzzle. It went down on its haunches and its arctic eyes pinned her with a glare, watching over her. Waiting.

But for what, she couldn't be certain.

She slowly angled her head. A cry caught in her throat and tears poured down her cheeks as she saw that the man she loved lay lifeless in a spreading pool of blood. Oh, God. Ray was dead. *Dead.* Emotions pained her heart, and it was all she could do to fight down a howl of panic.

In that moment, her arm started aching, and it occurred to her that the animal had killed Ray but it had only been bitten her—as if it wanted her alive.

Frightened, her glance strayed back to the beast, to the way its beady eyes observed her with careful precision.

Oh, good God.

What the hell was this thing, and what did it want with her?

Chapter Two

Sunray awoke with a start, her chest rising and falling in an erratic pattern as equal measures of nausea and dizziness overcame her. She widened her eyes and with her keen sense of sight, glanced around the small, dark room to gather her bearings. When the familiar outlines of her sleigh bed and mahogany dresser took shape, she shook the fog from her sleep-deprived brain and worked to stabilize her spastic breathing.

Ever since she—along with her shape-shifter friends, Jaclyn and Slyck—had fled their secret gated community in Serene, New Hampshire, where she had resided for the last hundred years, she'd found deep, restful sleep harder and harder to come by.

A result of her returning nightmares, she supposed.

She jolted upright in her bed and worked to bury the haunting memories of the night her lover Ray Bartlett had been viciously murdered—and she'd been *changed.* As she wiped the perspiration from her forehead, her blankets slipped from her shoulders and pooled at her waist, exposing her sweat-drenched skin, compliments of her vivid night terrors.

Perhaps the nightmares had returned because she was back in Chicago, near the neighborhood where Ray had been brutally ripped from her life forever. Well, that, and she'd recently gotten a whiff of his distinctive, familiar scent on her best friend's winter coat. Her hand went to her stomach as need gathered there in a twisted knot. God, she'd never, ever forget the intoxicating smell of Ray's skin, or the way it used to envelop her, drawing her into a cocoon of desire and making her feel so safe and cherished.

Ray . . .

Was it possible that he'd come back to her? That he'd been reincarnated? Here to fulfill a promise he'd made to her so many years ago?

Did she even dare to hope?

A few weeks ago, after she'd caught his scent on Jaclyn Vasenty's clothing, Jaclyn had quickly identified whom the aquatic aroma belonged to. Together they'd gone searching for him at Risqué, an erotic club that Jaclyn used to frequent before she'd fallen in love with Slyck, her mate. From what Jaclyn had explained to Sunray, Ray would often seek her out at the club. But other than his strong, dominating nature in the bedroom, she knew little else about him.

Unfortunately, Ray—or Kane, as he was known in this lifetime—had vanished. Disappeared from the club scene. Gone without a trace. But where he'd gone was anyone's guess.

After inquiring about him at Risqué, Sunray had come to learn that not only was he a dominant by nature—a replica of her Ray—but he was also a man who knew what he wanted and took what he needed. A fine shiver of excitement coiled through her. Even though she was now a strong, dominant wolf herself, she couldn't deny that thoughts of Kane as a powerful, take-charge kind of guy thrilled the submissive side of her.

Now as she considered Kane a moment longer, she had the sneaking suspicion that he was also a man who preferred to keep his identity hidden, and unless he wanted to be found, he wouldn't be found. But despite that, even after Jaclyn and Slyck had taken off to Florida to visit Jaclyn's parents over the Christmas holidays, Sunray had returned to the club a few times on her own, but had yet to find any man who resembled her long-lost lover.

With her stomach still in knots she stood, pulled on a warm cotton robe, and made her way to the bathroom. When she glanced in the mirror, haunted pewter eyes stared back at her. It was then that her thoughts raced to Serene, to the home she'd fled a little more than six months ago. Even though she'd made a life for herself in Chicago, and loved everything about her new job as marketing rep at Vasenty Cosmetics—well, everything except the conferences, that is, especially an upcoming one in Los Angeles, which she dreaded attending—a deep sense of loneliness fell over her. Her heart clenched as she thought about those family members she'd left behind.

Despite bonding with her panther friends, Jaclyn and Slyck,

she felt truly alone in this strange new world. Her pack, her brethren, were all living harmoniously in the gated town of Serene in an effort to keep their existence hidden from the rest of the world—and from bloodthirsty humans who were quick to hunt and kill anyone perceived as different.

After the Salem witch trials in 1692, the five species known as lycans, vampires, shifters, witches, and demons were forced to put aside their hatred and prejudice for one another and forge a truce. Covert communities were set up around the globe, and each species in each town had an overseer. These five overseers all worked together to keep their brethren in line and maintain order among their kind while keeping their existence a secret from the rest of the world.

Even though she missed her family dearly, there was one lycan she desired never to see again: Vall. Her alpha. Or, rather, her former alpha and Serene's former lycan guide. The beast responsible for her immortal gift, or as she preferred to think of it, lifelong curse. The man she'd recently watched die before she'd escaped Serene, leaving those residing in the small town believing that she, as well as Jaclyn and Slyck, had been killed, torn apart by Vall on shift night before he succumbed to his own injuries during the cat/dog fight with Slyck. Her stomach soured, and a cold shiver moved through her body just from thinking about him. She prayed that Cairan, Vall's first in command—Serene's new lycan overseer—would do a better job of leading the pack and keeping harmonious relations with the other species. Of course, both Cairan and panther overseer Drake, Slyck's replacement, knew the truth behind their escape, and kept it a secret for everyone's benefit.

Even though she loved Jaclyn and Slyck with all her heart, she couldn't deny that the wolf inside her craved to be with her own kind. She would like nothing better than to feel the cool grass beneath her paws as they ran together, to fall asleep in a mass of tangled legs and arms and wake up surrounded by others who knew and accepted what she was—what Vall had made her.

Her fingers fisted around her cool porcelain sink, and the hole in her heart grew, knowing those days were long gone and she could never ever go back. . . .

At least she didn't have to worry about Serene's security hunting her down. Even though Drake—who was also chief of security—had helped them escape, if anyone else knew she was alive they'd label her a rogue, search her out, and terminate her for fear that she'd somehow expose their secret community. After all, they were still primal beings ruled by instinct and survival of the fittest.

No matter how much she missed her brethren, she knew she could never return—despite the fact that the vicious alpha wolf who'd driven her away in the first place was dead. It did give her a measure of comfort to know that he was gone from this world, his thirst for young, innocent females snuffed out forever.

Of course, she still had to mask her true identity here in Chicago. Serene's security force wasn't the only group that hunted rogue creatures. The Paranormal Task Force, or PTF, officers were a constant danger—human hunters who were at the top of their game, killing everything and anything that went bump in the night, all while keeping the existence of those creatures a secret from unsuspecting humans, to prevent widespread pandemonium.

When paranormal beings were first discovered by humans ages ago, at a time when supernatural creatures hunted freely, the U.S. government set up the covert organization, with branches focused on hunting a particular species: vampires, lycans, demons, or any other immortal that invaded their human territory.

From intel gathered over the years by the overseers, Sunray knew these men were special, handpicked as soldiers in basic military training. They were highly intelligent, specially trained, and adept at reading others. Besides PTF officer training, the members were educated at the best graduate schools, where they obtained master's degrees in sociology, studying everything from social relationships to species interactions and deviances. The officers in the lycan branch were also trained by canine-behavior specialists. Detecting any wolf masquerading as a human was second nature to them.

Sunray's gaze moved from the mirror to her contact lenses, one of the many props she used to help camouflage the beast within her. She gave a heavy sigh and pushed all thoughts of hunting and bloodshed to the recesses of her mind, not wanting to reflect on those dark musings any longer.

In search of a distraction, she walked back into her bedroom and glanced around until her gaze settled on the windowpane. As if drawn by a greater force, Sunray padded to the windowsill. She glanced at the near-full moon, and her insides stirred to life.

In three days, the change would be upon her.

Contrary to what most folks believed, lycans could change at will. It was simply a matter of allowing the animal out to play. But during a full moon, there was no *will* about it. They had to change.

Sunray pushed away from her window and took note of the time. In forty-five minutes, Chicago would be ringing in the New Year. But for her, it was merely another year without Ray.

She hadn't planned on celebrating, especially since her only friends were out of town, and had chosen a restful night's sleep over partying. But since that restful sleep continued to elude her, she decided to take a brisk walk along the city's main street and watch the citizens ring in the New Year.

She ran her fingers through her mass of thick golden hair, threw on her favorite comfy jeans and a warm V-neck sweater, slipped in her blue contacts, and added just a touch of makeup to take away the tired, distressed look. A hint of her favorite floral perfume completed the package.

Of course, the floral scent had a twofold purpose: first, because she liked the bouquet, and second, it helped cover her natural canine smell. She also had to be careful with her body language outside the security of her home, taking care not to exhibit any signs of natural aggression, dominance, or reckless behavior, one of the many clues that could attract a PTF officer's attention. Not that Sunray displayed such traits during her everyday routine. For her, those behavioral variances only happened during shift night. But PTF officers were so damn good at their jobs that they could identify anything out of the ordinary during a simple conversation by facial expressions or body language alone.

And, of course, any astute paranormal creature could identify a possible PTF member as well, by the way they moved, scanning and studying each and every person they came into contact with.

After tugging on her boots, coat, and mittens, she made her way outside. The cool night air nipped at her flesh and turned her breath to cloud. But Sunray didn't mind the frigid city temperatures. In fact, she loved the frosty air, especially on a run night. She loved the feel of the cool grass, or even the soft snow, beneath her pads, and the way the fog rose from the ground and lit up under the silver moon. When she was in wolf form, she preferred the cold because she expended so much energy when running and had all that thick, downy fur to insulate her body.

Hurried steps carried her to the city's main drag, and she turned her attention to the lantern-lit streets, which were alive with activity. As light fanned the walkways, partygoers spilled out onto the sidewalks, their laughter bubbling up all around her. Despite her loneliness—not to mention how tired she felt— she found herself smiling. As she moved through the crowd, she pulled in the scents of the city and the people milling about: perfume, shampoo, alcohol, coffee, soap, arousal. And some not-so-pleasant ones: body odor, sewer drains, garbage Dumpsters, cigarette butts.

Nevertheless, the energy of the city was contagious and pumped through her veins like a powerful aphrodisiac.

Okay, speaking of aphrodisiacs . . .

She'd suddenly found herself standing outside Risqué, and deep in her gut she suspected she'd been subconsciously drawn to it. She slipped her fingers inside her coat pocket and wondered if she had her members-only pass with her. But did she really want to go inside? Could she handle the disappointment of not finding Ray in there?

Then again, maybe she'd stumble upon a hot man who'd be more than willing to fill the void inside her for a few minutes, or a few hours, if she was really lucky. And while he buried his cock in her, she could momentarily forget that she was different, that she could never live an ordinary life—a life as a mortal woman with a husband, 2.4 kids, and a nice bungalow nestled behind a white picket fence. Not when once a month she shifted into a nighttime beast and ran off to feed on animal blood. Sure, she had good control over her wolf form, keeping it tame and prohibiting it from acting on impulse. And she also took extra care to avoid humans during the full moon.

But what if . . .

What if she married a mortal man, and something went terribly wrong during shift night and she accidentally killed him? Even though she couldn't have babies with a mortal, what if he had a child already, or if he wanted to adopt? She couldn't risk hurting an unsuspecting, innocent youngster. That last thought made her shiver, and deep in her gut she knew she could never have what her heart longed for. Because never would she put any human at risk.

Which brought her thoughts back to Ray. Even if he had been reincarnated, what were the chances they could have a real relationship?

Just then, some dark-haired Adonis slipped past her and opened the door. She recognized him from her previous trips to the club. He smiled down at her and gestured with his hand. "Coming?"

Figuring nothing ventured, nothing gained, she moved past him and stepped inside, shutting out the din of the crowd as a burst of aromatic heat enveloped her.

The man's hungry blue eyes moved over her curves with appreciation, and the desire in his gaze didn't go unnoticed. They both showed their passes to the guard and stepped beyond the security doors and into the crowded establishment. As she shed her outerwear and handed it to the hostess, the scent of sex, seduction, and a heady mixture of pheromones hit her hard, her acute senses able to surf through the melee of aromas and distinguish their owners.

"Brian." He shot his hand out in greeting and brought her attention back to him. "I've seen you here a few times. You're a friend of Jaclyn's, aren't you?"

Sunray nodded and shook the offered hand. "Sunray."

He angled his head. "Such a . . . different name."

Sunray said nothing, not bothering to explain the story behind her name.

Brian nodded toward a booth full of gorgeous, scantily clad
women, all of whom seemed to be eagerly awaiting his attention.
Sunray took a moment to size him up, and wondered what it was
about him that warranted a whole harem. Without conscious
thought, her eyes went to his crotch, to see exactly what he was
packing down there.

"Care to join us?" Her gaze flew back to his face, and a
knowing spark lit his eyes.

"I'm meeting someone," she rushed out, slightly embar-
rassed by her blatant perusal, although in a place like this, not
only was ogling permitted—it was encouraged. To satisfy the
voyeurs in the group, she supposed.

As he turned his back to her and slid in next to his harem,
her stomach sank, and she took a moment to consider why she'd
rejected his offer. Hadn't she just decided that a hot man was the
answer to make her temporarily forget her worries? This guy certainly fit the description, so why the hell didn't she take him up
on his offer? But she already knew the answer. Deep inside her,
she suspected she could never be with another. Not now. Not
with the possibility that Ray had returned to her.

One thing she did know: She'd never willingly submit
herself to anyone. Inside the bedroom or out. Which was the
main reason her former alpha leader, Vall, had been so brutal
with her. A cub was always supposed to willingly submit to its
alpha. It was the way of the pack. But she'd made a promise

to Ray all those years ago, and it was a promise she intended to keep.

Sunray planted herself on a swivel bar stool and ordered a whiskey and coke. Once she had her drink in hand, she spun around on the seat and let her gaze roam over the hedonistic acts taking place around her.

Couples, all in various stages of undress, moved sensuously on the dance floor. Off in one corner, two well-built men worked in tandem to please a gorgeous brunette. Sunray inhaled deeply, pulling the woman's aroused scent into her lungs. As she watched the salacious act, she took a small sip of her drink and appreciated the way her body had begun to warm all over—but she was certain that burst of heat had nothing at all to do with the alcohol swirling around in her glass. Moisture dampened her panties and her clit swelled—a reminder that it had been far too long since she'd had any kind of male attention.

Okay, so she couldn't deny that she'd gone without sex for far too long, and watching those men work their tongues over that woman's shaved pussy excited her. After all, she was a lycan, a libidinous creature by nature, and even more so with the approach of the full moon. Soon enough it would take every ounce of strength she possessed to bank those primitive needs and keep her compulsions in check.

As heat prowled through her, filling her with a restless ache, baser instincts kicked in and there wasn't a damn thing she could do about it. Her wolf stirred, and the primal urge to join that threesome pulled at her. But since she prided herself on having control over the animal inside her—never giving in to its impulses—she watched the action from afar.

Just then, the front door opened, and when a tall, muscular man stepped through the threshold, a hush fell over the crowd. His mere presence seemed to mesmerize and intoxicate every member in the club—men and women alike.

Dressed in a pair of jeans that hugged his body in all the right places, and a dark, waist-length, hooded parka, he brushed his hand over his five-o'clock shadow in concentration. Hair mussed, he looked a little unkempt, a little disheveled, like he hadn't slept in days.

Even from her distance she could, thanks to her heightened senses, discern his features—the scar above his right eye; the prickly shadow on his jaw—and read the determination etched on his handsome face. As she took pleasure in the sight of him, it occurred to her that there was something about him that quite frankly fascinated her. Perhaps it was his confidence, the way he controlled the room, or the way his overwhelming presence seemed to swallow up the place. Or perhaps it was simply his virility. It had been a long time since she'd come across a red-blooded man as sexy as him.

He shrugged out of his jacket and passed it to the hostess. It was then that she noticed his long-sleeved T-shirt and the way it displayed broad shoulders and corded abs. He had a fit body, long and lean. The body of an athlete. His sinewy muscles tightened and relaxed again, dancing and rippling along his torso as he cut across the wide expanse of floor, his eyes scanning the patrons, seeking something. As she watched him, she realized that he moved like a predator. A hunter.

A PTF officer.

Oh, hell!

Sunray drew a shaky breath. Moisture broke out on her skin and her mind reeled in panic. Oh, God. She shot a glance around, but there was only one way out, and a lycan hunter was now blocking that path, caging her between himself and the door and making any kind of escape impossible.

With an air of command, he studied the medley of faces, his slow, sweeping glance carefully appraising each person before moving on to the next. Sunray watched him as he in turn watched the others. Just what—or who—the hell was he looking for? His gaze was calculating, shrewd, and far more astute than any mere mortal she'd ever encountered.

Sunray took a big slug of her drink and tried to shrink into the background. But before she had a chance, his dark gaze locked on hers and held her captive.

Her heart slammed in her chest and she drew a centering breath, suddenly feeling like a puppy among a pack of hyenas. Every instinct she possessed went on high alert and her flight-or-fight instincts kicked into high gear.

Fighting down the animal itching to claw its way out and flee, she drew on all her training and worked to show no outward sign of panic as he stalked closer.

He stepped up to her, and she immediately caught his scent. Oh. Sweet. Jesus. No!

She tried to calm her erratic heartbeat as his warm, familiar aroma seeped under her skin and drew her into a cocoon of need and desire.

Oh, God, it can't be. It just can't be . . .

Crowding her, he dipped his chin as his eyes moved over her face. "Hey," he said, his voice dark and seductive. Dangerous. His tone was . . . *familiar.* A low, sexy cadence that always got to her both sexually and emotionally.

I must be mistaken. Oh, God, I must be . . .

With her heart beating wildly and her head spinning, she made a move to stand. But when his gaze locked on hers again, those dark, piercing eyes burrowing into her very soul, it felt like she'd been sucker punched, and her legs refused to budge beneath her.

His sheer strength and magnetism made her breathless, and it was all she could do to keep a coherent thought in her head. Needing a moment of reprieve from those trained eyes, she finished off her drink and placed her glass on the bar before turning back to him. She looked past his shoulder and tried desperately to focus on something other than the riot of emotions erupting inside her.

He shifted, and his broad chest blocked her line of sight. Sunray resisted the urge to squirm. Instead, she stretched out her fatigued limbs to cover her discomfiture, and out of her peripheral vision caught his watchful eye and considered what he saw. Her golden hair was long, loose, and a little wild. Her jeans were snug, riding low on her hips and exposing the tattoo on the small of her back. A knit V-neck sweater exposed her cleavage, and was thin enough for him to see the telltale hardening of her nipples. Oh, boy! In conjunction with her formfitting clothes and blatant arousal, here she was, sitting all alone at a sex club, watching the action from afar. As if she were waiting for the right man, the one and only man who could satisfy her womanly needs.

Him.

With that last thought in mind, Sunray drew a fueling breath and angled her head to face him straight on. She immediately wished she hadn't, because the intensity in his eyes as he perused her turned her insides to mush. As she gave him her full attention, it occurred to her that he was standing over her with purpose, like he was waiting for something.

Her brain snapped back to reality, and she thrust out her arm and lenghtened her fingers to keep them from shaking. "Sunray." She forced herself not to show any reaction or give herself away to a hunter. "Sunray Matthews." Sure, she'd mastered numerous ways to camouflage her identity, but rarely could any wolf, including the elders, deceive a seasoned hunter. And she could only assume he was a veteran by the way he acted. What kind of chance did a puppy like her, who'd been around for only a hundred years, stand?

"Kane," was all he offered, confidence oozing off him in waves as his big warrior hand swallowed hers whole. She became acutely aware of the way she responded to his proximity, his touch, his ruggedness. Her skin came alive and a shudder worked its way through her body. His eyes fixed on her mouth, and in that instant—despite what he was—every fiber of her being ached for him to press his lips to hers, to thrash his tongue against the sides of her mouth, to taste the sweetness of her lips.

As she inhaled his scent, pleasure moved through her, and it took all her willpower not to throw herself at him, submit to him, to give herself over to him and let him take charge of her pain and her pleasure.

When he dragged his thumb over her flesh, she noticed that her hand was still in his. She snatched it back and examined her body's responses to his touch.

Oh, God.

Her strong response to him merely confirmed what Jaclyn had suspected. Sunray had only ever responded *this* strongly to one man. It was what every instinct she possessed was telling her. . . .

Kane *was* Ray.

There was just no denying who he was. Or *what* he was. Struggling for some semblance of control, her glance went to his, and something passed over his eyes. And as this PTF hunter—*Ray*—examined her responses, the hard lines of his face softened and he gave her a look she didn't understand. Then, for the briefest of seconds, she thought she saw a flash of pain in the depths of his eyes before he shook it off and once again presented her with a cool, hardened exterior.

Taking her by surprise, he asserted his dominance, cupped her elbow, and pulled her to her feet. He put his mouth close to her ear and inhaled, like he was pulling her scent into his lungs. He inched back until their gazes locked.

"I'm the man you're looking for."

Jesus, he has no idea.

Even though it was a statement, not a question, she swallowed hard and nodded in agreement. As she stood there staring up at him, taking in his roguish good looks, firm square jaw, and intense eyes, memories of the last time they made love came rushing back and shook her to her very core. An invisible band tightened around her heart.

Of all the things he could have come back as . . .

His grip on her elbow tightened and he gestured toward the back room. "Come with me." His commanding tone told her he wasn't asking; he was telling.

The wolf inside her barked a warning, and common sense dictated that she should run. Tuck tail and run as far away as possible. Because the one man she needed the most, the one man she'd spent the last one hundred years pining over, was suddenly the one man she needed to keep her distance from.

But common sense wasn't calling the shots.

As a sexual woman, she ached for him, cried out for him in ways that left her weak, needy. She refused to even contemplate the idea of fleeing.

Going against her own best interests and acting purely on impulse—something she swore she'd never do—Sunray blindly followed him to the back, never once stopping to consider the wisdom of her actions.

Chapter Three

Kane stole a sideways glance at the gorgeous woman beside him, as he escorted her to one of the back rooms, a private suite where he could have her all to himself and do delicious things to her voluptuous body. Although he had to admit, gorgeous didn't even begin to describe this woman's distinctive features. He wasn't sure what it was, but there was something about Sunray that set her apart from the others. And yeah, he'd been with enough others to know what the hell he was talking about.

He'd heard she'd been at the club, asking for him by name. But he had no idea who she was. Although in a few moments, once he had her tied up and at his mercy, he planned on rectifying that small problem. He planned on getting to know every inch of her perfect body with his fingers, his mouth, and his ever-expanding cock.

Oh yeah, most definitely with my cock, he mused.

His glance moved over her small frame and considered the natural, purposeful way she moved. As he examined her easy yet seductive strides, it occurred to him that there was also something very familiar about her. And that scent of hers, it had the strangest ability to get beneath his skin and warm his darkest corners.

As her aroma worked its way through his body and wove some sort of wicked spell on his soul, it seemed almost to dislodge a long-forgotten memory from the recesses of his brain. He concentrated, but the memories were too distant for him to grasp and bring to the forefront for a closer examination.

He panned her features a second time, and the officer in him committed her lush curves, the color of her tawny skin, and the sexy way she moved to memory. The man in him, however, drew in her sweet floral scent, acknowledged the creamy rise and fall of her cleavage, and took pleasure in the way her skintight jeans hugged her hot little ass. Jesus, she oozed sensuality in a way that made him shake with desire.

As his fingers itched to cup her perfect, heart-shaped backside, his gaze moved back to her face. He took note of her big blue eyes, flawless skin, and thick golden hair. Hair the color of a wheat field—the color of a lycan's fur.

Jesus, where the hell had that thought come from? He shook his head to clear it. Honestly, he'd spent so much time chasing lycans lately that it was becoming harder and harder to separate himself from his job. That last thought made him scoff. Fuck, who was he kidding? He *was* his job. It was what made him tick, what defined him.

Which was why a few years ago he'd separated himself from his parents, his two sisters, and their families—and anyone else that he had ever cared about. The last thing he wanted to do was drag those he loved into his dark world, and he couldn't afford to have his heart invested in anyone, for fear they would be used against him in battle. If there was one thing he'd been taught after joining the Paranormal Task Force, it was that love merely destroyed one's ability to think clearly. And when going up against a ferocious lycan, a man needed all his wits about him.

Of course, it wasn't just luck or skill during his basic training that drew the attention of senior PTF officers. With a strong sense of right and wrong, Kane had always gravitated toward law enforcement. And from the peculiar dreams he had about a wolf ripping into his flesh, deep in his gut he knew there was more out there. When he began asking questions, he was quickly brought into the secret government department and educated by the best.

A yawn pulled at him and he fought it down. Christ, he'd spent practically all of the last twenty-four hours hunting a deadly rogue who'd been terrorizing the streets, killing the men and turning the women—his calling card—and he was damn near dead on his feet. Unfortunately, the habitual swim he'd taken at the health club before coming to Risqué did little to rejuvenate him this time.

There was a time when the hunt used to rejuvenate him and he could go days on end without sleep. As of late, he didn't quite get that same adrenaline rush as he used to. But as long as those hounds of hell continued to invade his city, he'd made a vow to his department to pack silver and hunt every last one of them down. As far as he was concerned, the only good lycan was a dead lycan. He couldn't explain why he felt that so strongly, only that he did. Then again, perhaps it had something to do with his recurring adolescent night terrors, and his need to terminate each and every beast before that nightmare came true.

They reached the suite, and Kane pushed open the door to reveal a room with a BDSM theme. Sunray's big blue eyes widened, and that lost-puppy look that crossed her face reminded him of a scared and damaged stray. She glanced up at him, and for the briefest of moments he thought he spotted a hint of vulnerability. Something tugged at his insides and compelled him to wrap his arm around her and draw her in closer.

Yeah, he wanted to fuck her, but he wasn't going to force the issue. And the reality was, if she came looking for him, it meant she wanted one thing: total domination.

He dipped his head, his lips close to hers. "Second thoughts?" he asked.

Truthfully, Kane had come to the club tonight for one reason and one reason only: sex. With the approaching full moon, things were beginning to heat up in the city. And in order to give the hunt his full concentration, he had to satisfy all of his basic needs: food, rest, and, yes, even sex.

And this pretty lady—who'd been asking for him by name—was the perfect candidate for the job. A pretty woman who reminded him of a lycan.

He cursed under his breath. Jesus, if his thoughts continued in this direction, soon enough he'd convince himself she was a wolf. Then what? Would he draw his gun? Fuck, he was only thirty-two, but maybe he really was getting too old for the hunt. Because the truth was, a lycan would never come into the high-class members-only erotic club and hand herself over to him. Any wolf worth its weight in gold could smell a hunter from miles away; smell the gunpowder residue on his hands, the silver in his pocket.

No, Sunray was no lycan. She had a certain innocence about her. A strange purity that brought out some deep-seated instinct and did the weirdest things to him. Christ, maybe *he* should be the one having second thoughts. Then, suddenly, unease trickled along his nerve endings, and a disturbing theory hit him. Maybe Sunray really was a lycan, and the bizarre feelings she aroused in him had merely affected his ability to think rationally, throwing him off his game.

Sunray inched closer. The heat of her body called out to him in foreign ways as she brushed her tongue over her bottom lip. In the span of a moment, his cock thickened and rational thought flew from his brain with more speed than a round of silver from his .40 caliber. If she continued to lick her lips like that, he was likely going to shoot off quicker than his trusty Glock.

What the hell was it about her that had the ability to rattle him so much? He was an emotionless, heartless son of a bitch who maintained a cool, distant attitude at all times. It was what kept him alive on the Chicago streets and during his dangerous nightly hunts.

"Kane," she whispered.

Adept at reading others, he felt apprehension surge through her. He granted himself a moment to study her body language and facial expressions as she took in the BDSM room, complete with shackles, a bondage table, chains dangling from the ceiling, numerous floggers, and even a spanking bench.

As doubt filled her eyes, he felt something inside him give, soften. Pissed off at his temporary moment of weakness, he dipped his head and presented her with his best hard-assed face. Hands clenched, nostrils flared, he pinned her with a glare.

"If you want to play with me, Sunray, you have to play it my way. I figured you knew that since you came looking for me."

Unprepared for the bizarre mix of emotions those big blue eyes roused in him, he once again felt himself mellow around the edges. *Fuck* . . . He raked his fingers through his hair, blew a heavy breath, and rushed out, "Look, maybe we should just forget about it."

Taking him by surprise, she stepped back and opened her arms, palms out in surrender. Color bloomed high on her cheeks, and by small degrees her body relaxed.

"Take me, Kane. I'm all yours."

As he watched her hand herself over to him, he let out a breath he hadn't even realized he was holding.

"Do with me as you please."

Why the fuck did those words feel so familiar to him? After

all, he'd heard them a thousand times before, from a hundred different women. But this was the first time they made his stomach clench, his heart twist. *Jesus.*

Maybe I should just get the hell out of here.

Before he had a chance to back the fuck out the door and get his head screwed on straight, she flashed dark lashes at him and added, "Only you will ever be my master."

Her words felt deeply intimate, and oddly enough, as they pulsed through his brain, he began hungering for her in ways that left him perplexed.

What the fuck?

A thin sheen of perspiration broke out on his forehead, and he started to tremble. Almost violently. Kane pressed the butt of his sweaty palm to his forehead and tried to process the barrage of emotions attacking him from all angles. But as his balls constricted to the point of no return and his cock urged him to nail her up against the wall, coherent thought was damn near impossible.

He furrowed his brow and shot her a questioning glace. "Sunray . . ."

She lowered her head. "Only you will have the pleasure of spanking me." All doubt gone from her eyes, she kicked off her winter boots, glided across the room, and leaned over the spanking bench, offering herself up so nicely to him. "And it's been such a very long time since I've been spanked, Master."

Holy fuck!

And just like that, the inviting sight of her luscious ass

prompted him into action, rendering his ability to rationalize what his lust-drunk brain was struggling to tell him.

Since he ached to rub himself up against her, Kane moved swiftly across the room and slid his hand over her lush backside. "Such a beautiful ass," he growled. He drew his hand back and gave her a light smack, and listened to her excited intake of air.

He positioned himself directly behind her and leaned over her body, grinding his rock-hard cock against her ass as he pushed her sweater up to expose her silky-smooth back. Since her pants rode low on her hips, he also got a glimpse of the creamy crest of her buttocks. He bent forward, feathered his tongue over her flesh, and took note of her tattoo—a kitty-paw print.

Damned if he wasn't a fan of the pussy himself.

He slipped his hand around her body, stroked her cunt through her jeans, and then unhooked the button. The sound of her zipper being released cut through the air and elicited a soft mewling sound from her throat. Kane growled as his fingers itched to burrow inside her heat to discover just how wet she was for him.

"Wiggle your hips for me," he commanded in a soft tone.

As she wiggled, he ground his teeth together, need pulling at him so hard it was all he could do to slow things down. He slid her pants to her ankles and she lifted her legs one at a time to help him remove them. Once he'd shed her pants, her aroused scent hit him hard, and impatience to drive home with his cock and spend the rest of the night indulging in her warmth nearly drove him to his knees. God, never had he felt so edgy, so out of control. So frenzied. Commanding himself to get his shit together, he stood back and panned her body and the sexy lace thong that dipped between her buttock cheeks.

So fucking sexy.

"Open your legs."

Shivering in anticipation, Sunray immediately widened her legs, and his mind practically shut down at the sight of her wet pussy through her thin lace panties. Liquid desire dampened the fabric and exposed her curly hairs. His mouth watered in response. Blood pounded through his veins, and the overwhelming need to bury his dick in her made it harder and harder to draw in air.

"Kane, please . . ."

"Please what?"

"I want it hard."

Ah, Jesus . . .

Kane took two measured steps until he pressed against her. He sank to his knees, stroked a tender caress over her backside, and then pulled open her plump cheeks to expose her luscious ass and wet cunt.

He pulled her panties to the side, slipped one finger between her thighs, and parted her damp twin lips to test her readiness. Oh, fuck, she was ready all right. Primed and ripe for the taking. But he wasn't quite ready to take her over the edge just yet. The night was young and he needed this.

Oh, fuck, how I need this.

He slapped her ass. A bright red spot blossomed on a bed

of creamy white flesh. As the color deepened, he rubbed a gentle palm over her bottom to soothe the sting before giving her a whack on the other cheek. He continued to spank her until their moans of pleasure mingled. After a few more taps, he inched back to soak in the sight of her.

"No . . . please." She tipped up her ass and shook it at him, her body beckoning for his touch as the rich scent of her arousal swamped him.

Fueled by need and the desperation in her voice, he said, "Stand up and turn around."

Sunray lifted herself from the spanking bench, stood, and twisted to face him. The red stains on her face matched the stains on her plump ass cheeks, and the desire in her eyes as they met his nearly undid him.

He crooked his finger and bit back a moan. "Come here." Much to his delight, she blindly followed his command. "Now take the rest of your clothes off for me. Nice and slow." Sexual tension hung heavy between them as she stripped bare and stood before him, completely naked, his to do with as he pleased. His glance raked over her, and she shuddered.

"What is it you wish for me to do?" she questioned. The deeply intimate way she looked at him made his insides quake, and conveyed without words what she needed.

Pulse hammering, he took a moment to compose himself before saying, "Lift your arms and spread your legs. I want you at my mercy."

Her chest heaved with excitement. Kane grabbed her wrists

and shackled them above her head. "Spread your legs wider. Show me your cunt."

Once he had her legs chained to the floor, he stood back to examine her again. *Goddamn.* As his gaze skirted over her, hunger ripped through him with an intensity that made his dick throb. Before his passion-rattled brain could comprehend what he was doing, he tore open his jeans and gripped his stiff cock. He stroked himself hard, feeding the intensity of his arousal. Sunray drew a shaky breath and regarded him with wide eyes as he diligently worked his hand over his throbbing erection. Christ, he couldn't believe how turned on he was, how crazed this woman made him.

A little whimper of delight sounded in Sunray's throat. Her hair fell forward and her tongue swirled over her bottom lip as she looked at his dick with longing.

His body trembled, despite the warmth in the room. "What is it, Sunray? Do you want to suck my cock?"

"Yes."

He forced a quick laugh. "You're a very bad girl, aren't you?"

Her body shuddered. "May I show you how bad, Master?" Her voice was merely a breathless whisper.

Blindsided by lust, it took all his strength not to take her up on that seductive offer. To push her to her knees and ram his whole cock into her mouth. But he was certain he'd shoot his load off in seconds flat, and there were things he needed to do to her first. Like touch and taste every inch of her skin, drive his tongue into her sweet cunt, and drink in her syrupy release.

In one fluid movement, he peeled off his clothes. The sight of his naked body triggered a reaction from Sunray. She stiffened and her eyes widened, equal measures of apprehension and excitement dancing across her face.

It was then that he realized she'd seen all his scars. Unlike the animals he hunted, he wasn't gifted with regenerative abilities. At least they were only claw lacerations and not bite marks; otherwise, any one of his fellow PTF officers would have been quick to put him down. Rightfully so.

"It's okay," he whispered, addressing her worries. "Jet Ski accident."

Needing to ease her concerns and get her mind focused on more important matters, like fucking him, he stepped closer and parted her twin lips, his knuckles purposely brushing over her clit. Her broken gasp wrapped around him as he dipped into her liquid heat. Kane gave a low, throaty chuckle and stroked deep.

Jesus, she was aching for it.

She gyrated her hips. "I need you inside me." He was shocked at the urgency and emotion in her voice, and when her muscles clenched around his finger, there was nothing he could do to stifle the growl that ripped from his lungs.

Moving swiftly, his hands went to her breasts and he tweaked her pretty nipples between his thumbs and index fingers. They tightened into hard little buds, and the resulting shade of pink made saliva pool on his tongue. He lowered his head and clamped his mouth around one peak, sucked hard and deep and with a savagery that he didn't even recognize himself. Christ, he wanted—needed—her so desperately it scared the hell out of him. As he continued to ravage her breasts, Sunray gave a wild, animal-like cry and arched into him.

"More," she cried out, and he could feel the impatience thrumming through her.

He turned his attention to her other nipple and swirled his tongue around her pale orb, loving how it tasted and the way it fit so perfectly into his mouth. One hand went back to her cunt. He took note of her soft quakes and knew she was ready to go up in a burst of flames.

"You really do need my cock in there, don't you, sweetheart? You're hurting bad."

A wheezing sound escaped her mouth. "Yes, please, Kane. Feed it to me."

With a craving to sample her cream and to satisfy all her bodily urges, he sank to his knees and pressed a hard kiss on her pussy, his tongue sifting through silky strands until he found her hot little button. Using slow, skilled passes, he dragged his tongue over her hooded clit before spearing her channel with his index finger.

"Ohmigod, yes . . ." she cried out. She wrapped the chains around her wrists and held tight, the dual assault pushing her to the edge. "So good. So damn good."

Kane worked his tongue over her sex and manipulated her clit until it throbbed beneath his careful ministrations. He drew the engorged nub into his hungry mouth and raked it over his teeth. The chains rattled as she shifted and bucked against him.

When her body shuddered, surrendering to the pleasure, Kane drove his finger in deeper, brushing the soft pad over the sensitive bundle of nerves and giving her exactly what she needed.

What I need . . .

Fuck, he couldn't believe how much he wanted to make her come, how much he was loving the way she reacted to him—the way she wanted him.

Kane pushed another finger inside, and Sunray threw back her head. As he pumped in and out, in and out, her muscles contracted around his fingers and she exhaled a whimper of relief. "That's a girl," he said, coaxing her release. "Come for me."

She pulsed and throbbed and went wild as her orgasm tore through her. He held her tight and absorbed her tremors until her body stilled. Once her pussy muscles stopped spasming, he lapped at her cunt, drenching his mouth with her sweet cream.

A moment later he straightened, gripped the chains just above her hands, and used his height to loom over her. Breathing labored, he dipped his head and pressed hungry lips to hers. Their tongues tangled and played as they shared in the delicious taste of her cream. His cock slapped against her stomach, and knowing exactly what she was doing, she moved closer to squeeze it between their bodies. As her soft flesh massaged his dick, his tension grew to dangerous proportions.

"I need to fuck you. . . ." he whispered into her mouth. "So fucking bad, I can't think straight."

Kane released her from all four bindings and dropped into a chair. "I want you to ride me."

Sunray lowered her head to glance at his cock. She licked her lips. "Don't I get to taste it first?"

He growled and tugged at her. "Christ, girl, get the fuck over here and climb on my cock."

Her lips twitched, as though pleased by his gruffness, the way he was losing control.

She closed the small gap between them and threw one leg over his lap. Kane gripped her hips to guide her down, controlling the pace and depth as she tried to impale herself on him. He speared her with his cock, and her heat closed around him. His mind whirled, and much to his dismay, he couldn't ignore the intimacy in what they were doing. And for the first time in his life, for some inexplicable reason, he couldn't seem to separate himself from his emotions. What was it about her that prohibited him from hardening his heart?

Her hips began moving, rocking, pulling him in deeper and deeper with each thrust until his entire length was buried inside her. His balls slapped against her ass with each upward plunge. She tipped forward to rub her clit against his body, and her hands went to her breasts. She pushed her breasts together and lifted them to him in offering. He flicked his tongue out to lick and suck her hard nipples, and she threw back her head and cried out with desire.

Kane slipped one hand between their bodies to stroke her clit. "Baby, you're so hot."

He grabbed one hand from her breast and brought it to her cunt. "Touch with me."

Her soft chuckle curled around him. "You always did enjoy that, Ray," she murmured, but his lust-saturated brain was too far gone to comprehend anything she was saying.

The room grew stifling, aromatic, scented by their love-making. Her cunt clenched around him, and one palm closed over his face. Catching him off guard, a bizarre flash of posses-siveness zinged through his veins and he gripped her hips harder, his fingers biting into her flesh. Tomorrow she'd be bruised, but oddly enough, that thought pleased him. He wanted to leave his mark on her, wanted her to remember every minute of this night, every pump of his cock, every clench of her sweet cunt.

Her rich scent burned through his blood, and his cock pulsed to the point of no return.

Oh, God, I need . . .

Lost, mindless, crazed, he drove into her harder, powering his hips upward. It occurred to him he wasn't just seeking release; he was seeking something else. Something he couldn't quite put a name to. Pressure brewed inside him and he pumped harder, deeper, yet still couldn't seem to assuage this unfamiliar need flooding his veins.

"Kane . . . more . . ."

She grabbed the back of his chair and rode him hard, her gorgeous breasts swaying inches from his face as she came for him again. As their bodies fused, her juices poured over his shaft and singed his flesh.

Those needy words combined with her hot cream robbed him of his last vestige of control. His hands crushed through

her hair and a wave of tenderness overcame him. "Sunray . . .
kitten . . ." He opened his mouth, wanting to say more, but he
had no idea what he was trying to say.

"I know, baby. I know. It's been too long."

He wasn't exactly sure what she knew, or what she meant by
it being too long, and now certainly wasn't the time to ponder it.
Not with his brain shutting down and his semen rushing to the
finish line. His cock swelled, his mind took a hiatus, and he held
her tight as he let himself go. He threw back his head, splashed
his seed high up inside her, and was almost certain he'd found
heaven.

Heaven . . .

They both held each other tight, gripping on to each other
like their lives depended on it, as he pumped every last drop
into her. Moisture sealed their flesh together, and as bone-deep
warmth curled through his blood, Kane couldn't tell where his
body ended and hers began. Her cunt clenched around him, and
she worked her muscles until she milked him dry, leaving him
drained and sated, and feeling so damn fine he couldn't even
seem to remember his own name.

"So good." Sunray rested her head on his shoulder and held
him close. He didn't miss the note of satisfaction in her voice,
and it pleased him to know that he'd put it there.

Driven by a force he couldn't identify, he ran his fingers
through her long, damp hair and pulled her head back, needing
to see her. His eyes met hers and his gut twisted in response. *Oh,
fuck.* He had the sneaking suspicion that something was happen-

ing between them, and that even though he'd just met her, they were dangerously close to crossing some imaginary line.

Kane shook his head to clear it and worked to compartmentalize his emotions. Once he composed himself, he swallowed and asked, "You okay?"

"Yes," she assured him, but intuition told him otherwise, and he was starting to get a sense that they were playing a very dangerous game here. One he needed to put an end to right away. Because being with her felt different. Real. More emotional; less physical. But in his line of work, he had no time for emotions or relationships. A quick roll in the sack to take the sexual edge off was the extent of his personal affairs.

With that last thought in mind, he gave himself a quick lecture, pulled back from her physically and emotionally, and cursed himself for his stupidity. He should have bailed when he had the chance.

Passion receded as he tapped her ass to signal his intent and bit out, "I gotta go." His voice came out gruff, hard as nails, and his stomach clenched with a mixture of apprehension and disappointment.

Then he remembered something. Before she had a chance to climb off, he anchored her to his lap, his cock still buried deep inside her, and eyed her suspiciously. "How do you know me? Why were you looking for me?"

A pregnant pause lingered as she drew her lip into her mouth, and her voice hitched when she said, "Jaclyn told me you were the best."

Her moment of hesitation combined with the way she nibbled on her bottom lip spoke volumes. She was lying through her teeth. But why? What was she keeping from him?

"Well, am I, Sunray? Am I the best?" He shook his head, disgusted with himself for wanting to know, for wanting to hear her say it out loud.

"Yes . . ." Her voice was soft, breathless, and he fought the impulse to take her into his arms and show her again just how good it could really be.

Despite his better judgment, he cocked his head and in a harsh voice continued. "Has it ever been this good for you before?" Because he was damn sure it had never been this good for him.

What the hell was he doing?

She drew a deep, shuddering breath. "Yes, but only with one man, and it was a long time ago."

Unable to comprehend how that made him feel, or to handle the jealousy rising inside him, he eased her off his hips and went looking for his clothes, trying to keep his focus on something other than the reactions she drew from him. He tugged on his jeans and shirt and shot a glance at the door.

"Kane."

Her voice stopped him, and even though every instinct told him to bolt, he turned back around to face her. He widened his stance in a combative move and presented her with a cold, calculating look. But when he caught the softness in her eyes and the want evident in her lush body, his defenses crumbled like the toast he'd burnt that morning. She stirred things in him, things he didn't want to feel, things that as a PTF officer he had no business feeling, which gave credence to his logic to hightail it the hell out of there.

He grumbled, "What?"

"Thank you." One palm closed over his cheek, a gesture he was becoming increasingly familiar with, and she went up on her tiptoes to press a warm kiss to his mouth. That kiss was so achingly gentle and familiar, it took him completely by surprise. As a wave of tenderness stole over him, his whole fucking world shifted on its axis and he feared that life as he knew it would never be the same.

Neither said a word for a long time; then he cupped her hand and put it at her side, fully aware that sleeping with her was dangerous. In more ways than one.

The roughness in his voice gave way to softness, and with torment tearing at his gut he said with a quiet certainty, "Goodbye, Sunray."

Chapter Four

Here it was, three days later, and Kane's parting words were still spinning circles in her mind like a warped 1970s vinyl record.

Good-bye, Sunray.

Even though the bitter finality of those words stung like a thousand angry hornets, deep in her gut she knew they had no choice but to part ways, no matter how much it pained her, and no matter how much her heart ached with the knowledge that they could never be together. Ever.

Kane was a hunter.

And she was his prey.

She might have spent the last hundred years mourning Ray's death, but she hadn't dared to go back to the erotic club since her one blissful night together with Kane, and had diligently tamped down the deep-seated need to seek him out again. It was dangerous.

He was dangerous.

A warning shiver moved through her, and a lump lodged deep in her throat. Honestly, she must have taken a short reprieve from sanity to let her desires rule her actions and to have followed him into one of the private suites at Risqué. What if he had discovered what she was? Would he have killed her on the spot—without a moment's hesitation? She had no reason to believe otherwise.

But how could she possibly have stopped herself?

When it came to him, she was helpless, making it impossible to ignore her baser impulses. Sunray drew a deep breath and gifted herself with a moment of remembrance, recalling the way his lean, athletic body felt beneath hers. The way her hips had straddled his legs, and the familiar, intoxicating scent of his skin. The way his strong hands had so urgently touched her face, her breasts, between her legs. And the way his beautiful cock stroked deep inside her pussy, pushing open her tight walls and bringing her to orgasm again and again.

Oh, God, she could feel her nipples tighten and her sex moisten just from revisiting those delicious, intimate moments now. Her hand automatically brushed over her body with raw, primitive need, stopping to play with her nipples. But then, as the severity of the situation came crashing back in angry waves, his parting farewell once again hit her with the force of a storm surge.

Good-bye, Sunray . . .

Sunray cringed at those dark, ugly words, which felt more

final to her than a round of silver bullets. Emotions hardened her heart and a soft animal-like yowl broke through the silence of her condo. Even though Kane had turned a cold, calculating stare on her, she knew he hadn't left that room unaffected by their lovemaking.

Beneath the tough exterior that he presented to the world, she caught fleeting glimpses of Ray, her sweet, caring, giving Ray. And although he'd worked hard to keep his emotions in check, she had seen the need in his gaze as it locked on hers, and had felt the tenderness in his every hungry caress. When it came right down to it, Ray, or Kane as he was now known, had been gentle with her. His actions seemed caring as he took the time to satisfy her needs before he sated his own, traits deeply ingrained into his personality, she supposed.

Sunray linked her fingers together and squeezed. Perhaps she should just be satisfied to know that he was okay, alive, and thriving in this crazy, messed-up world. But something in the depths of his stormy gaze told a different story—a story that spoke of sadness, loneliness, and longing, like he wasn't really living at all.

Sunray blinked her eyes and pulled herself back to the harsh, immortal reality in which she lived, and worked double time to harden her heart. She let out a long, suffering sigh, and knew it was time to put a stop to her yearnings; she couldn't ever truly be with Kane, not the way she needed. Not now or ever. Nor could she tell him of their past and all the love and intimacies, secrets and fears they'd shared. He was now a ruthless hunter, and if he had any inkling of what lurked inside her, he'd kill her without a moment's hesitation. She was certain of it.

Deciding to shelve those memories in the recesses of her mind before her heart splintered into a million tiny pieces, she hugged herself and walked quietly through her condo, all too aware of the setting sun and the pull of the rising moon. She glanced outside at the shadows on the sidewalk moving beneath the moonbeams, knowing that soon enough she would become nothing more than a haunt in the darkness. Scuttling undetected along the city's wooded perimeter, a flash beneath the moon, gorging on animal blood.

She wasn't proud of what she'd become, but it gave her a measure of comfort to know that she didn't hunt humans or kill for the mere sport of it, like other lycans she knew. Despite what all PTF officers believed, not all lycans were monsters with their own best interests at heart. Heck, over the years, she'd seen less humanity in a few select humans. But she'd just bet Kane had a different theory. And he had numerous scars on his body to back up that argument.

Padding softly to her bathroom, she looked in her mirror and took note of her red eyes and tearstained cheeks. She sniffed and swiped at her face as she quietly refocused. Shift night was definitely *not* the time to lose concentration.

She took a quick glance at the clock and felt a moment of panic. Cripes, she desperately needed to get herself together and get to the outskirts of town before the change was upon her. As her bones began to ache and coarse hair began to poke out from her skin, she splashed her face with icy cold water, then ran a toothbrush over her teeth.

Once she had herself semicomposed, she turned off all her lights and made her way to the front hall, mentally preparing for the night ahead. If there was one thing she hated, it was when the full moon fell on the weekend. More innocent folks would be out wandering the streets, not tucked inside their beds at a decent hour, thus unknowingly putting themselves in grave danger. Shivering at the thought, she pulled on her winter coat and reached out to flick off her radio. But when the news of another murder/abduction in the south side came blaring through the speakers, it stopped her dead in her tracks.

Although crime was common in big cities and the statistics were rising at an alarming rate, it was the way these malicious acts went down that held her attention, and, quite frankly, scared the hell out of her.

Four men dead. Four women missing.

Sunray swallowed hard, and quaked with the familiarity of the crime descriptions. The anonymous voice on the radio continued to drone on about a reward for the return of the female victims, alive and unharmed. But Sunray knew the chances of them being found were slim to none. And if by some miracle they were identified and returned home, those women were already dead. Oh, sure, they might walk and talk and resemble their former selves, but they could never go back to living a normal life. Sunray knew all about that firsthand.

She rifled through the stack of newspapers that had been

piling up over the last few days as she huddled up inside and cursed the cruel turn of events. Heck, she hadn't even gone in to work; instead she took her time to sort through matters and process the knowledge that Ray was Kane, and Kane was a deadly hunter.

She'd also missed her kickboxing and strength-training classes down at the club, classes that helped keep her alert and alive on the dangerous streets, especially during her compulsory shift night. But, truthfully, after accepting the fact that Ray was forever lost to her, she found it harder and harder to maintain enthusiasm to continue on in this world.

A little over six months ago, before escaping Serene, Sunray had bought a gun and loaded it with silver bullets. After all, some things—like living with Vall—were worse than death. But after meeting Jaclyn, things had changed. Deep in her gut she had sensed Jaclyn was important to her, important to her future. It was only recently that she'd discovered why: Jaclyn had led her to Kane. And it was clear that that had led her into the arms of a hunter.

Sunray turned her attention to the matter at hand, and without bothering to flick on the lights, she scanned the front page of each paper. The murders were all too similar in detail to be considered random acts of violence. With this kind of pattern, most of Chicago would conclude that they had a serial killer on their hands.

But not Sunray. Oh no, not Sunray. She knew better. So would any good PTF officer. And, heck, they were all good.

This was the MO of a rogue lycan.

The city might be full of rogues who couldn't always be held accountable for their actions during the shift, but deep in her gut, Sunray suspected that this wolf knew exactly what he was doing. Any lycan on a carnal rampage would either have killed everyone in its path—men and women alike—or infected *all* its victims with lycanthropy and initiated them into the brethren.

Unless, of course, they were dealing with a "special" kind of rogue. Sunray knew of only one "special" kind of rogue that liked to kill men and turn women. The kind of rogue that was trying to grow his pack through careful selection. A fertile female could give her alpha a bountiful litter, producing offspring that would be loyal to their father, their master. It could be quite risky for a dominant wolf to bring a virile male into the pack, for fear that he'd grow stronger and challenge the leader for alpha position. Sunray could only surmise that the wolf responsible for the slew of murder/abductions wanted total and utter control of his submissives.

But there was only one wolf she knew of who would go to such extreme measures, only one wolf who left such a calling card. And that wolf was dead. She'd watched him die with her own eyes. Watched the silver pump through his veins. This had to be the work of a dangerous rogue she'd never crossed paths with before. There was no way Vall could be alive.

Unless, of course . . .

Sunray knew the only thing that could reverse the effects of the poison was the right combination of herbs administered by a powerful Earth witch. But surely Harmony—the coven guide in Serene and the only witch there with enough skill—would never use magic to revive Vall. Although, come to think of it, Harmony had been acting rather peculiar around Vall before his death.

Slyck's theory was that Harmony knew Vall had ulterior motives for shifting the power balance in the community, and she was forming an allegiance with Vall, should such a shift in authority take place. That way, she'd ensure her position of power on the council.

So why would she revive him? Because she still *wanted* the power shift to take place? Wanted to rule Serene with Vall?

A strange foreboding worked its way through Sunray's blood, and she gave herself a quick shake to push it down. Vall had to be dead. He just had to be. Because the alternative was too bloodcurdling to consider.

She turned her attention to the pull of the moon as the ache in her joints intensified. Primal hunger weaved its way through her veins and forced her to put all worries aside for the time being and make her way to her car.

As she put her vehicle into gear and pressed the accelerator, she had the strangest sensation that someone or something was watching. With her keen eyesight, she scanned the perimeter, then rolled her window down and tasted the air. If there was a hunter nearby, she'd sniff him out. But it wasn't the scent of a hunter that she'd picked up on; it was that of wet fur.

Peeling out of the parking lot before any lurking wolf identified her as family, she maneuvered her car into traffic. Even though she missed her brethren, the last thing she wanted to do was associate with a dangerous rogue.

She writhed beneath him in slow, seductive movements that drove him crazy and caused volcanic pressure to build within him, consuming his every thought, his every action. As her cunt muscles clenched and tightened provocatively around his rock-hard shaft, Kane soaked in her damp heat, sank his cock all the way up inside her, and once again was almost certain he'd found heaven.

Heaven . . .

The glow from the beeswax candle positioned beside their bodies reflected in her blue eyes, which softened with desire and met his. His body trembled as the need in her gaze touched his soul and knocked him off balance. He stole a glance around, noting that they were in some kind of run-down old building. A stack of blankets on the floor provided a makeshift bed. Aside from the flickering candle, their only other source of light came from the moonbeams peering in through the cracks in the decaying roof. With minimal luminescence, the room was hazy, her face a blur, but her eyes held him captive. Always. So blue, so full of want and need.

Mesmerizing.

It had been far too long since she'd come to him under the cover of darkness—her face always obscure, her features unidentifiable—and he wasn't sure what had prompted her to do so tonight, only that he was glad she'd returned. There was no denying that his need for her had grown to dangerous proportions, and his body threatened to go up in a burst of flames if he didn't soon have her—flat on her back, her sweet cunt milking his cock.

Fucking . . .

Her soft, silky flesh brushed against his body and the air grew ripe with the scent of their lovemaking. Kane caught a whiff of her alluring floral aroma as it danced along her skin. He pulled the enticing bouquet deep into his lungs to draw on later, to savor in its entirety when she disappeared into the shadows, leaving him with nothing more than wisps of erotic memories.

And disappear she would.

His eager hands raced over her hot, delicate flesh and spanned her waist as he reacquainted himself with her body, using his tongue, his fingers, and his cock.

God, he loved the feel of her sexy curves beneath him. Her muscles were toned and tight, yet soft and feminine just the same. She moaned at his touch and the sweet, melodic sound of her voice was like music to his ears. It was shocking how much he'd missed her visits while he slept.

Her sex clenched again and he slammed into her so hard he damn near drove her through the dilapidated wooden floorboards. Fuck, he ached to be even deeper, to bury himself inside her and stay there forever. With need burning through his bloodstream and sweat pebbling on his forehead, he captured her body in his arms and rolled under her without ever withdrawing his cock from her tight heat. He pulled her on top of him, desperately needing to watch this mystery woman ride him with wild abandon.

He couldn't see her mouth but instinctively knew she was smiling as she gyrated her hips and lifted herself higher and higher. As she dropped back down and impaled herself on his dick, her long, golden locks fell forward and brushed over her milky white cleavage. His mouth watered for a taste of those sweet cherry buds.

Kane shifted his focus. He leaned forward and feathered her hair away to expose her creamy shoulders and full, lush breasts. He thumbed her nipples before drawing one perfect pink pebble into his mouth. *So ripe; so fucking sweet.* He took her beautiful, natural breasts in his large palms and proceeded to tongue and nibble her tight buds until he nearly sobbed with pleasure.

A low growl rumbled in his throat and rang in his ears, a reminder of just how crazed and out of control he felt. Christ, he'd never lost control before. Not like this. Not with anyone.

Unable to help himself, he continued to ravish her, and she grew slicker with each of his upward strokes. His hunger and lack of discipline seemed to arouse her even more, pulling soft mewling sounds from her throat. Her nipples peaked with excitement and swelled inside his mouth. Jesus, she tasted so divine, delicious. . . .

Arching into him, she raked her long, delicate fingers through his tousled hair and held his mouth to her breasts.

"Yes . . . more . . ." Her voice was seductive and sensual and spilled over his body like warm summer rain. A tremble moved through him and urged him on.

He slid his hands over her flesh, shaping the pattern of her contours until his palms settled on her hips. With his fingers biting into her flesh and using her curves for leverage, he thrust deeper, then inched back and searched her face for answers. Much to his dismay, he was still unable to discern her features in the darkness. She let out a whimper, and their mouths were so close he could taste the sweetness of her breath.

"Who are you?" he murmured, but his mystery woman pressed her wet mouth to his and drank the question from his kiss-swollen lips. They traded hot, urgent kisses for a long time, and as her tongue pillaged his mouth, the erotic torture made him throb.

Attuned with her needs, he powered his hips upward and ravaged her dripping pussy. She threw her head back as soft, sexy moans slid from her lips and elicited a shudder from deep within him. Her hands went to her breasts and she played with her pretty nipples. Jesus, there was nothing sexier than a woman touching herself. As she stroked her breasts, Kane slipped a thumb between their bodies and brushed along her engorged clit. Her breathing was ragged, a moan caught in her throat, and her body quivered.

Electricity sizzled between them and practically lit the room as he pounded into her. Giving and taking, she met each needy thrust, and together they reached a fevered pitch that left them both breathless.

"Harder . . ." she cried out, and began rocking against him, smashing her clit against his body with each forward motion. Her pleasure resonated through him, and none to gently he began to fuck her. Hard. The way she liked it.

Jesus, he ached for her, burned for her in ways that left him perplexed. As unbridled desire gripped him hard, his skin grew tight and his balls constricted to the point of pain. No longer able to fight down his carnal cravings, he pitched faster, slamming deep inside her, and in no time at all she came apart in his arms. Kane shivered, reveling in the feel of her hot cream as it poured down his shaft and dripped over his balls. As she melted all over his cock, need streaked through him and pleasure like he'd never before experienced pushed him over the precipice.

Her body softened and she cried out, "So good, Ray. So good."

Beyond the point of comprehension, he gave himself over to his orgasm. He held her tight and exploded, splashing his seed high up inside her. His body pulsed and throbbed with the hot flow of release, and he gave a low growl that rumbled like thunder. Their bodies fused. Christ, his orgasm was so powerful and intense, it was almost frightening.

Satisfaction rolled off them in waves as they both found solace in each other's arms. Off in the distance, a train sounded, its piercing whistle cutting through the silence of the night. Kane took a moment to bask in the afterglow, enjoying the feel of his cock still buried inside her as he slowly came back down to earth.

A short while later, as his breathing settled into a steady rhythm, his mystery woman began to stiffen and a strange new darkness closed around them. It was a darkness unlike anything he'd ever felt before. It was cold. Evil. Menacing.

Inescapable.

Senses on full alert, Kane's body tightened and his blood pressure soared in warning. With the instinctive knowledge that danger was closing in from all angles, he felt a shiver run down his spine and jerked his head back to glimpse the girl who was still straddling him from above.

Her knees moved to his chest and prevented him from standing. Gone was the erotic mystery woman with the mesmerizing blue eyes. Instead, ruthless silver orbs met his and she began to morph, her face stretching and elongating, her cartilage transforming, an ungodly sound cutting through the air as her bones started to shift and take on the shape of a ferocious wolf. A silky-smooth coat of wheat-colored fur spread out over her lithe body to complete the metamorphosis.

Then, suddenly, her jaw dropped open and she drove one palm into his chest, knocking the air from his lungs. Sharp canine teeth clamped around his neck, and she let loose a loud howl before tearing into his flesh with vehemence.

He grabbed a fistful of fur and struggled. "No," he screamed out, and bucked upward in an attempt to knock the beast off.

Insidious laughter curled around him, and a heartbeat later, Kane awoke with a fright, gasping for breath as one hand went to his neck to check for puncture marks, and the other hand automatically went to his gun. Acting purely on instinct, he sat up and darted a glance around, sweeping his surroundings with his weapon, prepared to squeeze the trigger at the slightest of movements. He half expected to see a pack of lycans closing in.

For a long time he sat tense, not daring to blink or even breathe, for that matter. As his eyes shifted through the darkness and took in his barely furnished bedroom, his brain began to fill in the blanks and he understood it was just a dream. *A bad dream.* He was home in his bed, not sprawled out in some run-down building, and that whistling sound wasn't a train; it was a crow squawking outside his window. Kane threw himself back down on his sweat-stained sheets and relaxed his finger on the trigger as he pulled himself together.

Breathe, Kane, breathe. It was just a dream.

He flicked on his lamp and lay there a moment longer, the fear slowly ebbing away. Why the hell was he dreaming of her again? The dreams always started out sensual and erotic, but why the fuck did they always have to end in the same horrific way— with him being torn apart by a deadly lycan? Kane shivered.

Was it some sort of premonition? Christ, he hoped not. As a tremble moved through him, his fingers instinctively tightened for a second time around his cold steel gun.

Even though the nightmares had begun in adolescence and were undoubtedly the reason he'd found his way into the PTF, he hadn't dreamt of her in years. Why now? What had suddenly roused her from his subconscious?

As he continued to pant, his skin prickled in warning and

his mind raced, trying to make sense of everything. He set his gun on his chest and struggled to regulate his breathing as something niggled at the back of his mind. Something very important.

Kane swiped his forehead with the back of his hand, and when he shook his head to clear his thoughts, recognition flashed and the mystery woman had suddenly been given an identity. Now her features were as distinct and as bright as moonbeams peering in through his open curtains, taunting him.

Sunray.

For the second time in as many minutes, he sucked in a tight breath and bolted upright. Sweat poured from his body, and as his mind pursued answers, he kept reminding himself it was just a dream. None of it was real. Right?

But if this mystery woman was merely a figment of his imagination, then why, after all these years, had she suddenly come back to him? And why was he just now able to put a face to her ghostly image?

And why was that face Sunray's?

He paused to consider it longer. Why had the woman's identity been revealed to him now? Was it *because* he'd met Sunray Matthews that the woman now had an identity?

As frustration moved through him in rapid succession, his hands fisted at his sides and he clenched down so hard his jaw muscles ached and his teeth damn near shattered.

He needed to figure out who Sunray was and why the hell he hadn't been able to wipe her from his mind, get the taste of her from his mouth, or wash the scent of her off his skin after fucking her down at the club. Here it was, three days later, and not only was he still sporting a hard-on, but also she continued to plague his every waking thought—and now, so it would appear, even his sleeping ones.

Fighting down the sense of uneasiness, he climbed from his bed and let his blankets fall to the floor in a heap. Outside his small bungalow in suburbia, the light from the streetlamps poured through his window and created shadows on his wall. A quick glance at the clock told him he'd overslept. By hours. *Shit!* He'd been so exhausted lately, he'd dozed off earlier, hoping to catch a few minutes of shut-eye before a long night of hunting, but he hadn't expected it to be this late by the time he woke.

Moving swiftly through his sparse room, he rushed down the hall and hopped into the shower, attempting to wash away the remnants of his dream. Once complete, he tugged on a clean T-shirt and a pair of jeans, but still couldn't shake the uneasy feeling curling around him. Something else was bothering him, something he couldn't quite put his finger on. Christ, as if identifying the woman from his dreams as Sunray wasn't enough for one night . . .

The sound of his grumbling stomach called out to him. He walked to his kitchen and pulled open the refrigerator for a quick bite to eat. Suddenly, the reason for his unease hit him with more force than a sucker punch.

The woman from his dreams had called him Ray.

With a piece of leftover chicken halfway to his mouth, he paused and tried to process that new tidbit of information. As his brain chewed on that vital clue, he briefly shut his eyes, his mind revisiting his one and only wild night with Sunray. Something loosened in the back of his mind, triggering a forgotten memory.

Sunray had called him Ray.

What the fuck was going on?

He tore into his chicken. He needed to find her, and he needed to find her fast, because he wanted answers, and he wanted them yesterday. He shot a glance to his window to the full moon hovering over his city, mocking him and calling all the ferocious lycans out to play. Those answers would have to wait, because first and foremost, he was a PTF officer, and there were a few lycans out there with his name on them. *Soon to have my silver pumping through them*, he mused with a satisfied smirk.

Chapter Five

Sunray found herself on the outskirts of town, at her usual hunting grounds. A spot where there were plenty of deer and rabbits to feed on, and, most important, there were no humans around for miles.

She pulled her car off the main thoroughfare and onto a utility access road that she'd stumbled upon quite some time ago. After camouflaging her vehicle with tree branches and securing her keys in the wheel well, she moved deeper into the woods and let the cool evening air wrap around her. A few flakes of snow fell silently from the sky as she drew a rejuvenating breath and pulled the alluring scent of the night into her lungs. Off in the distance she picked up the faint smell of a raccoon, and listened to the sounds of a nearby owl. Up above, a shooting star that scuttled across the black canvas made her feel small and insignificant in the great, big world.

Lured by nature, she began to feel a little shaky, a little unstable, as she let her guard down and uncaged the animal inside her. Equal measures of apprehension and excitement surged through her bloodstream. Restlessness grew inside her.

Overhead, the moon shone into the black forest, the soft beams penetrating the thick canopy of leaves and lighting up the dark forest floor and scattered patches of snow. Not that Sunray needed the light to pave her way, not with her exceptional night vision. She drew in the scent of earth, the indigenous timber, and the nocturnal wildlife. As she took it all in, she shed her clothes and put them in a neat pile before letting the wolf guide her actions.

With unhurried movements, she dropped down onto her hands and knees and blocked her mind against the pain as her body flushed with heat and her nails extended to razorlike claws. Her nostrils flared and her mouth elongated, taking on the long, thin shape of a ferocious muzzle. Sharp fangs pushed out from her gums and she brushed them with the tip of her tongue to test the edges.

She began breathing harder, her pulse beating a quick and steady rhythm at the base of her throat. Chaos erupted internally and air exploded from her lungs as her muscles thickened, molded, and morphed until she began to resemble a member of the canine family. A moment later, a mass of soft golden fur covered her body. As her bones shifted and the cartilage slid into place, she let out a tortured howl of pain, climbed to her feet, and drew in her next breath as a wolf.

Christ, she'd never get used to that.

With her shift complete, she darted a glance around, hunger consuming her every thought; the need to feed, ravage, and fornicate controlling her actions.

Exhilarated, her wolf began to run, her streamlined body dodging in and out of trees, feeling the cool breeze against her face and reveling in the welcoming moss and snow beneath her paws. She ran harder, sprinting across an open field, following the delicious aroma of prey in an attempt to sate the incessant ache inside her. She felt ravenous, completely carnal, and wildly out of control. With single-minded determination, her legs pumped beneath her until lactic acid filled her sinewy muscles.

Up ahead she spotted a deer and slowed to a canter, her body quaking with renewed excitement. The breeze picked up and blew the delicious scent her way. She listened to the animal's blood pulse through its body and could almost taste the warm, coppery sweetness on the tip of her tongue.

Her quick run had caused her endorphins to kick in, and she welcomed the rush as it numbed her pain sensors. She angled her head and watched the animal lift its head and sniff the air. Did it sense danger? Would it run? Oh, how her wolf hoped so, anticipating the challenge, the thrill of the hunt.

Desire pumped through her veins as she cocked her head and studied the lone animal, which had suddenly tensed, as though fully aware of the approaching danger. The aroma of fresh meat had her wolf salivating, and heat moved through her blood like an aphrodisiac.

Enraptured, she crouched low, muscles shifting in preparation for another run and hunt to be savored; her wolf enjoyed drawing out the chase and feeding on the intoxicating adrenaline rush inside her. Feeling wild and untamed, she sensed dark need swirling in her guts and the urge to take chase and pursue her prey.

Moments before she bolted, the scent of another wolf came to her on the breeze and stilled her movements. She drew another breath, tasting the surrounding air. Her throat tightened and her stomach soured as that familiar aroma reached her olfactory system and triggered unpleasant memories.

Oh, God. She knew which wolf possessed that putrid stench.

Vall.

Everything inside her screamed danger and counseled her to tuck tail and flee. Instinctively, her mouth peeled back to expose her fangs, and her nails raked through the frozen forest floor as she scanned her territory. She had to be mistaken. She just had to be. Vall was dead.

When survival instincts kicked in, her legs quivered and she hunkered beneath a low-slung branch to cloak her presence, not daring to draw so much as a single breath.

A shadow moved between the trees and twigs snapped beneath its big beefy paws as the animal circled. Then, suddenly, it moved into the clearing. As her eyes penetrated the dark, Sunray gasped and her brain raced to catch up as she stood there stock-still, staring at a ghost.

The wolf moved and she watched the play of muscles along the hard lines of his profile. Strength radiated from his powerful body, and in that instant she knew it was none other than her nemesis, the bane of her existence. Standing before her was the beast that had robbed her of mortal life and stolen Ray from her forever. A beast she hated above all others.

Her brain was still struggling to make sense of it all when the alpha wolf lunged toward the prey with lightning speed. Vall was on the deer in seconds flat, his fierce jaw clamping around the animal's jugular and dragging it to the ground. He held tight, tossing the deer around like it was nothing more than a rag doll, until the animal drew its final breath. Roaring in victory, Vall licked his chops and tore into the animal with fervor.

Vall . . .

Oh, God, how could this be happening?

Incredulous, she continued to watch from afar, with memories of the night he'd killed Ray and turned her flooding back. A violent impulse to kill twisted her into knots. As she studied his ruthless silver eyes, years of suppressed anger prowled through her blood and caused her temper to go from simmer to inferno in record time.

She should be afraid, she knew, as he was bigger and stronger, and had taken out more powerful wolves than her. But before she could even consider the wisdom of her actions, and all the while ignoring the alarm bells jangling in the back of her brain, she bolted from her leafy cover. She ran long and hard until she closed the distance between them. When she reached Vall, she went up on her haunches and exposed her fangs in challenge, rage unfurling inside her.

Undaunted, Vall casually lifted his head from the deer, not at all surprised to see her. In fact, he seemed to be anticipating her company.

Had he been the one watching her?

Crimson blood dripped from his muzzle and roused the hunger inside her. Instead of retaliating, he offered her a lecherous smirk and gestured with a nod. "Sunray. Please. Come join me."

Her mind whirled, need and hunger consuming the beast inside her and driving her to distraction.

Focus, Sunray. Focus.

Tantalized by the inviting sight on the ground before her, she forced herself to concentrate on her anger and not on the thick, warm plasma beckoning her ravenous wolf, luring her to give in to impulse and take Vall up on his offer.

Her gaze flew to his face, rage welling up inside her. "How?" As the scent of metallic blood toyed with her wolf, she moistened her lips and made the mistake of sparing the lifeless carcass a quick glance.

In that split second that she'd dared to take her eyes from Vall, he pounced, promptly trapping her belly-up between the earth and his lean, powerful body. Frantic, she yelped and strained, refusing to submit herself to him in any way, shape, or form.

When he put his mouth near hers and inhaled, a look of

ecstasy flitted across his face. He was close enough for their breaths to mingle, for her to understand her fate.

A loud wail rose from her throat, and she cursed herself for that moment of weakness. She knew better than to allow herself to be distracted. She shook her head, gathered her wits, and gave herself a quick lecture. Okay, so she'd made a big mistake, one that could have cost her life, but it was also a lesson learned. Vall was dangerous and unpredictable, and she'd be wise to remember that. And the truth was, if he hadn't taken her by surprise, she would have at least gotten in a few good swipes before he knocked her to the ground. She hadn't spent a fortune on kickboxing and strength-training classes for nothing.

"How is it possible that you're alive?" she questioned, and bared her teeth. "I watched the silver pump through your veins."

As he flattened himself along her length, the sweet scent of blood wafted before her snout and she fought down the urge to lick the crimson droplets from his muzzle.

"Come on, Sunray. Is it really so hard to figure out?" His gaze drilled into hers, the message clear in his eyes.

"Harmony?"

"Yeah, Harmony," he confirmed.

Oh, God, why? Why would Harmony revive him? What the hell was going on in Serene? As she conjured an image of a town in chaos, her insides clenched. Just as soon as she figured out a way to free herself, she vowed to find out what was going on in her beloved town. Her pack all still lived behind that security gate, and she owed it to every wolf to protect them from the likes of Vall. But with the insidious look in his eyes as he climbed over her, she feared she wasn't going to be alive long enough to follow up on her concerns. Sunray struggled, her mind crafting an escape and strategizing her next move as she swiped her claws at his eyes.

Vall dodged her attack, and with a speed that impressed her, he clamped his jaw over her throat and pinned her down, a dominant hold that prohibited her from moving. She understood then that removing herself from his deadly clutches was going to be a lot harder than she'd anticipated.

She pawed at him but barely left a scratch as she connected with his snout. In that instant, she suspected it was time to change tactics.

Vall's tone was low, husky, and aroused when he inched back and snarled, "Still feisty, I see."

She began panting, panic setting in. "Come on, Vall," she cooed, in her best seductive voice. "Let's run together first. I know how much you love to run with me."

Astute wolf that he was, he laughed at her antics, aware of her attempt to lure him with charm. Her blood ran cold when she felt his erection pressing insistently against her stomach. She squirmed, desperate to get out from beneath him, but her efforts proved futile.

He growled softly and pushed against her, stroking his hard cock against her body. "It's going to give me pleasure to break you, Sunray."

She scoffed, and with much more bravado than she felt, she shot back, "Sure, you've taken me before, Vall. You're bigger and stronger. But you'll never get me to *willingly* submit to you. You haven't been able to do it in the last hundred years; what makes you think you can do it now?"

"Soon, Sunray. Soon. With the right motivation, you won't have a choice." He purposely pressed his paws into her chest, and breathing became most difficult. She sucked in air but couldn't seem to inflate her lungs. Vall lifted his head and howled, a triumphant bark.

What the hell was he up to?

She decided to humor him in a quest for information. "And just how do you plan on motivating me or narrowing my choices?"

His grin was wry, sinister, and Sunray didn't like the devious look in his eyes. Not one little bit.

"As long as I'm alive, I'm still your alpha," he supplied, hedging a direct answer as his fangs closed over her throat again.

"You're wrong. Cairan is now my alpha. He took over as lycan leader after you were terminated."

Vall laughed. "Cairan is dead, my little pet. I challenged him for leadership, and after I made short work of him, I resumed my rightful place as alpha. And soon, my little cub, you'll *willingly* submit yourself to me. And you'll come back to Serene to reign with me."

"Why me?" she whined, as his teeth threatened to tear through her skin. It was a question that had been plaguing her for the last century. Why couldn't he just let her go? Why did he insist she submit to him? Plenty of other women wanted him, willingly bowed at his feet, in fact.

Ignoring her, he softened his grip and began to nuzzle her face. His soft growl rippled on the air, and overhead a flock of birds took flight. Unease crept through her. Was it Vall's howl that startled them, or was it something else entirely?

His tongue snaked out and licked her mouth. Disgust roiled inside her and her heart thumped.

"Why do you always want to do this the hard way, my little cub? Just relax and give yourself to me. You know you want it. I can smell it on you."

No longer in the mood to humor him, and pushing down any fears she had, she retaliated, "What you smell is my disgust. I told you before: I'll never willingly give myself to you."

That outburst earned her a scowl. Vall growled deep in his throat and nipped at her with his razor-sharp canines, letting her know her disobedience wouldn't go unpunished.

His nails dug into her flesh and he leered at her body, all the while flashing his teeth. "I'm only here for you, Sunray, to offer my love and protection. And this is how you treat your alpha," he barked out.

Too far gone to back down now, she ignored the pain in her chest and added, "The only things you love are power and control."

His muscles tensed; then he drew his paw back and slashed her face with his claws. Sunray winced and turned, her heart racing madly, but she refused to soften her words, instead willing to accept the punishment that came with them. She met his arctic eyes straight on.

"It just pisses you off that you can't control me. You're like any other male, Vall," she spit out. "You simply want what you can't have."

He settled between her legs and pushed his cock harder against her, his eyes flashing wildly, his voice soft, threatening. "I can have you if I want you."

The whisper of a gun cocking with the grinding of metal against metal gained her full attention. Vall must have heard the ping of the chamber at the exact same moment. His ears perked up a millisecond before gunfire sliced through the air. Vall slid off her, severing the lecherous connection. As he sank to the ground, the bullet skimmed his fur before neatly embedding itself in a nearby tree.

With her hackles rising, Sunray gained purchase and flipped over. She sniffed the air, pulled in the acrid scent of silver and sulfur, and scanned the area in an attempt to pinpoint the exact location of the hunter. Jesus Christ, she'd been so caught up in her fight with Vall that her addled brain hadn't given any attention to her surroundings or to the danger lurking nearby. She should have paid heed when that flock of birds took flight. That, and clearly she should have positioned herself downwind.

With predatory precision, a man stepped into the clearing. Worldly, venomous brown eyes met hers. Like any good hunter, he moved with purpose and quickly narrowed in on his target.

Confident and commanding, he once again lifted his weapon and took aim. In the span of a heartbeat, Sunray found herself facing the barrel of a .40-caliber Glock. Her legs froze, paralyzed, beneath her, and her teeth peeled back as she stared him down while he balanced the gun on his arm and widened his stance. Her stomach lurched as recognition hit.

Oh, God. She knew him immediately from his imposing stance.

Kane.

Chapter Six

Kane grabbed his trusty .40-caliber Glock and headed out into the night, to an access road used by the power company, where surveillance had uncovered the remnants of a lone hunt after the last full moon.

As a senior hunter, Kane worked alone and was often given the more dangerous assignments. Like this one. Wolves usually ran in packs, and were selective when bringing fresh meat to the brethren. A rogue lycan hunting alone, however, could indiscriminately turn whoever it wanted, whenever it wanted, without having to consult with or answer to an alpha. And if Kane's suspicions were correct, and he assumed they were, he was well on his way to terminating the beast responsible for the recent carnage in his city.

A short while later, after parking his truck on the side of the highway, Kane threw his rucksack over his shoulder, pulled his hood up against the cool wind, and maneuvered through the dense forest to position himself downwind. Moving with stealth and precision, he pulled on his night-vision goggles, crouched low, and listened to the sounds around him, working hard to sort through the cacophony of noises and pinpoint those of a lycan: a soft growl, a heavy pant, the thump of paws hitting the frozen ground, or the howl of victory upon a kill.

After remaining motionless for half an hour, all the while cataloging the area, Kane was preparing to move deeper into the woods when off in the distance a low whine rent the air and stilled his movements. He breathed in deeply, catching the distinct, musky scent of wet fur as it tainted the air.

Jackpot.

He adjusted his night-vision goggles and carefully stepped over twigs, brush, and other fallen debris as he followed the low growls.

He advanced with purpose and soon came upon a tumbling cluster of fur and claws. Well, well. So it appeared he'd walked in on a lycan love fest. Perfect. Now he could kill the bastards before they had a chance to procreate and bring another hound of hell into the world. Damned if his night wasn't starting to look up.

He masked his body behind a huge oak tree, and that's when he noticed the clothing in a neat pile. He sank down and drew the clothes to his nose, taking note of the alluring, and oddly familiar, floral scent.

He stuffed the clothes into his rucksack—the wolf certainly wouldn't be needing them after tonight—and turned his attention to the fornicating animals. He pulled off his goggles and watched them for a moment as he considered the best angle. As he studied them, it suddenly hit him that they weren't mating at all. They were fighting. The alpha wolf had the female pinned beneath him in a dominant hold, and the whimpering sounds she was making were from pain, not pleasure.

Interesting.

With the wolves preoccupied, they hadn't sensed the approaching danger. Excited by the prospect of taking out two beasts with one shot, Kane eased himself into the clearing and tried to quiet his thumping heart.

Drawing on his years of intense training and professional experience, he steeled himself, secured the silencer on his gun, took aim, and peeled off an accurate shot. But just as the pin fired, the clicking sound caught the attention of the two lycans. The bigger one, the alpha with the dark fur and beefy paws, moved milliseconds before the bullet hit its mark. The smaller one, the female with the golden fur, gave a startled yelp, flipped over, and stared Kane down in challenge. Kane gave a silent curse as his precious silver embedded itself into a nearby tree.

With its hackles rising, the female wolf watched him as the alpha crept up beside her and analyzed the danger. Reacting to the threat before her, her mouth peeled back to reveal deadly fangs, and she crouched low, like she was ready to sprint toward him.

Hands steady and heart calm, Kane readjusted his stance

and prepared for the animal's counterattack. With nice, slow movements, he lifted his gun again and took aim. He sure as hell had no intention of missing the beast this time. Once he had his gun locked on his target, his finger prepared to squeeze the trigger. An instant before he sent the silver zinging from his pistol, the animal twitched, put its paws forward, and lowered its head in a submissive move that felt far too familiar to him and sparked something in his gut.

What the hell?

The big bad alpha wolf crawled on its belly until it was out of target range and then bolted into the woods. Kane flicked a quick look over his shoulder and could only assume it was circling, coming at him from behind. Which meant he had to work fast, kill this fertile female and reposition himself before the predator became the prey.

The glow from the moonlight lit on the lycan's smooth, well-kept pelt. As he readjusted the pistol in his hand, he took in the animal's submissive stance and the wealth of wild, golden fur on her streamlined body.

She had fur the color of a wheat field—the color of Sunray's hair.

The animal lifted its eyes to meet his and cocked its head to the side. Was it a ploy to communicate with him, to send some sort of silent message? Kane surveyed the animal and took in the lost-puppy look that reminded him of a scared and damaged stray. She looked frightened, not ferocious. Kane sucked in a tight breath as memories of Sunray came flooding back.

Jesus Christ, it couldn't be. It just couldn't be.

Could it?

He took a long moment to study the animal's stance and body language, and couldn't deny that there was something about those eyes and the way they stared straight at him that did the weirdest things to his insides.

A knot formed in his gut and blood rushed through his veins so fast it clouded his judgment, distracting him from what he was here to do. With his resolve evaporating like smoke from a barrel, his head began spinning and he held the gun tight, until his knuckles turned bone white. Tension hung thick in the air as Kane stood his ground in the distance, jaw clenched, barely able to draw in a breath as he counseled himself to pull the fucking trigger.

All lycans are heartless monsters.

As he continued to repeat his mantra, he momentarily blinked his eyes and every instinct he possessed screamed at him to react, prompting him to end this, and end it now.

With those words exploding inside his head, their gazes clashed and his chest rose and fell on a ragged breath. A nervous sensation gathered in the pit of his gut.

Jesus Christ, this is insane. Just shoot already.

Kane gave himself a mental shake and pushed down his apprehension, his indecision. Working hard to ignore the way his hands began to shake—and, goddammit, his hands never shook—he squeezed his index finger and discharged the gun, putting an end to her torment. Hot deadly silver rocketed from the chamber, and the sound fractured the silence, leaving behind the acrid smell of sulfur, a satisfying scent to Kane's nose, and a deadly one to a lycan's.

With his arms still extended and his heart hammering, he stood immobile and examined his target. The wind whipped at her fur, and as the silver closed the distance between them, a small, strangled sound rose up from the depths of her throat. With her belly flat on the ground and her paws splayed forward, she let out a long breath and shuddered, her big pewter eyes still staring up at him.

Chapter Seven

He'd missed!

Oh, God, he'd missed.

By some small miracle, the silver had zinged past her head, and with a soft thump embedded itself into a distant maple tree. Incredulous, Sunray remained motionless, staring up at him. How the hell he'd missed her was anyone's guess. After all, Kane was a seasoned hunter, and seasoned hunters never miss a direct target.

Unless he'd missed on purpose . . .

Sunray worked to get the blood flowing back into her numb extremities, and decided she wasn't about to hang around in a quest for those answers. Earlier that day, she might have openly welcomed the silver and accepted her fate, because maybe, just maybe, she'd find the peace she was seeking in the afterworld.

Heck, who was she kidding? She was a damned dog—

damned if she did, and damned if she didn't. Nevertheless, now, after finding out Vall was alive, she had a new purpose. She had a family, a pack, to protect.

But could she sneak back to Serene to observe the goings-on from outside the protective gate with Kane tight on her tail? The last thing she wanted to do was lead a hunter to her family.

She remained still, bracing herself, and tried to gather her wits, along with the ability to run, as she watched Kane watching her—a silent exchange. His guarded gaze bore into hers, but there was something in the stormy depths of his chocolate eyes that called out to her, something so dark and troubled it made her tremble. In that instant, as their eyes held and locked, she instinctively knew she could never control her emotions where he was concerned. Loving him felt right, in her heart and in her head, and she'd just have to find a way somehow to deal with the reality that he could never be hers again.

A breeze blew around her, and a flash of Vall in the distance jolted her out of her reverie and snapped her into motion. Never taking her eyes off Kane, she inhaled a rejuvenating breath, cautiously climbed to her feet, gave a swish of her long golden tail, and bolted into the thick forest. Using the dense cover of the foliage to camouflage her body, she ran long and hard until she was miles and miles away from her clothes, her car, and the man she loved, a man who'd just spared her life—for reasons she couldn't begin to understand.

What would have compelled him to miss the shot? Had he recognized her as the woman from Risqué? Surely to God, that still wouldn't have been enough to stop him from shooting. Was it possible that he knew who she *really* was? That since he'd been with her physically, it had somehow awakened memories and touched him emotionally, and he'd been able to figure out that she was his lover from another lifetime?

She dodged in and out of towering trees while her mind raced. A few low-slung branches hooked her fur, burrowing deep and slicing into her flesh like cold bloodthirsty claws, but she didn't dare slow down, for fear that he would change his mind and come after her. That, and she also needed to shake Vall, and hinder his remarkable ability to follow her scent.

Sunray ran until she couldn't run anymore. Many hours later, she finally came to a grinding halt. Breathless and completely spent, she dropped down onto her belly, licked her dry mouth, and closed her eyes in distress. When she opened them again, she glanced up at the full moon and gave a low howl of frustration, strategizing her next course of action.

As much as she wanted to curl up and root herself for the remainder of the night, she knew she couldn't stay hidden among the dense bush and wait until sunrise to embark on her mission. If she came crawling out of the woods, stark naked, in the light of the day, any passerby would call the authorities. Then what? She couldn't even begin to guess what would happen to her, especially since the PTF had stumbled upon her hunting grounds.

No, she needed to pull herself together and get her ass back to her clothes and her car. Both Kane and Vall should be long gone by now. The sun would soon be up, and they'd both have sought shelter. Deciding to take a chance, she gave a quick glance around and coaxed herself to move.

Branches snapped and echoed in the cold, dark night as she lifted herself from the frozen ground and began backtracking, carefully scanning the area and using her heightened senses to identify anything out of the ordinary.

A long time later, she came across the spot where she'd neatly placed her clothes, only to find them missing. Her heart lurched. Had Kane taken them? Had Vall?

Forgetting about her clothing for the time being, she ran to her car and hunkered down next to the front end, where she impatiently waited for dawn. Senses on alert, she brought her paw to her mouth and groomed her fur, counting off the minutes as they slowly ticked by. Her stomach rumbled, a reminder that she hadn't sated the hunger inside her. But come morning, the cravings would subside until next time. Yes, feeding drove a wolf's primal behavior, but it wasn't necessary for survival by any means.

Finally, in the far distance a pretty pink hue touched the sky, putting the full moon to bed for another month. But as soon as that bright silver orb disappeared and the sun made its ritual ascent, Sunray knew the cycle had already begun again. In a mere thirty days, she'd have no choice but to give in to her primal urges, transform, and hunt.

Sunray took a moment to compose herself and mentally prepared for the shift. For some reason, turning back to her human form never hurt quite as much. She went back on her haunches, held her breath, and envisioned herself as a woman. A moment later, she morphed back. She stood and stretched out her fatigued limbs. After finger-combing her long locks from her face, she pulled the branches from the roof of her vehicle. The cool air rushed over her naked flesh and brought on a shiver as she reached under the wheel well to retrieve her keys, pleased that she hadn't left them in her jeans. Working quickly before hypothermia set in, she went straight for the trunk, to where she always kept a spare change of clothes.

She pulled on a clean pair of jeans, a sweater, and sneakers, then climbed into the driver's seat. Blasting the hot air, she put her car into gear. With so much to consider, she frowned in concentration and pulled out onto the quiet highway. As her mind raced with the recent turn of events and she struggled to plan her next move, a yawn pulled at her, demanding she shut her body down and rest. Not a bad idea. After nourishment and sleep, maybe she'd be better able to concentrate.

A short while later, she pulled into her assigned parking spot outside her downtown condo, where warm rays of sun were just beginning to spread their far-reaching fingers over her home. It was still quite early, which meant that the residents of her complex were all likely asleep at this ungodly hour. Asleep or not, Sunray wasn't about to take a chance on stumbling upon a neighbor. She grabbed her dark shades and pushed them on, covering her silver eyes. The squeak of her car door as she opened it reminded her to oil the hinges. She pushed on it gently and cringed, not wanting to rouse her neighbors.

The frigid morning air hit her hard and turned her breath to fog. A shiver raced through her, urging her to move quickly. Gripping her keys, she wrapped her arms around herself to keep warm and made a mental note to keep a spare coat in her trunk. Hurried steps carried her to her front door, but a movement at the side of her building gained her attention.

She tensed, half expecting to see Vall lurking nearby, but she knew that like hers, his body would need rest. But where would he be resting? In Serene? If so, how was he sneaking past the security gate? That thought made her worry about Drake, Serene's new panther guide and chief of security, and his ability to command his species and oversee the town's security.

She gave a heavy sigh and thought more about Vall. Where and when he would strike next was almost impossible to predict. Sunray would have to stay on extra alert and keep her senses finely tuned at all times. Not that she didn't already, but still . . .

Turning slowly, she let out a breath of relief when she spotted her young neighbor Tanya MacPherson walking her new toy poodle. Goodness, that little pup looked like a fluffy white snowball, and wasn't much bigger.

Sunray pitched her voice low. "Tanya, what are you doing out so early?"

Tanya pulled out her earbuds and turned off her iPod as her heavy-lidded eyes met Sunray's. With a wave of her gloved hand, she gestured toward her new puppy as it yipped at Sunray's feet. Then Tanya narrowed her tired eyes and took in Sunray's attire, or lack thereof.

She pursed her lips knowingly. "I suppose I could ask you the same question. Or better yet, maybe I should be asking why you're out so *late*, and so underdressed," she teased.

Sunray resisted the urge to roll her eyes. Instead she forced a chuckle and made light of the situation. Honestly, seventeen-year-old girls were far worldlier today than they were decades ago. Compliments of the Internet, she supposed.

"Working late," she said, not wanting this beautiful teenage girl to get the wrong idea about her. Plus, Tanya sort of looked up to her, always asking her about makeup and boys, and Sunray didn't want to set a bad example. "And I was so tired when I left the building, I forgot my coat. Then I didn't want to hike back up twenty flights of stairs to get it." She was rambling, she knew, but heck, cut her some slack—she'd had one hell of a night.

"Uh-huh," Tanya said dubiously.

Sunray scanned the area, then turned the conversation back to her. "You shouldn't be out alone."

Tanya crinkled her nose, an indication that she knew exactly what Sunray was talking about. "I know, but Molly really needed to go. If she goes on mom's floor again"—she paused to swipe her finger across her throat—"I'm toast."

Sunray gave Tanya a once-over and kept her distance from Molly, who really didn't like her. Most dogs didn't. Tanya was a sweet young thing with a killer body, and not much younger than Sunray was when Vall had turned her. She fit all the requirements for Vall and was a prime target, which reinforced Sunray's belief that Tanya shouldn't be venturing out alone.

Brow furrowed to show the seriousness of the situation, Sunray pressed, "Still, I don't want you wandering around outside by yourself. And keep those buds out of your ears. Anyone could sneak up on you and you'd never know. Come and get me next time, okay? Or lay down some newspapers for Molly until other tenants are milling about."

Tanya nodded, and Sunray walked her to her front door before making her way back to her place. She slipped her key into the lock and pushed open her door. The second she stepped inside her warm condo, the phone rang and she immediately stiffened, startled by the intruding sound, even though she'd been fully expecting the early-morning call. Not a "morning after" went by without one.

She grabbed the receiver and pressed the phone to her ear, aware of who it was on the other end of the line. Sunray dropped into a comfortable chair, cleared her throat, and worked to sound casual. "I'm home."

"Glad to hear it," Jaclyn responded.

"Safe and sound," she added.

"Good. Now that we have that out of the way, there are other things we need to talk about."

God, it was shockingly good to hear her friend's voice, and the normalcy of their conversation helped ease the tension from her body, making her feel human again. Well, as human as she could possibly feel.

"Such as?" Sunray asked.

"Such as Kane." The hope and excitement in her friend's

voice gave her a moment of pause, and in that instant she knew what she had to do. "Have you found Kane?" she asked eagerly.

Something in Sunray's voice hitched when she said, "No." Christ, she'd never lied to her friend before, and was shocked at the amount of guilt that gnawed at her in doing so now. But she didn't want to talk about Kane. Not only was it too painful; she didn't want to drag Jaclyn and Slyck into her mess. The less they knew, the safer they'd be. Whatever Vall was up to had something to do with her, which made her feel responsible for his actions. This was her fight, not Jaclyn's and definitely not Slyck's. They'd found their freedom and were just now settling into a wonderful life together. And she refused to drag them into this crisis, no matter how much they'd want to fight at her side. But Slyck had only one of his nine lives left to live, and there was no way she'd let him gamble with it, or take a chance on Vall snuffing it out once and for all.

Sunray squared her shoulders and a new calmness settled over her. As her mind cleared, she knew what she had to do. Take Vall out herself. She had the gun. And she had the silver bullets. Plus, she knew how Vall worked, hunted, and played. Maybe he was still stronger than she, but she'd simply amp up her training and avoid another sneak attack like the one in the woods last night. Next time she'd be prepared for him—gun in hand.

"Hey, are you still there?" Jaclyn asked, concern evident in her tone.

Sunray leaned forward, planted her elbow on her knee, and rested her forehead in her palm. "I'm fine. Just tired."

"Sunray, are you okay?"

"Peachy. So, are you back in town?" Sunray expertly redirected the conversation, and even though she suspected Jaclyn knew exactly what she was doing, she was thankful her friend didn't press.

"Just got in last night."

"How was Florida?

"Hot."

"Speaking of hot, I decided to go to the conference in Los Angeles next week."

"Really? You were so adamant about not going before."

Sunray could just picture the frown on Jaclyn's face, the worry lines crinkling her brow, and she really didn't want her friend to fret. Addressing her unspoken concerns, she went on to explain, "They're doing a whole session on guerrilla marketing, and I think it really would be beneficial to the company if I sat in on it."

A short pause, and then, "Are you sure there isn't something on your mind, Sunray?"

Sunray heard the rustle of sheets and Slyck mumbling something in the background. "Say hey to Slyck for me."

She listened to Jaclyn give Slyck her message; then Slyck muttered something about shutting the hell up so he could go back to sleep.

"He says hey right back."

Sunray let out a bark of laughter and shook her head. So it appeared that Slyck was settling into marriage quite nicely and had become a lazy cat on the weekends. Even though Sunray was a bit envious of the two, she knew they deserved a happily-ever-after. And Slyck deserved every bit of happiness Jaclyn brought his way, especially after acting as Panther Overseer in Serene for the last four hundred years, alone and unmated.

"I'd better get some sleep, and it sounds like Slyck needs his too. I'll call you when I get back."

She heard Jaclyn purr. "Slyck can forget about going back to sleep. I have other plans for him."

Sunray chuckled. "Have fun. I'll let you get at it, then."

"Take care, Sunray."

That said, Sunray hung up, took a much-needed shower to wash the forest from her skin, and practically crawled into her bedroom. Exhaustion pulled hard at her, and she drew the blinds. It occurred to her that she couldn't stay in her condo for long, not with the chance that Kane was aware of her identity—and she was pretty certain he was. He might have let her go once, but he could change his mind anytime about letting her live and could easily track her to her complex. She couldn't let that happen. What if one of the tenants got caught in the cross fire? She knew she would eventually have to deal with the situation, but that could wait until she'd taken out the rogue wolf—unless Kane found him first.

Kane . . .

She set the clock, climbed into bed, and closed her eyes. As she drifted off to sleep, she allowed herself a moment of remembrance, reliving their night down at the club. She moved restlessly against her mattress and recalled the look in Kane's eyes when he'd made love to her. It was the same look he'd given her tonight in the woods.

Which brought her back to the question, Did he know who she *really* was? Did he know she was his lover from another lifetime?

After only a few hours' sleep, Kane pulled himself out of his bed, took a quick shower, and made his way into the precinct to find some answers. Being nocturnal, a night hunter, rising at the crack of dawn didn't bring out the pleasant side of him. Not that he had a whole lot of pleasant in him anyway, but he was damn anxious to get on his computer and get into the secure database to do a little research on Sunray Matthews.

He swung his truck into the underground parking garage and reached beside him to grab the rucksack with Sunray's clothes still in it. He tossed it over his shoulder, climbed from the driver's seat, and darted a glance around the near-empty garage. He drew a breath, and the remnants of oil and exhaust still lingering in the air assaulted his keen senses.

He moved quickly, his military-issue boots slapping against the ground, cutting through the silence, and echoing off the walls as he darted across the wide expanse of concrete floor. After swiping his identification card through the computerized lock, he made his way up the back stairwell.

He stepped up to the security desk and greeted the guard

sitting behind it. "Morning, Neil," he said, taking in the fatigued look on the man's face.

"Kane," Neil said, and handed him a clipboard to sign. "You're up early."

"No rest for the weary," Kane announced. As he signed in, they exchanged a few more pleasantries, small talk about the weather and Neil's hot date last night, which accounted for the tired eyes that stared back at Kane. Kane was pretty certain he mirrored that run-down look himself.

Neil pressed the security button beneath the desk, granting Kane access to the secret underground quarters, a private area available only to those with the highest security clearance.

As Kane hastily moved down the long, narrow corridor to his office, the delightful smell of freshly brewed coffee wafted before his nose and he wondered who was in the office this early. Most officers would be home, sleeping the day away, having reported the time and location of their kills before hitting the mattress.

With the aroma of coffee pulling hard at him, and his addled brain in dire need of caffeine, he walked into the brightly lit kitchen and squinted as the overhead fluorescent light glared down on him. He surveyed the room upon entering, a habitual response.

"Morning." He gestured with a nod to his fellow officers, cousins Jaret and Toby Darkland—both empaths—who were sitting at the table, tallying their kills.

Pompous assholes.

Both men had recently transferred in from the western branch to help with the sudden influx of lycans. But there was something about the two of them that rubbed Kane the wrong way. They were great hunters, and both were calculating, coldhearted, and decisive—which was more than Kane could say for himself last night—but there was something troubling about them. Perhaps it was the self-righteous sneers they always wore, walking around the office like a couple of young punks who thought they were better, and knew more, than the precinct's seasoned hunters.

Jaret smirked. "Well, well, what's got you up so early, old man? Piss the bed or something?"

"Yeah, something like that," Kane shot back and went straight for the coffee, trying his best to avoid a confrontation. He was just too damn tired for it.

Toby stood, empty coffee cup in hand, and in a few short strides he closed the distance between himself and Kane. He slapped Kane on the back, his brow furrowed in genuine concern. But Kane was no fool. He understood that look; it was one that questioned Kane's age and abilities.

"How'd you make out last night, Kane? Did you get your target?"

Kane reached for a clean mug and took a moment to weigh his words carefully, all the while working to block his mind to their probing. It wasn't like him to miss a target, and these two empaths knew it. The last thing he wanted to do was raise their suspicions.

"Grazed him," he muttered, owing them no further explanation. If there was one thing that Kane understood, it was that this alpha wasn't any ordinary wolf. He was smart, stealthy, and old, which made him all the more dangerous. It would take careful consideration and planning to take him down. If Captain Cavanaugh asked, he'd willingly explain the circumstances. But these two clowns? Forget about it. As far as he was concerned, they were on a need-to-know basis.

Out of his peripheral vision, Kane watched Jaret's head jerk back with a start.

"Grazed him, huh?" Jaret questioned, his lip curling in aversion and sparking Kane's temper.

"That's what I said." Kane cocked his head and stared at Jaret—a tactical showdown. The tension grew and would have been palpable to anyone within fifty yards. Kane narrowed his eyes and studied the brawny man seated before him. "What is it that you didn't understand?" he asked quietly, and stretched his words out. "Did you need me to talk slower, using shorter sentences?"

Okay, so maybe he wasn't so tired, after all.

Having said that, Kane refocused his thoughts and completely blocked his emotions and the images of Sunray from his mind, as he waited for Jaret to react. Dammit, he could almost feel his comrade probing around inside his brain, sifting through all his dirty little secrets. He shivered to think what they'd find in the dark corners of his mind. Fuck, if they ever got an inkling of Sunray or that Kane had spared her life, they were both as good as dead.

As Toby leaned against the counter and refilled his coffee cup, Jaret stood and folded his arms across his barrel chest, a challenging gleam in his dark, shrewd eyes.

"So maybe the captain didn't send the right guy for the job after all." He scoffed. "I suspected as much."

And maybe you should fuck off.

Jaret smirked and casually scraped a hand over the gun holstered to his side. "You got something on your mind, Kane? Something you'd like to say? Or are you too much of a chicken-shit to say it?"

Knowing it was not the time or place for this, and he had more important demons to fight at the moment, Kane lifted his coffee cup in salute—a friendly fuck-off—and met Jaret's gaze straight on. "Just getting my coffee, Jaret."

Heck, those two might be the empaths, but Kane could feel the fury bubbling up inside them, and couldn't deny that he found it oddly entertaining.

With that, Kane exited the kitchen and made his way to his back office, feeling far more satisfied with the encounter than he should have—it was juvenile of him. Once inside, he locked his office door, shed his coat, and dropped down into his chair. He took a swig of coffee, pulled Sunray's clothes from the bag, and inhaled her floral scent. His mind revisited his time with her at the club, and he immediately hardened. *Jesus.*

Marshaling his lust, he refocused, striving to get his mind off his libido and back onto the case. As he booted up his computer, he glanced at his closed door, half expecting his captain to come barreling through it at any moment, certain those two assholes would run and report their confrontation. If there was one thing Cavanaugh didn't tolerate, it was in-house fighting. They were all supposed to have each other's backs. Unless one of them got bitten, of course. Then it was game over.

As the minutes ticked by, Kane focused on his computer screen and blocked his mind to everything and anything but the information in the database. The satisfaction he'd felt earlier was short-lived as he pored over years' worth of files, going as far back as a century ago, but was still unable to come up with anything on a Sunray Matthews. The only information he had was a current address, and that she'd been living there for six months. Where had she been all this time?

He did, however, come up with a Sunni Matthews. Thanks to exemplary record keeping over the years, he was able to read the fine details of her case.

One hundred years ago, in October, on Chicago's south side, Sunni Matthews had been reported missing by her mother. That exact same night, her boyfriend had been murdered—killed by a rabid dog. But Kane knew it was no rabid dog; it was the work of the alpha ruling Kane's city.

Like a gang, each territory had its own alpha that ruled inside their boundaries, but this particular alpha wolf was smarter than most. Not only was he stealthy and lethal, but despite their efforts, the PTF had been unable to identify and kill him. Over the last century, said wolf would show up on occasion, leave his mark, and disappear without a trace. But something in Kane's gut told him he'd encountered that wolf last night in the woods.

As Kane read on, his heart began to race and his stomach tightened. The murder/abduction felt familiar in far too many ways. An uneasy feeling closed in on him. He tapped his pen against his desk as nausea welled up inside him. He drew a deep breath and let it out slowly. He blinked his tired eyes back into focus and read the entire case a second, and even a third, time, solidifying every single detail in his memory.

Kane leaned back in his chair and shook his head, his mind sorting through the barrage of information. So, it appeared that not only had the crime taken place in an old abandoned building near the train tracks, not at all unlike the one from his dreams. And the boy Sunni had been with, the one who'd been killed, was none other than Ray Bartlett.

Ray . . .

Jesus Christ!

Kane jumped from his chair and grabbed his parka and rucksack. As he bolted out the door, he knew it was time to talk to Sunray face-to-face, to hear the answers directly from her mouth. And hell, once he was done, ridding the Earth of another bloodthirsty, fertile lycan sounded just about right.

Chapter Eight

Sunray's alarm went off at six o'clock, and as day gave way to night, she stretched out her fatigued muscles and rolled over in bed to glance out her window. Snowflakes fell from the darkening sky and blanketed the ground in a soft bed of white; not great for covering her tracks, she decided.

With her emotions still a tangled mess, she glanced at her phone. She longed to call a member of her brethren in Serene, to find out what kind of chaotic state Vall had put the town in, but she knew she couldn't, not without the threat of security tracing the call and coming after her.

As a feeling of loneliness enveloped her, she climbed from her bed, grabbed her suitcase, and haphazardly threw clothes into it. She made her way to her bathroom to grab a few toiletries, and the ghostly image staring back at her in the mirror took her by surprise. Her hair was in total disarray, fine lines crinkled the corners of her bloodshot eyes, and her skin looked red and raw, like that of a sailor who'd just weathered a fierce storm.

With little time to spare, and knowing every moment would count in her hunt for Vall, she took a second to smooth down her hair, and run a cloth over her face and a toothbrush over her teeth. Feeling slightly more human, she grabbed the rest of her supplies, padded back to her bedroom, and tossed them on top of her clothes.

With her hands planted on her hips, she stood back and cataloged her suitcase. She took stock, mentally ticking off the items that she'd need for the next week or so. Of course, there was one thing still missing from the case. She reached under her mattress and grabbed her pistol, which was already loaded with silver bullets.

As she tossed that onto the heap, her stomach rumbled, but she didn't want to waste time preparing food. Instead she would grab takeout, or, better yet, call room service from the hotel, once she settled herself into one.

When she was satisfied she had everything she needed, she dressed in dark clothes and a dark jacket, opened her front door, and descended the stairs. With her suitcase in hand, she peered into the night and tasted the air for danger.

Under the cover of darkness, she made her way to her car, but her forward momentum stilled when she sensed a movement in the shadows. A quick flash of anxiety rushed through her. She sucked in a fueling breath and crept to the side of her house. She peeked around the corner, and it was then that a set of piercing pewter eyes met hers.

Oh, hell!

Heart racing in a mad cadence, her senses went on full alert as she looked at the powerful wolf positioned a mere six feet away, his lips peeled back to threaten her with sharp fangs.

Sunray's fingers tightened around her suitcase, while a shiver of fear raced down her spine. She darted a glance around, her gaze going from Vall's to the young girl and puppy he held hostage between his massive body and the condo's exterior wall. She could hear Tanya's blood racing over the music coming from her iPod earbuds, and smelled her fear as it saturated the air. Sunray's mind raced. If only she'd had her gun in hand and not in her suitcase, then she could have ended this once and for all. There was no way she could get the gun now. If she reached for it, it would raise Vall's suspicions, and then she had no idea how he would respond to the threat. She couldn't take a chance on him tearing into Tanya. She had to think of something else. Some other way to distract him and free his captive, because she'd be damned if she'd let him hurt her.

Tanya squirmed and Sunray held one hand up, palm facing out. "Easy, Tanya." Molly let out a little yelp, and the sound gained Vall's attention. In a threatening move, Vall turned back to Tanya and inched closer, pushing his muzzle between her legs to draw in a deep breath. He gave a low growl and lapped at her through her pants. Tanya shivered when Vall's tongue made contact with her jeans.

Her body trembling uncontrollably, Tanya's frightened, watery eyes met Sunray's, tears spilling out of the corners and staining her cheeks. Molly whimpered in her arms, and Tanya proceeded to carefully tuck her inside her coat for safekeeping. But Sunray knew nothing or no one was safe from the likes of this wolf.

Tanya pressed herself against the wall and turned away from Vall, her eyes blinking rapidly. "Sunray, please . . ." she whimpered in a breathless tone.

At the sound of her soft sobs, rage welled up inside Sunray, ripping through her like a raging forest fire. That burst of anger was so fierce and so powerful it shocked even her. As she took in the horrific scene before her, it occurred to her that this was likely how Vall had planned on convincing her to willingly submit to him. By hurting those she cared about. Not fucking likely.

Using slow, easy movements, Sunray put her suitcase on the ground, took a measured step forward, and widened her stance. Eyes locked in concentration, she spoke quietly. "Let her go."

The wolf smirked, his grin reckless. Ignoring Sunray, he extended a paw and stroked the girl's damp cheek, as if reveling in her fear. When his claws connected with her face, her small dog yelped, stuck its head out of Tanya's jacket, and nipped at his hand. Vall let out a roar and drew back his paw, preparing to hit Molly, but Sunray's voice stopped him.

"Stop. I'll do whatever you want."

Vall gave a low growl of satisfaction as his pewter eyes lit on her. He sat back on his haunches, and Sunray eased herself between his body and Tanya's. "Walk away slowly," she whispered. "I've got this under control. Go inside, lock your door, and wait for me." Just then, the song coming from her earbuds changed, and Justin Timberlake's voice filled the air.

"Sunray . . ." Her voice was shaky and apologetic.

"Just do it," Sunray bit out.

"Should I call—"

"No. We don't want anyone else involved. Trust me, Tanya. I can handle this." Without voicing any further argument, Tanya slipped out from behind her back and, following Sunray's exact orders, slowly backed away. It wasn't until after she heard the click of a door lock that Sunray let out a relieved breath. She turned on Vall.

"What the hell are you doing?"

He sat there staring at her, watching and waiting, and she knew exactly what he was waiting for. She glanced at her suitcase, and the wolf caught the movement. With a swish of his dark tail, he bolted and pounced on her bag, which, with her exceptional speed, gave her time to hastily rip off her clothes, tearing them in the process, and quickly remove her contacts. Without her gun, the only way to take him on was in her primal form.

Vall lifted his head and let out a howl, his eyes trained on her as she morphed. Playing coy, Sunray began circling him, waiting for the opportune moment to strike. She could see the excitement in Vall's eyes, feel the heat in his gaze.

He cocked his head. "Come here, little cub, and bend down before me."

Heart racing, Sunray took a cautious step forward and extended her claws. If she could just catch him off guard . . .

"Move."

The voice came from behind. Sunray spun around and nearly stopped breathing when she spotted Kane standing there, gun pointed at her head, his eyes gleaming dangerously.

Their gazes clashed, and eyes as cold as the ground beneath her swept over her face. "Move," he repeated.

She angled her head to the side and whimpered, communicating with him the only way she knew how.

"I can't kill him if you're in the way."

Kane took aim but couldn't pull the trigger with Sunray's body blocking his target. "Drop," he yelled out.

In the time it took her to comprehend and drop to the ground, the alpha had taken off, a swish of black in an even blacker night. Paw prints in the snow gave away his location and identified his exact escape route. Kane could give chase, but he wasn't taking a chance on this one getting away. He had a million questions, and she was the only one holding the answers.

He glanced at the suitcase and then back at her. Bending slowly, he unzipped it and scanned the contents. He picked up the gun and unloaded the bullets. Silver. Interesting.

Just what the hell was going on between Sunray and her alpha? What had he done to make her want to flee town? To kill him? This was the second time he'd caught them in a standoff. He knew that wolves were pack animals who readily bowed to their alpha, and in turn he offered them love and protection.

"Shift," he demanded.

He stuffed her gun into his pocket and hovered closer. Snowflakes fell over his body and danced along her fur as he watched her morph back to her female form. Once complete, she carefully stood still, then shook out her long locks. Her fresh floral scent curled around him, and despite himself, he groaned.

She nodded to the gun. "Do you want to get that out of my face?"

Kane scoffed, but didn't lower the pistol. Instead he let his glance flicker over her body, taking a long moment to gaze at her nakedness. As he registered every delicious detail, fire pitched through him and his cock tightened. Jesus, she was beautiful. Her pretty nipples puckered in the cold air, and goose bumps pebbled her smooth, silky flesh, flesh that he'd touched with his mouth and his hands. Flesh that he'd salivated over.

Was *still* salivating over now, goddammit. Disgusted with himself for ogling a lycan, he shook his head.

As though suddenly realizing she was naked, Sunray put an arm over her breasts and a hand between her legs.

Gun trained on her, Kane eased the rucksack off his shoulder and tossed it to her. "I think these will fit."

She arched a brow and waited, but when he didn't move, she asked, "Do you think you could turn around?"

He gave her a wry smile. "We're a little past modesty, don't you think, Sunray? After all, I've been inside you."

She leveled him with a stare. "And here I'd mistaken you for a gentleman."

"You shouldn't mistake me for anything other than what I am."

She pulled her clothes from the bag and arched an inquisitive brow. "And what's that?"

"A hunter." To prove his point, he gave a slight shake of his gun.

He watched her throat work as she swallowed, but despite her apprehension, she squared her shoulders and tilted her chin in defiance. Good for her.

Her body began shivering from the frigid temperature. With the barrel of his gun, he gestured toward her clothes. "Get dressed."

"If you're a hunter, then why did you spare my life?"

"Don't get used to it." He watched her hurry into her clothes. "Just because I did it once doesn't mean I intend to do it again. Especially if you don't give me the answers I'm looking for."

Her hands paused over the button on her jeans, and her head came up with a start. Silver eyes met his. Surprise and something else, something that looked like love, lingered in their torrid depths.

A noise came from deep in his throat and his voice sounded tight when he asked, "So, you know exactly what I'm talking about, then, *Sunni* Matthews?"

Appearing to steel herself, she wet her plump lips, and his gaze settled on her mouth. In that instant, something sparked between them and the air around them changed. She wrapped her arms around herself to ward off the cold.

He picked her coat up off the ground, shook off the snow, and handed it to her. "Put this on."

"Kane . . ." Emotions passed over her eyes and chipped at his hardened exterior. He drew a breath and filled his lungs with her arousing scent, all the while fighting his natural inclination to press his hungry mouth to hers.

What the hell was the matter with him?

As anger segued to passion, he mentally kicked himself. *She's a goddamn werewolf, and werewolves don't feel emotion. They live to feed, kill, and fornicate.*

Scowling, he asked, "Why are you running?"

She gave a heavy sigh and struggled to zip her coat, her fingers too cold to work the teeth properly. "Look, if you're not going to shoot me, put the gun down. Or I'll take it from you, and I don't think you're going to like that."

He clenched his jaw, frustration moving through him. "I should just kill you now."

Zipper forgotten, she planted her hands on her hips. "Then do it. But you'll never find Vall without me."

So the alpha's name was Vall. That was more information than his precinct had secured in a century. But why was she running from him? In that instant, a million other questions went through his head.

"Who are you, Sunni Matthews?"

She studied him. "You really don't know?"

He tapped the tip of his gun to his temple. "Why are you in my head?"

Once again he caught a flash of affection in her eyes—her silver eyes, a reminder that she was a wolf. And he was a hunter. Christ, he really should just fucking kill her.

As though she'd read his thoughts and didn't like where they were going, she redirected the conversation. "If you want to catch Vall, you'll need my help."

His gaze skirted over the spot where the wolves had circled. "From the looks of things, I'd say you need my help."

When her eyes went to her suitcase, Kane stepped close. "Don't even think about it. The only place you're going is with me."

He repositioned the gun in his hand and helped her with her zipper. The hiss of the metal teeth meshing together filled the air. As he pulled it to her neck to keep her warm, she stood there staring up at him. Her eyes were so full of desire and need that it caught him off guard. Goddammit, she somehow had the uncanny ability to crawl past his defenses without even trying. He felt a flash of possessiveness and quickly cleared his throat, rattled by the emotions she brought out in him.

Hardening himself to her, he cupped her elbow and gave a tug. "Let's go."

She didn't even try to struggle as he picked up her suitcase and led her to his truck. "Where are we going?"

He took in her chattering teeth. "Do werewolves drink coffee?"

"Are all hunters assholes?" she shot back.

He shook his head and gifted her with an amused look. He

had to hand it to her: she could hold her own in a verbal spar. Likely in a physical one too.

"I need to check on Tanya first."

"Tanya?"

"Yeah, Vall had her pinned before I intervened, and I want to make sure she's okay."

Uncertain, he stopped and stared at her for a minute. Did she really care about this girl? Weren't all lycans self-serving monsters? Or was this some ploy of hers to escape his clutches?

Pleading eyes met his. "I just need—"

"Make it quick."

She gave him a grateful smile. "Thanks."

When her big pewter orbs blinked up at him, he shook his head and wondered when he'd gone soft.

Kane walked with her to Tanya's door and stood in the shadows as Sunray took a pair of sunglasses from her coat pocket and put them on. When Tanya answered the knock, Sunray went to work on assuring the teen that she was okay and the rabid dog was long gone. She also warned the girl not to venture out alone again. Tanya continued to apologize profusely, but Sunray tried to ease her mind and make light of the situation by saying the incident had given her a chance to put her self-defense classes to work. After a hug and a promise that she'd lay papers out for her puppy next time, Tanya closed the door, and Sunray turned to Kane.

Twenty minutes later, they sat inside Rosie's café, Sunray with a big fruit-filled muffin and a steamy latte. Kane had a coffee, black. She sat across from him, a small round café table separating them, not far enough away to keep their knees from bumping every other minute. A few people milled about, but all in all, the place was pretty quiet, good for conversation.

Without preamble, he pitched his voice low and got right to the point. "Who's Ray?"

She searched his face and bit down on her bottom lip, as though unsure of how much to say. Silence stretched on for a long moment.

"Look, we're not leaving here until you tell me everything, Sunray. So you'd better start. Who's Ray?" he asked again.

Dark lashes shut briefly, and she whispered, "You're Ray."

Taken aback, he jabbed his thumb into his chest. "Me? You think I'm Ray?"

"Yeah. You've been reincarnated."

He almost laughed at the ridiculousness of her statement. "I don't believe in reincarnation," he said flatly, giving her a look that suggested she'd better come up with some other explanation, something less ludicrous.

Her voice rose in challenge and she gave a roll of her slender shoulders. "Why wouldn't you believe it? You believe in werewolves, don't you? Why can't you believe in reincarnation?"

"I've dealt with werewolves. They're concrete. I've never dealt with reincarnation."

"You are now," she said with a quiet certainty. "So you'd better start dealing." She peeled the paper back from her muffin, took a huge bite, then sipped her latte, all the while giving him a moment to deal. As he watched in mute fascination, the froth pooled on the tip of her nose, making her look damn adorable. She tore off the muffin top, popped another large chunk into her mouth, and around a mouthful of food said, "I never thought a guy who hunted supernatural beings would be so closed-minded."

Kane blinked his mind back into focus and gave an impatient sigh. "Maybe you're just using me, toying with me to let you live and help you hunt your alpha," he said, although he had to admit, there was nothing calculating in her tone.

"And maybe I'm telling you the truth. I don't lie, Kane."

"A werewolf with a conscience. How refreshing," he mocked.

"How do you account for the dreams, then?"

His heart thumped, his muscles tensed, and he shot her an accusatory glance. "How do you know about the dreams?"

"Let me guess: They started in late adolescence?"

He leaned forward, his gaze panning her face in search of answers. His teeth clenched and he glared at her, a sober look that told her he meant business.

"How do you know, Sunray?"

"I don't know a lot about reincarnation, but what I understand is this: You died at nineteen, so when you reached nineteen in this lifetime, you started getting flashes of your old life, from the end back to the beginning. Like a movie playing backward."

Kane flattened his hands on the table and scrutinized her. "But how do you know about the dreams at all?"

Their legs bumped and she quietly explained, "I have the exact same dream."

He decided to humor her. "Because you were reincarnated?"

"No, because I was there and it still haunts me."

"And do you kill me in your dream too?" he questioned.

With a look of surprise spilling across her face, she blinked rapidly and shook her head. "No, it wasn't like that. Your memories are jumbled." She paused for a long time before continuing. "I watched you die," she whispered. Her voice was laced with undeniable pain and anguish, and it momentarily shocked him.

Jesus, he'd never seen anyone look so scared and fragile. So damaged. Vall must have done a hell of a number on her.

"It was the worst day of my life," she elaborated. "And even though it was you who died that day"—she paused to put her hand over her heart—"I died too, in here." For some peculiar reason, the honesty in her eyes and the sadness in her voice ripped through his protective shield and touched something inside him—something deep down. As tenderness stole over him, he forced himself to ignore it. He couldn't afford to get distracted. She was a damn werewolf.

Striving for normalcy, he studied her. And even though his gut told him she wasn't lying, he reminded himself that she *had* tricked him once at the club when he mistook her for a human, not a monster.

"So that's why you were looking for me at the club? You thought I was your reincarnated lover?"

She picked up a napkin and began curling it around her fingers. "I *know* you're Ray."

"And after you met me, how long did it take you to figure out I was a hunter?"

"Seconds."

"But you slept with me anyway." He arched a curious brow. "Quite a risk, don't you think?"

"Yes, quite a risk." Dark lashes blinked over expressive eyes, and her voice was soft and seductive when she added, "But it was worth it, because no one can make me feel the way you do, Kane."

His mind reeled. Just hearing her say those words brought back sensual memories and roused the hunger in him. As his eyes devoured her, he thought about how good she felt between his legs. Lust prowled through him and his cock reacted instantly. Unable to ignore the sensations, and angry with himself for feeling such need and desire, he worked to contain his emotions.

"What is it about me that makes you think I'm Ray?"

She leaned in to him and inhaled. "Been at the pool lately?"

His throat tightened. He narrowed his eyes and worked to stay focused. "What are you talking about?"

"Are you still swimming?" A slight smile touched her cheek and her eyes went a bit hazy, like she was recalling happier times. "You loved to swim. You were on the school's varsity team, and sometimes we'd sneak into the complex late at night for a dip. Afterward we'd always make love in the shower." Warmth and desire flitted across her face as her hand unconsciously reached out and touched his.

As their fingers entwined, creating an instant intimacy, Kane rubbed his temple. "Okay, Sunray. You're starting to freak me out here." How was it possible that she knew so much about him?

She pulled her hand back, as though realizing what she'd done. "You should be freaked out." She paused to blow on her drink, and the way she puckered her lips was so damn erotic he nearly hauled her into the nearest alleyway and had his wicked way with her. Perhaps that wasn't such a bad idea. If he just fucked her, maybe he could get her the hell out of his system and get his thoughts back on the job at hand. "You've got a lot of information coming at you," she continued. "A lot to take in at once. But everything I'm telling you is true."

He gave her his best hard-ass face and tried to ignore the heat rising in him. He needed to be thinking with his head, not his cock. He drew a breath to center himself. "Yeah, bullshit information you could be feeding me to throw me off my game and lead me to your alpha. Maybe you two are really working together to take out hunters. I'm sure he'd like to see one less PTF officer in the world."

Her eyebrow shot up at his accusations. "I told you I don't lie." When he gave her a dubious look, her lips twisted and she offered, "You know, Kane, you might be tough and hard on the outside, but underneath that you're kind and gentle and giving, no matter what you think."

Kane scoffed. "Don't be so sure about what you think you know about me. I'm not your guy. I'm not Ray."

So exactly how do you account for the dreams, then?

"Yes, you are," she countered. "I'd know you in any lifetime, Kane."

Kane refocused and asked her, "Where is Vall's den? His pack?"

Her glance went back to her cup. She exhaled slowly and her lids fluttered. "I don't know," she murmured under her breath.

"I can't help if you don't tell me everything."

A long pause, and then, "I'm telling you everything I can." That moment of hesitation told him she'd chosen her words very carefully. She obviously knew more than she was telling him. What was she holding back, and why?

Vowing to get to the bottom of it, he asked, "Why aren't you with your pack?"

"It's better this way."

"Wolves don't travel alone." When she didn't answer, he sat back in his chair and stretched out his legs, careful not to connect with hers. "What has Vall done to you to make you want to kill him?"

Silver eyes flashed. "Do you mean besides kill you?"

"Yeah." He decided to humor her again, figuring it was the only way to keep her talking.

Concern reflected in her eyes. "He's murdering innocent people, Kane. Don't you think that's enough for me to want to stop him?"

An elderly gentleman walked by their booth, and Kane waited until he'd passed before he leaned in and asked, "How come I have no record of a Sunray Matthews until a little over six months ago?"

"I've led a quiet life."

Unconvinced, he opened his mouth to ask another question, but she glanced at the clock on the wall and cut him off. A second later, she pinned him with a glare, and there was a note of desperation in her voice when she asked, "Look, how long is this interrogation going to last? I need to go after Vall."

"I didn't think wolves killed their own kind."

She cocked her head and gave him a humorless smile. "You know, Kane, at times I've seen less humanity in humans than in lycans. We're not all cold, calculating beasts with our own interests at heart."

Kane folded his arms and traced the deep scar above his eye, his message crystal clear. He gave a derisive twist of his lips and in a mocking tone said, "Now, that I didn't know."

She lifted her chin. "I'm sure there are a lot of things you don't know."

Ignoring her jibe, he continued. "One more question. Why do you go by Sunray now?"

Her glance met his, and when she moistened her lips nervously, he suspected he hit a nerve. Emotions danced in the depths of her solemn eyes. "It's a combination of our names. Sunni and Ray. A way for me to keep you with me at all times after Vall killed you."

Hyperaware of the vulnerability in her tone and how it touched him, he clutched his coffee cup, took a sip, and watched her for a long moment, assessing her as his brain processed everything she'd said.

He was Ray?

Reincarnated?

Jesus, it was crazy. Everything she was telling him was crazy. Wasn't it?

"Do you want my help or not?" she asked, her forehead creasing with anxiety.

"I don't need your help." He sat up, and his coffee mug hit the table with a thump at the exact same time their legs connected. He watched her suck in a breath as the air around them changed. "I can track him on my own."

"Well, you've been doing a piss-poor job so far," she lashed out. "How many people have been killed, Kane? How many more will get killed because you're too arrogant to accept my help?"

Was she for real? A werewolf who cared about others?

He pitched his voice low. "I don't work with werewolves, Sunray."

"That's right: You're a hunter and I'm a lycan." She scoffed and mumbled her next words under her breath. "And once again, I'm on the wrong side of the tracks."

"What the hell is that supposed to mean?"

"Nothing." Frustrated, she threw her hands up in the air and jumped from her seat. "Forget it, then. I'll track him on my own."

"Like hell you will." Kane jumped to his feet and stood over her, blocking her escape and gaining the attention of those around them.

She met his gaze unflinchingly. "So does that mean you'll help me?"

"No. It means *I'll* let *you* help me."

They stood there eye to eye, and he leaned in to her until they were merely a breath's distance away from each other. "But when we're done, I'm going to have to kill you, you know."

She stared at him and moved an inch closer. "Not if I kill you first."

Chapter Nine

With an uneasy truce between them, Sunray followed Kane back out to his truck. After he opened her door and tucked her inside, he circled the front of the cab. Never taking his steely eyes off her, he climbed into the driver's seat. He turned the key, and as the engine purred to life, he flicked off the radio and blasted the heater. With his full attention on the road ahead, he pulled out of the parking lot.

Silence hung heavily as she shot him a sideways glance and took in his hard features and even harder physique. Her own body grew needy at the mere sight of him, and her heart clenched with longing. She cleared her throat and tried to keep her voice tempered when she asked, "Where are we going?"

He continued to stare straight ahead, as though lost in his own thoughts. It wasn't until he took the next exit leading to the highway that he answered her. "My place. We need sleep," was all he offered before tightening his hands around the steering wheel until his knuckles turned bone white. He was no doubt trying to sort through matters and come to terms with everything she'd told him.

Sunray shifted her glance to look at his rugged hands for a moment, hands that were so strong and powerful, yet so damn gentle when they touched her. Her eyes strayed to his and she spotted tenderness there, a glimpse of the inner man so well hidden behind a tough exterior.

Aware this was not the time to let her mind wander, Sunray shook her head, sagged against the seat, and stared out the passenger's window. Minutes ticked by as she watched the trees and road signs fly by. A long while later, he pulled off the highway and into a quaint subdivision. He turned onto a quiet cul-de-sac and eased his vehicle into his short driveway. Reaching up, he pressed a remote control button attached to his sun visor, and drove his truck into the garage of a cute little cedar-sided bungalow in the suburbs. Honestly, Sunray wasn't sure what to expect, but she didn't take him for a bungalow-in-the-burbs kind of guy. Maybe Ray, but definitely not Kane.

Once inside the garage, he shut the steel door behind them, jumped from his seat, and came around to her side. He opened the door, and she climbed out. Before she even realized what he was doing, he slapped a pair of handcuffs on her.

"What the hell?"

Ignoring her, he led her through the garage and pulled open the door leading into the kitchen.

A light over the range lit the room in a soft glow and illuminated the length of Kane's body. Despite the situation she'd found herself in, the soft luminescence took her back in time and made her think about romantic candlelight, strewn blankets, and hot, sweaty bodies. By small degrees, her flesh tightened, and she suspected Kane felt the erotic shift. He turned to her, and when his dark eyes locked on hers, she shivered.

"Do you need anything?" he asked, and kicked off his boots.

Oh, she needed a lot of things. Like his body moving under hers again, his mouth kissing her, his hands touching her and loving every inch of her body. Oh yeah, she needed a lot of things, none of which required these handcuffs, she didn't think.

As if he'd read her mind, his eyes settled on her mouth, and the air around them immediately grew more charged. His nostrils flared and he pushed the hair off his face. Sunray could feel his sexual need as it reached out to her.

"A drink? The bathroom?"

His raspy voice sent a barrage of emotions rushing through her. "Bathroom."

He gave a slight nod, then bent down to help remove her boots. He placed them beside his on the rubber mat, and with a touch that was commanding yet soft, he led her down the hall. "There's a spare toothbrush in the cabinet." He pulled the door behind him to give her privacy, but didn't click it shut.

Once inside, Sunray went to work on preparing herself for bed, not an easy task with her wrists locked together and her winter coat still on. She shook her head, hardly able to believe she was in Kane's bathroom or the circumstances that had led her there. Her mind reeling, she washed her face, brushed her teeth, and left her facecloth and toothbrush on the edge of the sink. Her heart thudded as she thought about the man who stood outside the door—a man who didn't trust a single thing about her. God, if only things between them were different. If only she weren't a werewolf and he weren't a hunter—a hunter who thought she was spinning an elaborate tale to lure him into some trap.

A hunter who promised to kill her when this was all over.

With the water still running, she took a moment to stare at her disheveled image in the mirror. After a heavy sigh, she tightened the taps and prepared herself to face Kane.

"Done?" he asked through the crack of the door when she turned off the water.

Sunray opened the door to find him casually leaning against the wall, and she was completely unprepared for the emotions that washed over her. With his legs crossed at the ankles and his hands jammed into his pockets, dark, intense eyes met hers. He had shed his coat, and his long-sleeved T-shirt accentuated his broad muscles. Oh, God, seeing him standing there, looking so damn hot and sexy, turned her legs to rubber. How could she possibly spend time with him and not touch him?

"Done," she managed, surprised her voice was working properly.

He packaged her into his strong arms, led her to a small

bedroom, and tossed her suitcase—minus her gun—onto the bed.

He released his tenuous grip and gestured with a nod. "You can sleep in here."

She glanced into the room to see the single bed, neatly made, a small wooden bureau, and a tiny window with black metal bars on it. Metal bars? Jeez, and here she thought it was a nice neighborhood. Then again, he was a hunter who had to take extra precautions. And wasn't it a little ironic that those bars were in place to keep wolves out, yet tonight he was using them to lock one in?

She rattled the handcuffs. "I can't sleep with these on."

"And I can't trust that you won't tear my throat open in the middle of the night."

She shot him an indignant look. "If I wanted to kill you, I would have done it already."

He stared down at her for a long time, his eyes watching her carefully as though mulling something over. Then he left her standing there for a moment, disappeared into the other room, and came back with a screwdriver.

She tensed and took a small step back. "What are you doing with that?"

He went to work on the door knob. "Locking you in."

"You don't think I can break it down?"

"It'll buy me some time."

She blew a heavy breath and shot back, "I'm not going to go anywhere. You know, we both need each other's help if we want to catch Vall."

"Yeah, we're quite the team, you and me, aren't we?"

Exasperated, she said, "Kane . . ."

He paused and rolled one shoulder. "Look, it's either the cuffs or I lock you in."

For a long moment neither one spoke; they just stood there staring at each other. As his large body loomed over hers, she searched his face, and it became apparent that he was waiting for her decision.

"Lock me in," she said reluctantly, and held her arms out for him to remove the cuffs.

Kane went to work on switching the doorknob around until the lock was on the outside. Then he grabbed a set of keys from his pocket and gave her his full attention. He took her arms into his hands to release the cuffs. When skin touched skin, heat instantly arced between them, creating an air of intimacy. Distracted by him standing so close, her libido roared to life. A shiver moved through her and her nipples tightened in anticipation of his touch.

In response, Kane's muscles tensed, his teeth clenched, and a strange, strangled sound caught in his throat. Sunray knew he felt the potent connection between them every bit as much as she did.

Thrown off-kilter, she cleared her throat. "You okay?" she asked, her voice a little shaky.

His gaze slid over her, and the look on his face was intense. "What, exactly, is it that you're doing to me?"

Without conscious thought, she reached out to him, needing in some unfathomable way to tell him everything was going to be okay, even though she knew it wasn't. "Kane."

His fingers twitched at his side; then he stepped back. "Night," he said, and closed the door. Her heart twisted as she listened to his footsteps on the hardwood floors and the click of the bathroom door.

As she found herself all alone in Kane's spare bedroom, locked inside, she couldn't quite believe she was here. With him. She pulled off her winter coat and moved to the window to test the bars. She pulled open the pane and a breeze whipped over her face as she gripped the metal. Nice and solid. After tightly shutting the window, she carefully pulled back the blue bedspread and flopped down onto the comfy but squeaky bed. She lay there listening to Kane wash up in the bathroom, then make his way to the bedroom next to hers.

Hours slipped by, and despite her efforts, she couldn't shut her mind down and sleep. Unable to toss and turn any longer, she gave up. Frustrated and uncomfortable in her jeans and sweater, she climbed from the bed and pulled on her nightie. After neatly folding her clothes and placing them on the bureau, she began to pace—not at all unlike a caged animal—all the while listening for signs of Kane in the adjacent room. With her superior senses, she could hear his soft, regulated breaths, and the ping of the bed springs as he shifted in his sleep. Once she was certain Kane had fallen into a deep slumber, she grabbed a bobby pin from her cosmetic bag and made short work of the lock. Too bad Kane's effort to lock her in had been for nothing.

She'd been around long enough to know how to work a simple piece of hardware like that one. Surely to God he would have suspected that, or, like her, he was so flustered by the heat between them that he couldn't think straight either.

She slipped from her room and tiptoed down the hall, briefly pausing outside Kane's room. She pressed her hands to his door and listened. Honestly, it was hard being this close to him and not *being* with him. Everything from the way he looked at her to his scent, his voice, and his sensuous, confident strides filled her with intense need.

She quietly passed his room and thought more about their conversation. She didn't want to lie to him, but there was no way she could tell him where Vall's den was. Not without leading him to Serene. She couldn't—wouldn't—put her secret town in danger.

Following a desire to learn more about Kane in this lifetime, Sunray moved through his living room. Without bothering to flick on the light, she took in his big-screen TV and trailed her fingers over his leather sofa. Even though it was a nice house in the burbs, with its manly furniture and lack of warmth, it was easy to tell it was a bachelor pad. This place needed a woman's touch to take it from a house to a home.

A blanket strewn over his sofa had her mind wandering. Was Kane the kind of guy who came home and prepared himself for bed, or did he simply throw himself down on the sofa and flick on the TV while he caught a few hours' sleep? She picked up a square cushion, brought it to her nose, and inhaled his warm, familiar scent. She glanced around his sparse room and hugged the cushion to her chest as she absorbed every essence of his being.

Childhood pictures hung on his walls, and she thought it odd that a guy like Kane would have put them there. She stepped closer for a better look, and it tugged at her heart when she saw the happy faces of the people she assumed were his mom, dad, and two older sisters. Perhaps it was one of his sisters who had tried to make his place a little homier for him.

Sunray smiled and wondered what it was like for him to grow up with two older girls in the house. He was an only child in his last life, and she knew he'd always longed for siblings. So much so that they'd spent numerous nights talking about having a big family together. After he had finished school, they had planned to elope to a place where social status didn't matter, and have a brood of kids.

As she thought more about their lost plans, the smile fell from her face and her heart clenched. She instantly knew she had to earn his trust and convince him that he *was* Ray, and that it wasn't she who had killed him a century ago. Partly because she didn't want him to believe she was capable of such bloodshed, and partly because she wanted him to remember, because then maybe, just maybe, he'd love her again. Even if only for a little while.

Down the hall she heard Kane's bedroom door squeak open. She stood stock-still while he moved into the kitchen and went to his refrigerator. He pulled open the door, and the soft light from inside fell over his half-naked body and lit his hewn muscles. As lust saturated her brain, her thoughts careened in an erotic direction, and desire slammed into her hard. Sunray drew her bottom lip between her teeth as his masculine essence completely overwhelmed her.

He pulled out the orange juice and turned in her direction. Kane took a swig from the container, but didn't notice her standing there in the dark. As he faced her, his position afforded her with an unobstructed view of his body. When her eyes flitted over his magnificent athletic frame, the need to lose herself in him became too powerful to deny.

She reveled in his washboard abdominals and the way his pajama pants rode low on his hips, enough to expose his oblique muscles—the sexiest part of a man, she decided. As she took in the sight of his virile body, there was nothing she could do to fight down the whimper of need that bubbled up from her throat. Her flesh tightened and she began to shake, in search of his touch, his comfort.

The sound gained his attention. His head snapped up; their eyes met from across the dark room. Kane immediately tensed, his fingers tightening on the container. For a moment, shocked silence lingered.

As he stared at her, they both realized he didn't have his gun. Unease passed over his handsome face, and she could feel his tension as if it were her own. Sunray smiled at him, put his cushion back onto the sofa, and folded her arms across her chest. This was the perfect opportunity to gain his trust.

"So it seems the big bad cop isn't so tough without his gun." They both knew she could tear him to shreds if she wanted to. Except she didn't. She wanted to feel his mouth and hands on her again. She wanted to feel him inside her, pushing, pumping, taking them both to the moon and back, over and over again. And for just a little while, she wanted to forget that he could never really be hers again, not forever like he'd always promised, and just enjoy this moment and this man while she could. Desire bombarded her body and heat rushed to her pussy, and in no time at all her aroused scent filled the room.

She took a step closer and watched his nostrils flare as he inhaled. His expression troubled, he leveled her with a stare.

"So it seems the big bad wolf is in heat, then?" he countered.

That brought a smile to her face. Even unarmed, he wasn't about to back down from her. She had to admit, she loved Ray, but she also loved the man he'd become.

Then, as if he suddenly remembered something, he glanced down the hall at her bedroom door. "How did you . . . ?" His gaze went from her room to his room to the front door. "Why didn't you . . . ?" Silence fell between them as he eyed her uncertainly.

In a bold move, she stepped closer, took the orange juice from him, and set it on the counter. "Kane . . ."

"What?" His rich baritone sent a barrage of erotic sensations through her body.

"Why are you up?"

He tapped his temple and in a soft voice said, "You were in my head again."

"Were we making love?"

She could feel his body stirring to life in remembrance, and sensed his mounting desire. "Yeah."

As the sexual tension sparked between them, she added, "It doesn't have to just be in your dreams, you know."

Wound so tight she feared he'd snap, he shot her a weary glance and pushed a shaky hand through his hair. The need between them was palpable, all consuming, and so damn powerful not even a dangerous, deadly hunter like Kane could deny it. Whether he accepted it or not, they truly were meant to be together, in every lifetime.

His jaw muscles twitched and the confusion on his face tore at her heart. As she gauged his responses, she knew she should just walk away and try to make this easier on him. After all, sleeping with a lycan went against everything he believed in. But how could she possibly flee and deny her body and heart what they had been missing for the past century?

With need fueling her actions, she stepped in to him, their bodies colliding, molding together. Oh, God, she ached for him, craved him with an intensity that rocked her world and derailed her ability to think rationally.

She could hear the urgency in her voice when she said, "Take me, Kane. Love me the way only you know how."

In one swift move, he shackled her wrists roughly, and the warmth of his fingers as they closed over her arms ignited a fire inside her. Delirious with need, she pressed her breasts against him and rocked her hips. She could almost feel the shift inside him as she offered herself up, completely, thoroughly, unapologetically.

With his resolve melting, he backed her up until she was pressed against the wall. He propped his arms on either side of her head, and as the energy reached out to her, she soaked in his desire. Dark, turbulent eyes met hers as he captured her legs between his and pinned her in place. His arms shook as he braced them against the wall and held her captive.

He took a breath and let it out slowly. "What the fuck are you doing to me?" he rasped, his voice hard, low, and tortured.

As she stared up at him, watching him come apart before her, she found it hard to believe that she could reduce this big bad hunter to such quivering mess of need and lust.

His warm, arousing scent filled her with want, and his heat scorched her. As flames surged inside her, firing every inch of her flesh, she slipped her arms around his waist and pulled his body to hers, until she could feel his hard cock pressed against her stomach, an indication that he wanted her every bit as much as she wanted him. She went up on her toes, lightly feathered her mouth over his, and kissed away his reserve.

With her back still nailed against the wall and their bodies meshed as one, the attraction between them demanded their full attention. Kane groaned, and with a tone that she'd never heard him use before, he whispered, "Sunray . . ."

Aching deep between her legs and hungering for so much

more than his touch, she lowered her voice to match his. "I know. I feel it. . . ."

His lips crashed down on hers before she could complete that sentence. His mouth was both cold and sweet from the orange juice, and hot and wet from desire. Moaning in delight, she savored his distinctive flavor as their tongues dueled and played.

By the way his dark eyes smoldered with want, it was easy to tell he was losing control. No longer able to fight down his carnal hunger, his muscles tightened and he pushed his cock against her stomach, the heat between them tremendous. Sunray was certain if they didn't soon tamp it down, his bungalow would go up in a burst of flames.

He inched back, smoothed her hair from her face, and breathed into her mouth. "This is fucking crazy," he muttered, his voice soft, intimate.

Conflicted.

Sunray shifted and put her hand between their bodies to cup his cock, conveying without words exactly what she wanted. "Yes, crazy . . ." she agreed, and felt him shiver under her invasive touch. "But so right. So damn right. You can't tell me you don't feel it too." Kane groaned and threw back his head in answer to her question.

"But, Sunray, I'm not Ray. I'm Kane."

"I—"

She sensed the jealousy in him when he said, "I want you to want me for me."

"I do," she assured him.

The hungry look in his eyes spurred her on. As pleasure raced through her, her body trembled almost uncontrollably, and she slipped her hand inside his loose pants to stroke his impressive length, loving the way he swelled in her palm.

Feeling weak with need, she whimpered, and the erotic sound filled the room and seemed to unleash something wild inside him. His eyes flashed, his nostrils flared, and perspiration broke out on his skin. He let loose a low savage growl and buried his face in her neck, where he ravished the hollow of her throat before raining kisses over her earlobes, chin, cheeks, and eyes.

She continued to stroke him, her hand easily gliding over his smooth, stretched skin as she reveled in his hunger, his urgency. Small droplets of his liquid heat pooled on the head of his penis, and her mouth watered for a taste of him. As she dipped into his precum and rubbed it over his crown, she broke his kisses and shimmied lower, deciding to follow her impulses.

He gripped her shoulders. "Sunray, what are you doing?"

Making her intentions clear, she dropped to her knees and dragged his pajama pants lower, releasing his beautiful cock. As it jutted out at her, she flicked it with her tongue. When it throbbed in response, she made small, sensuous circles and lightly brushed his engorged head. His breath came in jagged bursts, and she could hear the blood racing through his veins in preparation.

He pulled her hair from her face. "Sunray, kitten . . ."

She tipped her head to see him, and something tightened around her heart. He looked so sweet, so vulnerable, and the softness in his voice when he called her kitten took her back in time. Memories flooded her brain and shook her to her very core.

"Kane," she murmured. Their eyes met and held a long, lingering glance that spoke of want and unchecked emotions.

Needing him now more than ever, she turned her attention to his throbbing cock, drew him into her mouth, and moved her head back and forth, intent on giving him pleasure like he'd never before experienced, intent on giving him . . . *everything.*

His loud moan thrilled her, and as he gripped her head to follow the motion with his hands, warmth pooled between her thighs. If she didn't have a mouthful of his hard, thick cock, she would have cried out in ecstasy.

She sucked him in deeper and gently massaged his balls. His hips began swaying, and she knew he was struggling for control. God, she'd missed the taste of him, the silky texture of his cock, and the way it felt sliding in and out of her hungry mouth.

He stiffened, his thigh muscles going tight, and she knew he was close. "Sunray . . . Jesus," he murmured, and gripped her hair tighter to ease her off.

Undeterred, she moaned and encouraged him to release in her mouth. But she sensed his restraint, his unwillingness to give himself completely over to her.

"Come here." He grabbed her shoulders and hauled her to her feet. He wrapped one arm around her waist to anchor her to him; his other hand stole under her nightie. When his fingers connected with her sopping-wet pussy, he groaned.

"You're so damn wet."

A wheezing sound escaped her lips when he twirled his finger over her swollen clit.

"You like that, do you?"

Since she was well past the point of vocalizing anything intelligent, she merely squirmed, shamelessly forcing his finger to press harder against the spot that needed it the most. His gruff chuckle brought on a shiver, and he pushed one thick finger inside her, answering her unspoken needs. Unhinged, her pussy muscles clenched around his thickness, and she was so close to coming, she damn near dropped to the ground in a quivering mass of need.

He stepped out of his pajama pants as his mouth found hers. With a slight nudge, he backed her up until her knees hit the table. He slid his hands around her waist and effortlessly lifted her, gently placing her bare ass on the wooden top.

"Open for me."

Shaking with want and moist with need, she watched him as she slowly inched her knees open, giving him only a small glimpse of her sex.

"More," he growled. He gripped her thighs and widened them as far as possible. God, his virility frightened and excited her at the same time.

Excitement coiled deep in her belly when he stepped back to stare at her, his cock standing at full attention. The gleam in his eyes turned wicked. "Stay like that and don't move an inch."

He turned his back to her, and she cried out in sweet agony as she watched his tight ass disappear down the hall. Blood pounded through her veins and she shook, both loving and hating how he prolonged the seduction, feeding the intensity of her arousal.

A moment later, he came back with two pairs of handcuffs, and his eyes raced over her body. Her breath caught as she tracked his every movement. "I thought—"

He shot her a scalding look, and she flushed hotly. "I want you at my mercy." He licked his lips as his eyes settled on her hard nipples and the way they were brushing against the thin cotton of her pajamas. "Now get naked."

As she made short work of her nightie, he gripped one ankle and secured it to the leg of the table, then proceeded to do the same with another. Once she was sufficiently bound, he began circling her, his gaze caressing her as he splayed his big hand over her stomach. He lightly traced his fingers over her trembling flesh, going lower and lower until the soft pad of his thumb hovered over her clit.

She arched upward in an unsuccessful effort to force his fingers to her cunt. Tossing her head to the side, she said, "Kane, I need . . ."

"You can touch yourself."

Her sex pulsed and she moaned in response. With single-minded determination, her fingers went to her pussy; his eyes dimmed with desire as he watched her begin to pleasure herself. As she worked her finger over her slick clit, he placed his mouth on her breast. He brushed his fingers over the underside, drew in one nipple, and gave a long, hard suck. With his mouth doing those delicious things to her, she could feel soft quakes deep between her legs.

"Yesss . . ." she hissed. "That's it."

He slipped a hand between her thighs and pushed one finger inside her. Her pussy throbbed. "Mmm, so nice. And so close." He angled his head until his mouth was only a breath away from hers. The dark desire she saw on his face made her breath catch. He gave her a wicked grin and commanded, "Don't come until I tell you to."

Ruffled, she gave a broken gasp and begged, "Kane . . . please . . . I want to come now."

He abandoned her breasts and pressed his lips to her mouth. "Such a greedy girl," he murmured, and gave a soft chuckle of amusement.

As she continued to work her fingers over her clit, he kissed a path down her body, stopping to pay homage to her breasts, her belly button, her hips, and her inner thighs. He pushed his nose against her clit. The sweet stab of pleasure had her arching into him and crying out shamelessly. She tipped her ass up, and the chains securing her legs to the table rattled, which excited her all the more.

Kane moved around the table and settled between her legs. Using slow, skilled passes, he licked her sex with the soft blade of his tongue—long, luxurious laps that had her feeling wild and frenzied and desperate to have him inside her. His bangs fell forward and brushed along her thighs and tickled all the way to her toes. Writhing beneath his erotic assault, she reached down and raked her fingers through his hair.

"You taste so fucking good," he murmured from deep between her legs. Heat ambushed her cunt and it was all she could do to hang on.

As pressure brewed deep within her, he brought her to the edge and kept her hovering there. Her body cried out for release and she began panting, the sensations too much, too intense. With her body on overdrive, she flipped her head from side to side, frantic, a woman on a mission.

"Sunray . . ."

"Yeah," she answered, breathless.

"You can come now."

In tune with her body, he pressed his thumb over her clit and worked his finger around the bundle of nerves on her pussy.

"Oh, God," she cried out. And just like that, he took her over the edge, allowing her to tumble into a much-needed, powerful orgasm. Pleasure pulsed through her, and dragging in air was almost impossible as the rippling waves took hold. Trembling and panting and entirely lost in the moment, her body shook and she cried out in ecstasy. Kane helped her ride out her release, and remained pressed against her until her raging tremors subsided.

Then, before she even realized what he was doing, he unhooked the cuffs and pulled her to her feet. His hands were all over her, giving, taking, pushing, and pulling as he released a lusty groan. Good God, he looked like he was going to eat her alive. He grabbed her around the waist and lifted her onto his hips.

She snaked her arms around his neck and locked her legs around his back. "Did you want me to ride you?"

"No, I want you under me."

"Bedroom?" she asked.

The air around them sizzled with electricity, and the fire in his dark eyes licked over her flesh. "Too far." He carried her into the living room, hauled the blanket off the sofa, and threw it onto the floor. As he laid her out on the makeshift bed, Sunray doubted he even realized what he was doing, even though it was so obvious to her. Undoubtedly, with his subconscious at work, Kane was taking her on the floor the same way he'd used to take her so many years before, in the abandoned building.

"I really need to be inside you. Now," he confessed.

He pressed himself over the length of her and propped himself up on one elbow, while his other hand greedily kneaded her breasts. She could feel his heart race in a mad cadence, and his body practically shook as he positioned his cock at her entrance. Jesus, she'd never seen him look so edgy, ravenous, carnal.

Perspiration matted his bangs to his forehead, and she reached out and pushed them to the side. His breath came fast, his nostrils flared, and as he breached her slick opening, he shot her an apologetic look.

"This might get a little messy, kitten," he confessed in advance, his voice wavering, easily conveying his rattled emotions, his frantic needs.

Seeing him this aroused, this needy, touched her deeply and bombarded her with primal hunger. "I like it a little messy," she assured him, and raced her hands over his hot skin, sharing in his urgency and the new, unspoken intimacy between them. He pushed his tongue inside her mouth in a frenzied move, and at the same time, he thrust forward and drove his cock all the way up inside her.

He gave a low, tortured moan when she clenched her sex muscles around him. "Christ . . ." he whispered, and slowly began to pump. As he indulged in her heat and took full possession of her body, she gyrated her hips, a new pressure building inside her.

She opened herself up to him. "Take me the way you need to," she encouraged, wanting him to lose his control with her, to give himself to her the same way she was giving herself to him. Kane inched back to see her. His smoldering gaze panned her face, and when their gazes collided, she added in a soft tone, "No advance apology needed."

With that he crushed his hands through her hair and pumped hard and deep, driving her against the floor. She held him tight, her fingers tangling in his hair as he rode her feverishly, until her warm wetness covered his shaft and dripped down her legs.

"God, yes . . ." she cried out, and bucked forward to meet and welcome each needy thrust.

As she concentrated on the sensations, her tangy, intoxicating aroma saturated the small room, and it seemed to push him over the precipice.

"Kitten," he cried out, and as though seeking an even deeper intimacy, Kane's mouth found hers again. His kiss was so achingly tender and passionate, she completely lost herself in him. As her heart clenched, he pushed his cock deep inside her and stilled his movements. A sound caught in his throat as his cock pulsed and throbbed with release.

Her thighs hugged his hips, holding him inside her while she concentrated on each throb. "Yes, come inside me," Sunray murmured, as he let himself go and released his hot seed into her. Kane gave a low growl of satisfaction and held her tight, his fingers biting into her flesh.

Breathing labored, he stayed on top of her for a long time, and she reveled in the feel of his weight pressing down on her. Something about the way she was pinned beneath him felt so incredibly intimate and right.

After a long while, he slid beside her, and her breath caught as he slipped a hand between her legs to stroke and soothe her well-ridden pussy. He exhaled slowly. "Jesus, I didn't mean to get so crazed."

With contentment washing over her in rippling waves, she moistened her dry lips and said, "I wouldn't want you any other way."

He angled his head, his eyes full of tender concern. "I didn't hurt you, did I?"

There was a new fullness in her heart when she cupped his face and whispered in a soft voice, "No."

He blinked, his look sheepish. "Like I said, messy . . ."

"It was perfect. You were perfect."

He shot her a glance and the look in his eyes spoke volumes; there was a need inside him he couldn't seem to assuage. She understood that feeling all too well. Sunray pulled him closer, knowing she'd never be able to extinguish the insatiable hunger in her. Not where Kane was concerned.

She opened her mouth to speak, but he cut her off. "I know, kitten, I know . . ." Hard, hot, and hungry, his mouth closed over hers once again. And oblivious to every reason that they shouldn't be together, and knowing that they had no future, they became lost in each other's arms.

Chapter Ten

Sometime during the night, Kane had taken Sunray to his bed, where he made love to her again and again, until early-morning rays filled his room with warmth and bright light. He glanced at the woman snuggled beside him, and even after all the heady sex they'd indulged in, the overwhelming need to be inside her pulled at him once more. It was mind-boggling, really, especially since he hardly knew her. And what he did know about her dictated that he should terminate her on the spot.

He gave a low, frustrated groan.

Goddamn. What the hell was it about her that got to him? He was beginning to think she'd been put on Earth just to torture his soul.

With daylight upon them, Sunray blinked her eyes open, shimmied closer to him, and rested her head against his chest. Kane stifled a yawn, tucked a wayward strand of golden hair behind her ear, and lay there trying to remember how to breathe. Honestly, he could hardly handle the wild, passionate night they'd just had, or believe the things she'd unearthed in him.

Things that made him feel alive.

Dangerous emotions.

Things he had no business feeling.

"Sunray."

She tilted her head and blinked up at him. "Yeah?" she asked, her voice drowsy, sexy.

Even though he knew he should just get her the hell out of his bed and start thinking with his head, not his dick, curiosity got the better of him. He wanted to know more about Ray. What kind of man was he to deserve the love of a woman, even after a century apart?

"Tell me more about Ray."

Shifting, she rolled onto the pillow beside him, her hair falling around her shoulders in a wild mess, making her look so warm, cozy, and seductive. Sunbeams spilled over her body and her flesh glistened, forcing Kane to draw a quick breath to center himself.

Kane levered himself up on one arm to bring them face-to-face, then adjusted the blankets around their waists, leaving his chest and Sunray's beautiful breasts exposed. Yeah, yeah, he knew. Not a great way to start thinking with his head.

Sunray was naked and completely comfortable in her own skin. A slow smile touched her lush mouth, and her expression was one of love and devotion as it met his.

"Where do I start?"

"At the beginning." He brushed her hair from her flushed cheek. "How did you two meet?"

"Well," she paused, and jabbed her finger into his chest to emphasize her point. "*We* met one beautiful summer day when I went into town with my mother to run errands. As I walked by Bartlett merchant clothing shop, your father's store, and peeked out from beneath my hat, I spotted the most gorgeous man on the face of the Earth staring back."

Her excitement was contagious, and Kane couldn't help but smile. "Yeah?"

"Yeah." She put her hand over her heart and squeezed her shoulders together. "It was love at first sight."

He gave a quick shake of the head and ran his thumb up and down her arm. "I don't believe in that."

Sunray made an annoyed face and rolled her eyes playfully. "Well, there are a lot of things you don't believe in, now, aren't there?"

He ignored her smart-ass remark and nudged her to continue, acutely aware of the new comfort between them. "Go on. So, you started dating right away."

She looked down, and her long lashes shadowed her emotions. "Not exactly."

He put his thumb under her chin and tipped it up until their eyes met, because he desperately needed to see her face, to read her expression. "Why not?"

"It wasn't as simple as that, you see. You were from an affluent family on the Gold Coast, and I was merely the girl from the wrong side of the tracks."

His mind raced back to their conversation at the café, and he nodded in understanding. "'And once again, you're on the wrong side of the tracks.'"

"Yeah. And because of that, we weren't supposed to be together."

Just like we're not supposed to be together now . . .

"It was quite unacceptable, really," she continued. "My mother thought you were slumming, and your parents forbade you to associate with anyone from my neighborhood, anyone of a lower class."

The cabin on the outskirts of town flashed in his mind. Kane pinched the bridge of his nose, once again finding this all too much to believe. But some small part of him couldn't discount the significance of those recurring dreams, or that Sunray was the leading character in them.

Or the way she kills me, he reminded himself.

"You and Ray had to sneak around."

It was a statement, not a question, but she answered anyway. "Yes." She paused to wag her finger back and forth between the two of them. "*We* had to sneak around."

"Stop saying *we*." His gaze stole over her face, and his chest tightened with the candid sadness he met there. His hand brushed against hers without conscious thought, and as their fingers entwined he gave a slight squeeze, prompting her to continue. "Tell me about the abandoned building near the tracks that you two used to go to."

"Well, I found it one day while I was out looking for my cat. She'd wandered off, and I found her in the building, along with a dozen or so others." Her eyes lit up and a smile touched her mouth. "You always used to bring a can of sardines for the strays."

"*Ray* used to always bring sardines," he reminded. "So, you were a cat lover?" he asked.

"So were you."

"Stop saying *you*." He leaned in to her and slid his other hand down her back to the crest of her buttocks. His thumb traced her tattoo. "Is that why you have a kitty paw print?"

"Yes, another way for me to remember our time together."

"A wolf with a kitty tattoo. How ironic." A pause, and then, "And stop saying *our*."

Her lips twitched, and she ran her finger along his chest to trace one of his many scars. "We had such good times together, Kane. You were so sweet and loving and we shared so much. We were going to get married and run away to a place where our folks would have no control or influence and social status didn't matter. You promised me that we'd be together forever."

"What were you two waiting for?"

"*We* were waiting for you to finish school."

"Stop saying *we*." He considered that a moment, and then asked, "Why didn't Ray get you off the dangerous streets earlier, Sunray? Why would he let you continue to live like that?" He jabbed his thumb into his chest. "I sure as hell wouldn't go back to my rich neighborhood and leave you all alone to fend for yourself—which proves that I'm not, and never was, Ray."

Her warm smile reached her eyes, and it was then that he realized he'd given away too much of himself.

"You know, Kane, you're really not as hard as you think you are."

Ignoring her, he probed, "And you're positive Ray wasn't slumming."

Her expression turned serious. "You wanted to elope right away."

"You didn't?"

"No. I wanted you to get your education first. That was more important to me."

He lowered his head, struck by her selflessness. "How noble of you," he murmured quietly. As warmth settled in his stomach, he examined the sheets and felt something inside him soften. As he considered that curious shift, he blew out a breath and shook his head in awe. "*Ray* must have been one hell of a guy, Sunray."

She pressed against him harder, and snaked her arms around his waist. "You are."

"You must have loved him very much."

He could feel her heart pounding against his body, and her voice hitched when she answered, "I do."

His pulse leapt, and understanding exactly what she was

saying, he dug deep to summon a defense against her allure. "Sunray . . ." he warned.

She feathered her lips over his chest, and he shivered. "Why do you think you call me kitten?"

"I don't."

"Yes, you do. When we're having sex, you always call me kitten."

He shrugged. "Maybe I do; maybe I don't. Christ, Sunray, in the heat of the moment, who knows what I'm going to call you?"

"I do." Her fingers slid to his stomach and marched up his chest to play with one of his nipples. "Because you always used to call me kitten. It was your pet name for me." She reached higher and lightly tapped his temple. "I think that memory is lodged in your subconscious."

For some inexplicable reason, he asked, "Was Ray the only man you were ever with before you were turned?"

"Yes."

"When we were together at the club, you said it was good with only one other man, and that it was a long time ago. You were referring to Ray, I take it."

She gave a lazy catlike stretch. "And once again, you've proven to me that you are the best." She chuckled. "Well, maybe not *once* again; more like four times again. But, hey, who's counting?"

Despite himself, he felt his chest puff up. Jesus, it really was ridiculous how good that made him feel. "Tell me what happened the night Vall turned you and Ray was murdered. Give me the exact order of events."

Her smile faded, an indication that those memories were hard for her. "Why do you think you're a PTF officer, Kane?"

"It was my calling."

"Because of the strange dreams that began in adolescence?"

"I guess."

"And we already know why you started having those dreams, right?"

Kane studied her, wondering why she was so reluctant to give him a detailed account of the events. Because maybe his dreams weren't so jumbled, after all. And maybe it really was Sunray who'd killed him.

He redirected the conversation. "I understand why you hate Vall, but why is he so angry with you?"

Exasperation sparked in her eyes, and her voice was bleak as she said, "Because he's my alpha, and I've never willingly submitted to him."

"You mean, you've been in his pack for a hundred years and you've never willingly submitted to him?"

"That's right."

"But you submitted yourself to me, every inch of yourself, in fact. The first night we met, remember?"

"Of course I remember, Kane. I remember everything from the feel of your lips on mine to the way your rugged hands touched me and the way you tied me up and took control of my pleasure."

As those erotic memories took shape in his mind, he felt his cock harden. He shifted, suddenly uncomfortable. "So why submit to me and not him?"

Sunray rolled her eyes and gave him a look that suggested he was rather dense. "You still don't get it, do you?"

"What?"

"I promised *you* a hundred years ago that I'd never give myself to another in the way I gave myself to you. And I didn't."

"Stop saying *you*." He thought more about her devotion to Ray, and let out a low whistle. "That's one hell of a promise to keep."

"I keep my promises, and I don't lie."

Kane narrowed his eyes and scrutinized her. "What is it about you, Sunray? What is it about you that Vall wants so badly? Why is he so determined?"

The pain and the confusion in her eyes haunted him. "Honestly, I've spent the last hundred years wondering that myself." She shrugged a slender shoulder. "He's very dominant and craves power, so maybe it's simply that he wants what he can't have."

Not all that convinced, he rolled his neck and said, "Maybe."

Lips pursed in thought, her pewter eyes moved over his features, and she tucked a long golden lock of hair behind her ear. The simple gesture was so damn erotic, his cock throbbed.

Fuck . . .

He fisted his hands. He really needed to curb his overwhelming attraction to her and get out of this situation before she seduced his heart. If she hadn't already. Christ, it was unnerving how real this all felt.

Her stomach grumbled, and his immediately joined in the chorus. "Should I make us something to eat?" she asked. "Or will I find only beer and ketchup in the fridge?"

He pushed down his apprehension, tapped her ass to get her moving, and then rolled out of bed. When his feet hit the floor, he glanced around for last night's pants, then remembered Sunray had taken them off him in the kitchen.

"My fridge is stocked," he shot back over his shoulder.

"So you cook?"

"I get by."

He turned in time to see something pass over her face—her eyes went dark, turbulent, and her mouth turned down in a frown.

"What?" he asked, even though he was pretty certain he knew what she was thinking.

"Nothing."

He studied her body language and the way she tugged on the sheets, sliding the material through her fingers. "What? You think cooking is more intimate than sex?"

Her nose crinkled. "In a way, I think it can be."

"If you need to know, you're the first woman I've ever brought here." He jabbed his thumb into his chest. "I don't sleep with women in *my* bed, and *they* don't cook breakfast for me in the morning."

He saw something blossom inside her, and at the same time his stomach clenched, angry at himself for feeling emotional. For feeling anything.

He took a quick moment to lecture himself. They could never be together the way she wanted, and no matter what the circumstances, he would never completely give himself over to her, heart and soul, like she'd said. They were on opposite sides of the fence. And that was where they needed to stay.

Backtracking, he cursed under his breath and tried to harden himself, not wanting her to get the wrong idea. "Look, you're only here so I can keep an eye on you."

"And the fucking is an added benefit?" she asked.

"We shouldn't be fucking." Christ, he had to stop thinking with his dick.

She blinked several times, and the vulnerable look in her eyes nearly did him in. "Kane."

"Look, Sunray. I don't date and I don't do relationships. I fuck and I hunt, okay?" He battled his conscience, aware that he was being a prick. She didn't deserve to be treated this way, but there couldn't be anything between them, and she needed to know that.

When she slipped from the bed, his eyes panned over her beautiful body. He swallowed a low, tortured groan; all he could think about was tossing her back onto the mattress and burying himself inside her again.

He bit the inside of his mouth and mentally kicked himself. Ever since he'd met Sunray, his even-keeled temperament had gone haywire. His emotions were all over the place, which had him acting like a deranged smack addict.

It took all his effort to pull himself together and say, "Let's eat out. Then I'll drop you back here so I can check in at work. If we're going to pull this off, we need to keep up the status quo; otherwise, my colleagues will get suspicious." Under his breath he added to himself, "And the Darkland cousins are already leery of me as it is."

She eyed him carefully and planted her hands on her hips, determination etched on her pretty face. "I'm not staying locked up in here for the day, Kane. Not when I can be out tracking Vall."

Adamant that she stay put, he gave her a cold, calculating stare and began, "It's not a good idea for you to go wandering around the city. You could get—"

"It isn't up for debate."

As he took a moment to chew on that, they exchanged a long, heated look. "If you try to lock me in, I will escape," she continued, and gestured toward the bedroom door. "I'm a master with locks."

Well, she did have a point there. "I still have the handcuffs."

She pursed her lips in defiance. "Kane . . ."

He gave a resigned sigh. "Fine. Come with me," he reluctantly conceded, not trusting that she wouldn't eventually find a way out of the cuffs and get herself into trouble. "At least this way, I can keep an eye on you. But you damn well better be sure no one figures out what you are. Otherwise, it's game over. For both of us."

"I outsmarted you, didn't I?"

"Yeah, well, maybe I'm just getting too old for this shit." Either that, or his emotions were fucking up his ability to think straight.

A short while later, Sunray sat in the cab of Kane's truck as he maneuvered through traffic. When they reached the downtown center, he pulled his vehicle alongside the curb and turned to her, the material on his black parka brushing against his leather seat and cutting through the silence. It was then that she noticed he looked a little rumpled, a little sleepy, and a whole lot conflicted.

"Can I trust you to stay here?"

Despite the way her heart reached out to him, she pulled a face and shot him an impatient look. "I think we've already established that you can."

With that, Kane pulled the keys from the ignition and, as though unable to help himself, tossed a final warning over his shoulder. "Stay put."

Sunray sank low in her seat and observed him as he climbed from the vehicle. With confident strides, he hurried across the busy road. A tall glass building towered over him, and she assumed it was headquarters. Just knowing she was so close to the main office—an office filled with dedicated PTF officers who'd kill her without a moment's hesitation—made her shiver in apprehension.

Two men with similar features came from around the building and approached Kane; she assumed they were the Darkland cousins Kane had mentioned earlier. One was taller, with a slightly thicker build than the other. But with their dark hair, dark, shrewd eyes, and firm, square jawlines, it was easy to tell they were related. And from the confident way they moved, it was also easy to tell they were fellow PTF agents.

Kane stopped to exchange words with them, but by the looks on their faces, she'd hazard a guess that it wasn't a pleasant conversation. Sunray cracked her window, sorted through the cacophony of noises, and zeroed in on their intense discussion.

"Where were you last night?" the tall one with the barrel chest asked, looking a little self-righteous, a little too pompous for Sunray's comfort.

Kane widened his stance in a defensive move, his muscles bunched. "Hunting Vall."

"Vall?" The shorter man asked.

"Yeah, our rogue wolf," Kane offered.

"How'd you find out his name?"

With palpable annoyance, Kane shoved his hands in his pockets and scoffed. "You know better than to ask that, Jaret. I don't give out the names of my snitches."

"So, I take it you haven't caught him yet," Jaret shot back, his disgust apparent in his tone.

"He's a lycan elder."

"Yeah, and you're a PTF elder," he countered. Jaret narrowed his eyes and gave Kane a hard, cold glare, but Kane didn't flinch under his scrutinizing stare. "You should have killed him by now." Without shifting his smug gaze from Kane, he spoke out of the side of his mouth, asking, "Don't you think he should have killed him by now, Toby?"

Sunray could tell that there was definitely bad blood between them. But weren't they supposed to be a brotherhood, with all officers having each other's backs?

These two were toying with Kane, purposely trying to draw a reaction from him. Even though she could smell Kane's anger, he refused to react—a testament to his strength of character.

She found it difficult to sense anything from the other agents. She studied them a moment longer. There was something different about those two. Something she couldn't quite put her finger on.

Jaret glanced at the car, and Sunray slunk down even lower, certain he hadn't seen her. "Are you sure he's that good, Kane, or does something else have you distracted?"

As she hid, she watched them in the side-view mirror and continued to listen. "Don't you have somewhere else to be?" Kane asked. "Someone else to bother?"

Jaret smirked. "The captain's been asking for you."

"Probably putting together your retirement package," Toby added.

With that, Kane pushed past them, and Jaret and Toby moved down the sidewalk and disappeared into the coffee shop.

A few minutes later, they came out, coffee cups in hand. They walked back toward the building, climbed into a black SUV, and peeled out of the parking lot.

Following Kane's orders, Sunray waited in the vehicle. As cold penetrated the cab, she zipped her down-filled coat higher and hugged herself. Twenty minutes later, she spotted Kane exiting the building. Face set in a grim line, he bolted across the street, yanked open the truck door, and climbed inside.

She took in his hard profile, and his scent filled the cab. "Everything okay?"

"Yeah. We got a new lead." He turned the engine over, glanced out his window, and eased the truck into traffic.

Sunray waited for him to enlighten her about his conversation with Jaret and Toby, but when he remained silent, she asked, "Who were those two guys?"

"Weren't you listening?" he asked, instinctively knowing that, with her sharpened senses, she must have tuned in to their less-than-pleasant exchange.

"Yeah."

He spared her a glance, and she saw concern in his dark eyes. "Did they see you?"

"No. I'm pretty sure they didn't."

"Good. Because they're both empaths."

It suddenly occurred to her that Kane knew werewolves and empaths—descendants of witches—were real. So why couldn't he believe in reincarnation? That *he'd* been reincarnated? Was it because he didn't want to believe he'd been killed, unable to save his lover during the battle? After all, he was a protector.

"The last thing we need is for an empath to sense your wolf."

His voice pulled her back, and she nodded. "I knew there was something strange about them, but I couldn't pinpoint it."

Rich, intense eyes turned on her. "Can you block yourself to their probing, Sunray?"

She nodded. "Yeah, Lily taught me."

"Lily?"

Damn, she'd said too much. Lily was a witch from Serene, but she wasn't about to tell Kane that. Lily, along with the coven guide, Harmony, had taught the townsfolk how to block their minds to probing. One never knew when an empath would stumble upon their secluded town and discover their deadly secrets.

"Who's Lily?" he asked again, his gaze searching her face for answers.

"Just a friend." She waved a dismissive hand. "Someone I used to know."

"Speaking of friends, if you stay with me until we catch Vall, is anyone going to miss you?"

"No."

"You work at Vasenty Cosmetics, don't you?"

"Yeah, but I'm supposed to be at a marketing seminar in Los Angeles."

"What about Jaclyn? Will she try to contact you?"

"No. I told her I'd contact her when I got back."

"So, you two are friends?"

"Yeah."

"You met through work?"

She hesitated, aware he was prying. "Uh, yeah." It wasn't exactly a lie. She'd met Jaclyn at the department store in Serene when Jaclyn had moved there to try to turn around cosmetic sales.

"And you found me through her?"

"Yes."

"How?"

She nodded. "About a month ago, I picked up your scent on her coat."

His brow furrowed in thought. "I haven't seen her since before Christmas, when she gave me a hug outside Risqué. She was hurrying home to be with her husband."

"That must have been the day."

He got quiet for a moment, and then asked, "How is she anyway?"

Sunray didn't miss the genuine concern in his voice. "She's in love."

He angled his head. "Is he a good guy? Is he good to her?"

Sunray smiled as she thought about her friend Slyck and the lengths he went to to save both Jaclyn and Sunray from Vall. "Yeah, he's an amazing guy. Why do you ask?"

"Last time I saw Jaclyn, she seemed . . . *different*. But not in a bad way."

"I guess that's what love does to a person."

He scoffed. "I wouldn't know. Nor do I plan on finding out."

The sobering reality of his cold words moved through her and turned her blood to ice. As she glanced out her window, her heart turned over in her chest and she knew it was time to turn the conversation back to Vall.

"Now what?" she asked.

"We patrol."

"What's your new lead?"

"Last night, outside Candy Cane, a strip club in the city's south side, one of the dancers went for a smoke and was cornered by a rabid dog. She hit it on the nose with her shoe and it ran off."

Surprised, Sunray furrowed her brow in concentration. "A girl from a strip club," she murmured, and considered that a moment longer. "That's odd."

"Why?"

"Vall normally goes for the sweet, innocent types."

He arched a curious brow. "Like you."

"Yeah. I was a good girl who never got into trouble. I followed my mother's rules, except where you were concerned, of course." She lifted her hands, palms out in surrender. "What can I say? I was a love-struck teenager."

"And look where that got you." His eyes darkened. "You never would have been attacked if you hadn't met up with Ray that night."

Sunray linked her fingers together and shifted in her seat to face him. "You have no idea what you're talking about. We were committed—"

"Yes, I do know what I'm talking about," he intervened. "Which is precisely why I live my life the way I do. No commitments; no mistakes."

"Oh, is that what you think you're doing, Kane?" she challenged. "You think you're living?"

"Yeah, I'm living." He turned to her. "And what about you? You're a lycan, Sunray. You call that living?"

"I know it's not an ideal life, and I merely go through the motions while I chase the next moon, but at least I'm willing to admit it." She sagged against her seat, tired of sparring with him. "Believe me, you're just as damaged and just as lost in this world as I am, Kane."

"And what about your pack? Why aren't you with them? It's nature's way, isn't it?"

"What about you? You're a thirty-year-old man who lives alone. Why don't you have a wife? It's nature's way," she countered. "And where's your family, Kane? I saw the pictures on your walls. Let me guess: You separated yourself from them too."

At the mention of his family, he cast his eyes downward and the color drained from his face. "How old does Vall like his victims?"

"In their teens."

His fingers tightened on the wheel; a muscle in his jaw clenched.

Sunray eyed him. "What?"

"It's just—"

"It's just what?" she probed, a wave of unease moving into her stomach.

"Nothing," he said. Her stomach dropped when it occurred to her that he didn't trust her enough to share his secret. But honestly, could she blame him? He'd spent a lifetime killing rogue lycans, who were all monsters in his eyes. And he had the scars to prove it.

She was about to probe, but Kane shook it off and fixed her with a look that told her to drop it. "So, why do you think Vall let the stripper go?" he asked. "I hardly think she scared him off with her shoe."

"No, a shoe to the muzzle would only infuriate him, and actually would have prompted him to attack."

"So why did he let her go, then?"

As understanding dawned, Sunray's eyes widened. "He's toying with us."

Chapter Eleven

As they waited for the nightclub to open, they talked about everything and nothing over soup and sandwiches at Rosie's café. After a night of lovemaking and their honest conversation earlier that morning, Kane couldn't deny there was a new level of comfort and intimacy between them—no matter how hard he tried to ignore it.

Once their bodies were nourished, they spent the remainder of the day driving around the downtown area. As day turned to night, Sunray observed the neighborhood and tasted the air, looking for any signs of Vall, or any other lycan's presence in the city.

Kane tapped the steering wheel restlessly while he scanned the busy streets and continued to mull over and dissect all his conversations with Sunray. He wondered who Lily really was and why Sunray had quickly dismissed her when he pressed for information. And where, exactly, was Vall's den? He was pretty certain she knew. Why wouldn't she just tell him, so they could track the bastard and take him out once and for all? Kane suspected she was still keeping something from him, but for what reason? Was she protecting someone or something?

Either way, it made him very uneasy and had him questioning his sanity for agreeing to work with her. It also made him think more about his nightmares and their horrific finale.

Was it a premonition?

Hell, it had to be, because the alternative was beyond his comprehension. He believed in a lot of things, had seen a lot of shit, but no matter how much Sunray tried to convince him, he wouldn't believe he'd been reincarnated. That he had been killed and had allowed terrible things to happen to the woman he loved. That he'd been unable to protect her. Shit.

As night closed around them, Kane pulled his truck into Candy Cane's busy parking lot, a rather seedy establishment where rules were merely a suggestion and anything went. NAKED GIRLS flashed on the neon sign above the door. Actually, it was AKED GIRLS, since the *N* was burnt out.

He glanced into the dark alleyway beside the strip club, and a cold foreboding chill moved through him. Kane turned to Sunray and observed the way she was scanning the area, her blue contacts glistening in the fluorescent light from overhead.

"You want to wait here?"

Her gaze flew to his and she flashed him a smile. "Why? Are you worried about my sensibilities?"

Kane smirked, realizing what he'd said. After all, he *had* met her at Risqué. Even though it was a high-class establishment that catered to a discerning crowd, it meant that she wasn't opposed to watching, or offended by open displays of eroticism. Not to mention the fact that she was a powerful lycan who could easily rip him from limb to limb if she wished. But despite all that, there was an innocence about her, a vulnerability that brought out his protective instinct.

He curled his mouth up at one corner and shook his head. "Never mind. It was stupid."

Dark lashes quickly blinked up at him. She cupped his face, a familiar, intimate gesture that rattled him, and leaned so close her warm breath pushed back the cold. "No, it was sweet," she murmured softly. "Like you."

Fighting down the barrage of emotions that somehow managed to shake him to the core, he clenched his teeth and muttered, "Not sweet. Have you forgotten what I do for a living?" When the smile fell from her face, he pocketed his keys and said, "Let's go."

She circled the cab to meet him, and Kane led the way.

"Should we check the alleyway first?"

Kane nodded and closed his hand over his pistol. Moving with stealth and precision, they entered the darkened passage. With his back pressed to the wall, Kane peered into the black channel and glanced around. Expect for the huge Dumpster over-flowing with rancid garbage, it was empty. He turned to Sunray for her consensus.

"Nothing," she whispered.

"Let's go inside."

With his hand on the small of her back, he guided her to the front of the run-down building, pulled open the heavy door, and ushered her inside. Loud dance music filled the air, and the pungent scent of alcohol and cigarettes hit him hard. With Sunray's heightened senses, he could only imagine how putrid the odor was for her.

He glanced around, taking stock of their surroundings. Since it was still early, and it was a weeknight, the place was relatively quiet. Good. The club had a reputation for fights breaking out, and Kane didn't want any trouble while he was there with Sunray. Not that she couldn't handle herself. But still: He just wanted to get in, get his answers, and get out.

Up on stage, the stripper was sliding down a red-and-white-striped pole, her too-perfect breasts swaying with each seductive movement. At least now he knew where the name Candy Cane had come from.

Sunray waved a cloud of smoke from her face, put her mouth close to his ear so he could hear her over the music, and asked, "What was the name of the stripper?"

"Vanessa," he answered.

"I'll ask around."

He cupped her elbow and drew her close. "Maybe I'd better do it."

"I think it might be less threatening coming from me." She nodded toward the bar. "Grab us a soda, and I'll be right back."

Kane grabbed two sodas and slid into one of the grimy vinyl-covered booths at the back of the room, away from the strobe lights, which were already starting to give him a headache. With his back pressed against the seat, he watched Sunray speak with one of the guards near the rear exit. The burly guy nodded toward the girl onstage. With that, Sunray came back and slid in beside him.

"Vanessa's onstage," she said, and shed her winter coat. "We have to wait." She examined her glass, holding it up to the light before taking a small sip.

Kane pulled off his coat and shifted restlessly as he watched Vanessa writhe against the pole. In a seductive move, she spread her long legs and slid to the floor. Then she shimmied across the stage to accept bills from the slew of men sitting front and center. Kane shifted again, but there wasn't a goddamn thing he could do to deter his cock from rising to the occasion, clamoring for its own front-row seat.

As though sensing his discomfort, Sunray commented, "She's very sexy."

"She's okay."

"Come on, Kane. She's better than okay. Look at those breasts; they're perfect."

"They're fake." Despite the hard-earned battle to concentrate on the job at hand, his gaze roamed to Sunray's chest. Beneath her sweater, he glimpsed her nipples and noted the way they'd suddenly hardened under his visual caress. His mouth watered, remembering the sweet, creamy taste of those luscious buds.

He cleared his throat. "I don't like fake." His traitorous dick, however, didn't agree.

Sunray moved closer, until their thighs touched. "Well, I find it all very stimulating."

They watched the show for a bit longer, and once again, there was nothing Kane could do to marshal his growing erection. Beside him, Sunray moved slightly, and by the way her chest rose and fell in an erratic pattern, it was easy to tell how turned-on she was. He could feel her heat reaching out to him, her body beckoning his in the most provocative ways.

He glanced down at his lap to find her hand on his leg, and he wondered when she'd put it there. As though moving of its own accord, his hand closed over hers, and he squeezed. In that instant, her eyes met his, and sexual energy leapt between them. Jesus, he couldn't deny how much he wanted her, how much he wanted to take full possession of her mouth and her entire body, right there in the booth.

Conflicted, he blinked and forced himself to focus on the job as he removed her hand. He felt unable to wrap his brain around how much he craved her—and how utterly distracted it made him feel.

"Sunray, this isn't a good idea." His voice lacked conviction, and they both knew it. "We have a job to do. And if we don't start thinking with our heads, we're going to get ourselves killed."

The music stopped, pulling them both out of their erotic daze. Drawing on every ounce of strength he possessed, he inched back from her and whispered in a shaky voice, "Go find out what you can. I can't get up right now." He gestured to his lap. "For obvious reasons."

Bewitching blue eyes met his. She nodded slowly, ran shaky fingers through her hair, and sucked in a breath, clearly as rattled as he was. "Right."

Kane sat there, trying to tame his arousal, as he watched her cross the floor and meet up with Vanessa. As they exchanged words, Vanessa opened her arms wide, then grabbed her shoe to imitate her actions from the previous night.

Vanessa disappeared for a moment, then came back with a sweater. She handed it to Sunray, and when Vanessa turned her back for a second, Sunray brought it to her nose and inhaled. Sunray angled her head and gave a slight nod as her glance met his. She handed the sweater back and made her way across the room.

As he watched Sunray move toward him, something tightened inside his chest and he knew he was getting in too deep. She was a lycan. He was a hunter. This thing between them, whatever the hell it was, was completely insane. Suddenly tense, he rolled his shoulders in an attempt to loosen the painful knots in his muscles.

As though she sensed his unease, Sunray didn't sit next to him. Instead, she remained standing and said, "It was Vall. It was definitely Vall."

The vinyl seat squeaked as Kane grabbed their coats and

hastily climbed from the booth. He handed hers over, and she slipped into it. "Let's go."

He pushed the front door open, and it slammed shut behind them as they stepped outside. The cool breeze whipped over his face and helped push back the lust. As his head cleared and his passion receded, he glanced around the quiet parking lot. An uncomfortable silence fell over them as they made their way back to his truck.

She walked beside him, keeping pace, their footsteps echoing in the still, cold night. When they reached the vehicle, he slowed, and she continued to walk, moving past him. He scrubbed a hand over his chin and watched her for a moment longer before saying, "Sunray, about us . . ."

She spun around to face him and opened her mouth, but when their gazes clashed her words died on her lips.

His heart was beating in a mad cadence. Kane swallowed, and every reason he had for staying away from her instantly seemed so insignificant, so irrelevant.

Sexual energy hit them hard, and his body trembled. "Sunray . . ." he murmured, a note of desperation in his voice.

He didn't even know who moved first, but in the next second their bodies were colliding, their lips were meshed together, their tongues were thrashing, and their hands were racing over each other with fevered passion.

With little finesse, Kane pulled her against him, anchoring her hot little body to his. Her hips swayed every so slightly, grinding against him to let him know, in no uncertain terms, that she felt the pull every bit as much as he did. As urgent need overcame them both, the desire to fuck her and mark her as his overruled any rational thoughts.

Lust exploded inside him, and with a single-minded pursuit, he ripped at her jeans. "Get your pants off."

Panting and moving swiftly, she tore her jeans open and climbed out of them. As they fell to the ground, Kane pulled down his zipper to release his raging cock. He gripped her hips and lifted her onto his waist, firmly packing her against his body. His cock brushed over her soft mound, and in that instant some small, coherent part of his brain warned him to take heed, because the minute he entered her, he knew it would somehow change everything, and the future as he knew it would be forever altered.

Understanding his intent, she immediately put her long legs around his back and squeezed her thighs around his body, offering herself up to him and granting him access to her most private parts.

Kane inhaled her scent, buried his face into the soft hollow of her creamy neck, and backed her up until she was pressed against the door. He positioned his hands on her ass to keep her bare skin from connecting with the cold metal truck, and with one quick thrust, he pushed inside her.

"Oh, fuck." His entire body convulsed as her moist heat closed around him. His blood pressure soared, and despite the frigid temperatures, sweat broke out on his skin.

Her eyes clouded, and her lush mouth opened in a silent gasp as he pushed open the tight walls of her cunt. She pressed her lips to his, and when she gave a little erotic whimper, he deepened the kiss and slipped his tongue inside for a more thorough exploration.

Jesus Christ, he'd never felt such passion for anyone before, and for a moment he couldn't think, couldn't breathe. He could only feel. He held her tight, reveling in the way she felt in his arms and luxuriating in the feel of his cock inside her. Like it was where he was always meant to be. Forever.

"Sunray, kitten," he whispered into her mouth, and there wasn't a damn thing he could do about the longing in his voice.

Tension grew within him, and as much as he wanted to just stay buried in her forever and savor the sweet sensations, he knew he was so damn close to erupting. With need skyrocketing through his veins, he'd be lucky to last a full minute.

She moaned in bliss as he pumped deeper and harder, unable to get enough of her, unable to curb his desires where she was concerned.

She pitched forward, grinding her sensitive clit against his body. "More," she cried out, her breath jagged and labored. "Harder, Kane . . . please."

As she became pliable in his arms, he shifted for deeper thrusts. He rammed his cock into her so hard he feared he was going to drive her through the passenger's-side window, but he was too far gone to slow himself down. And control—hell, control was a thing of the past.

"You always know how to touch me just right." Her tight muscles clenched and pulsed around his cock, and ecstasy flitted across her face as she tumbled into an orgasm. "So damn right."

"That's my girl."

"Kane. Oh, Jesus, Kane."

He pressed his lips over hers and muffled her cries of pleasure. Sensual overload fried his brain as her hot cream dripped over his shaft and trickled down to his balls, singeing his skin along the way.

Every nerve in his body was on fire. His legs weakened beneath him, and it was all he could do to remain upright. "Fuck, I love it when you come for me."

With her every movement purposeful and sensual, she thrust her pelvis forward, grinding against him. Exquisite pleasure closed around him as she rode out her climax, wildly thrashing about in his arms.

He held her tight until the spasms passed.

"You're so wild, kitten," he whispered.

Smiling, her fingers moved over his face, tracing the scar above his eye, and he leaned in to her gentle touch. "Kane . . ." Her voice was soft, breathless, and coaxing as it seeped under his skin and produced an unfamiliar fullness in his heart.

Flustered by the emotion in her voice, his eyes went to hers. "Yeah, baby?" he asked, his breath turning to fog in the chilly night air, a reminder that he was so goddamned crazed he was actually fucking her in a parking lot. A parking lot! And, dammit, she deserved better than this, better than him going at her like an animal in heat.

"I love when you come for me too," she responded, and squeezed her sex muscles.

He growled. "Keep that up, and I'm going to lose it."

"I want you to lose it with me, Kane. The way you used to."

"Sunray . . ."

"What is it?"

Once again, ribbons of jealously whipped through his blood. "Who is it you want—me or Ray?" he asked, desperately needing to know.

"I loved Ray, but I especially love the man he's become."

She kissed him on the mouth, her lips hot against his as her hands moved over his body, palming his muscles. As pleasure poured through him, his balls clenched and he buried every damn inch of his shaft in her hot, tight sheath.

"Give yourself to me, Kane."

As a battle raged inside him, he pitched his voice low. "Sunray, I can't—"

Her eyes smoldered as her gaze flitted over his face. "Yes, you can," she murmured. "Because you're Kane, and I love you for who you are today, not for who you used to be."

With that, every ounce of resolve he had melted, and he completely and utterly gave himself over to her. Lost in a haze of emotions, he poured his seed into her and branded her as his. No matter how much he'd lectured himself on keeping his distance, knowing that they couldn't be together the way she wanted, none of that seemed to matter right now. All that mattered was this minute and this woman.

Discretion aside, he groaned out loud and didn't give a shit who heard him. Not when all he could think about was how good and how right it felt to be inside her.

After he depleted himself, breath rushed from his lungs and he remained buried in her hot sheath. He gathered her tighter in his arms, and for the first time in his life, he knew it for sure. He'd found heaven.

Heaven . . .

He stayed there for a long time, until he became aware of the cold nipping at their flesh. Knowing she had to be chilled, yet desperate not to leave her heat, he made a move to inch back.

She placed her arms around his neck and held him tight. "Not yet."

Without censor, he found himself whispering under his breath, "Not ever." As he kept her trapped between his torso and the cab of the truck, he suddenly felt her entire body go rigid.

He positioned his mouth close to her ear. "Are you okay, babe?"

A low animal-like growl came from the depths of her throat. "Don't move," she warned.

Oh, sweet Jesus! No!

With his senses on high alert, the fine hairs along his nape prickled and vivid memories from his nightmares came flashing back—memories of the way her body had tightened after making wild, crazy love, and moments before she tore into his flesh.

He inched back and took in her savage, feral look. Her eyes widened, her face paled to a cream color, and she ripped her coat and sweater from her body as she began to morph into a creature of the night.

"Holy fuck!" It was all happening so fast, he didn't even have time to think. Kane pulled in a quick breath and stepped back, but before he could put any distance between them, she grabbed him by the collar, and with a strength no mere human possessed, she spun him around until he was pressed against the door. His head smashed against the window with a thump, nearly blinding him with pain. Ignoring his injury, Kane readjusted his pants in preparation for a fight.

Once she had him up against the truck, she dropped to the ground on all fours. As she completed her metamorphosis, Kane reached for his gun.

She lifted her head and pewter eyes met his. "Sunray, what the hell are you doing?" The cop in him took aim, but the man deep inside wouldn't allow him to pull the trigger. He briefly pinched his eyes shut and tried to wrap his mind around the turn of events.

It took him by surprise when she flashed her long golden tail and turned her back to him. What the hell? He glanced up and spotted another wolf nearby, closing in on them.

"Oh, shit."

He waved his gun toward the brown-haired lycan, but before he could get a shot off, Sunray bolted across the parking lot and went up on her haunches. The rogue counterattacked, and the two dropped to the ground, their growls and yelps curling around him as they rolled across the asphalt, both fighting for purchase.

Catching flashes of sharp white teeth, fur, limbs, and claws, Kane lifted his gun again. With steady hands, he took aim, sifting through the assortment of golden and brown fur, until he was able to narrow in on his target. He squeezed the trigger, and the sound serrated the quiet as the bullet embedded itself into the wolf's shoulder.

The rogue gave a loud cry before dropping to the ground on its belly. A moment later, it shifted back and took on its human shape.

Careful not to sneak up on Sunray in her primal form, Kane dropped his gun to his side and made sure his boots smacked against the pavement to herald his approach.

Sunray inched back and remained crouched on all fours. Her body went still, almost lifeless, as her wolf examined the deceased young girl.

"Sunray," Kane whispered, trying to pull her out of her stupor.

She took a measured step toward him. Her long nails clinked on the pavement as red lips peeled back to reveal razor-sharp teeth.

"Morph," he commanded in a soft voice, not at all certain she could understand him.

Her body shook all over, and a moment later she returned to her human form. Cold and naked, she crawled across the ground until she hovered over the girl.

She finger-combed the young teen's auburn bangs back into place. "She's just a girl." Her voice was so low, Kane struggled to hear her. Tears welled in her eyes, and Kane reached out to her to bring her to her feet.

"Come here." He gathered her into his arms and held her tight, doing his best to comfort her, but he was unfamiliar with the process. She shivered, and it was then that he realized she was still naked. Kane guided her back to the truck, pulled open the door, and ushered her inside the cab. After gathering her clothes off the ground, he handed them to her and hurried around to the driver's side.

As she dressed, he put the heat on, grabbed his cell phone, and called in the shooting. Once complete, he turned to her and gave her his undivided attention.

"You okay?" he asked.

"As well as I can be under the circumstances."

He had to hand it to her: She was one heck of a strong woman. As admiration kicked in, he rubbed the goose egg on his head and said, "You know, you scared the shit out of me for a minute there."

Still shaken, she conjured a slight smile. "Sorry about that."

He put his hand on her shoulder—a calming gesture. As they exchanged a look, warmth passed between them. The depth of desire he felt for her was incomprehensible. He cleared his throat and said, "Thanks."

She sniffed and stole another glance at the body through her frost-covered window. "I could say the same to you."

"That was a close one." Kane raked his fingers through his hair and let loose a whistle.

"Yeah, we nearly had our asses handed to us."

He gave her an apologetic look. "I guess I kind of got carried away."

"*We* got carried away," she corrected.

He brushed her hair back and ran the pad of his thumb over her cold blue-tinged lips. They'd been so caught up in each other, that wolf had easily snuck up on them, which gave credence to his logic that he needed to keep his distance from her both physically and emotionally.

With his voice low, he said forcefully, "We need to start thinking with our heads, Sunray. Otherwise, one of us is going to end up dead." And, truthfully, the thought of anything happening to her turned his blood to ice.

She got quiet for a moment as she mulled that over. "You're right. And we can't let anything happen to either one of us, because we need each other to catch Vall. I'll be damned if I let another innocent person get hurt." She tapped her temple. "From now on, we think with this."

As his gaze panned over hers, he instinctively knew he hadn't been thinking with his dick or his head when he fucked her. He was thinking with his heart.

Bloody hell . . .

But, Jesus, hadn't he always been taught that lycans were monsters who only acted in their own best interests? The cop in him told him to tread carefully where Sunray was concerned. Hell, who was he to say that once they found Vall, she wouldn't turn on him? Maybe she was really working with Vall to bait the hunter.

But he recalled the way she'd checked on Tanya at her condo. The genuine anger that sparked in her eyes at the thought of Vall killing another innocent. The tears in her eyes after they'd discovered the lycan was just a young girl. And the way she'd protected him, putting herself between him and the wolf.

Not to mention the way she'd always given herself to him, handing herself over and trusting that he'd take care of her, body, heart, and soul.

Was it possible that he'd been wrong all these years? That not all lycans were coldhearted monsters? That the world as he knew it was falling apart?

"Where the hell are they all coming from, Sunray?"

Her eyes went wide, like she had a lightbulb moment. She slid her fingers through her hair and groaned. "Vall is building an army."

"Why? What is he planning?" An array of emotions— everything from anger to sadness—passed over her face, but she said nothing.

Exasperated with her secrecy, he said, "Sunray, you have to tell me everything you know."

She lowered her head, and he felt her resistance soften. "I can't," she said honestly. "I wish I could, but I just can't."

"Are you protecting someone?"

A long pause, and then, "Yeah, something like that."

Kane blew a breath and backed down. "Okay, for now I won't probe, but if you're holding something back that can help us find Vall—"

"I'm not."

"Sunray—"

"Kane, you'll have to trust me."

His heart kicked into gear, and it suddenly hit him that he did. He did trust her.

Chapter Twelve

Sunray glanced out the small bedroom window and looked up at the sliver of moon hovering over Chicago. Four days had passed since the night at the club, and they were still no closer to finding Vall than they were when this had all begun. At least there hadn't been any more murders in the city. Which made her wonder if Vall had gone back to Serene. She'd like nothing better than to make the long trek to New Hampshire herself, to observe the town she'd left behind, but she couldn't, not without leading Kane there.

She thought some more about their passionate rendezvous in the parking lot. Even though Kane had been rough with her, like he'd been trying to fight a few of his own demons, there was no denying that their encounter had been more emotional, less physical. She knew it, and whether he wanted to admit it or not, Sunray believed he knew it too.

As much as she wanted to be in Kane's bed again, she also knew he was right about keeping their distance, because they easily could have been killed outside Candy Cane. If they wanted to catch Vall, they needed to keep their heads clear.

With a new understanding between them, they remained civil and kept their distance, both physically and emotionally, despite the insurmountable tension building around them. She was sure anyone within a hundred feet could feel it.

But still, she fought it down. And no matter how hard it was to share his house with him, no matter how hard it was to cook and eat breakfast with him or to ride around in his truck all night with him, she kept her emotions in check—when all she really wanted to do was love him the way he needed to be loved, the way only she knew how to love him.

The knock on her door drew her attention. She tightened her robe around her waist and spun around. "Come in."

Kane inched the door open, and his dark eyes were somber when they met hers. Her heart leapt and everything inside her reached out to him, needing him in ways that left her breathless.

"You okay?" he asked.

"Yeah," she lied, and nodded toward the neatly folded clothes on her bed. "I'll be ready in a second."

"Make it quick." He tapped his side, where his gun slumbered. "We need to move."

Her stomach sank. "Not again."

Kane shook his head and gave a heavy sigh. "Afraid so."

"Where?"

"Another seedy little spot on the south side."

"Was anyone hurt?"

"Yeah." He stepped into the room, and his brow furrowed with worry. "Sunray, I've been thinking. You should have your gun." In a show of trust, he reached behind his back and drew her gun from his belt.

He took two long strides and closed the short distance between them. As he stood over her, she could hear his blood rushing through his body, hear his heart pound hard against his chest. Fighting not to lose composure and throw herself at him, she closed her fingers around the metal and nodded in understanding.

He slipped his finger under her chin and lifted her head until their eyes met. His voice was low and soft when he asked, "You do know how to use this thing, don't you?"

"Of course." Her voice came out a little shakier than she would have liked.

His mouth turned up at the corner, softening his features and making him look so adorable. "I wouldn't want you to accidentally shoot yourself with it."

"I haven't yet," she assured him. As she gave him a small smile, she wondered why he wasn't worried about her—a vicious lycan—shooting him.

With that, he chuckled and fingered the lapels of her robe. His gaze raked over her body, then went to the pile of clothes on the bed, before his attention drifted back to her. His fingers clenched, and she didn't miss his moment of hesitation. With energy arcing between them, she opened her mouth, but wasn't sure what to say.

Fortunately, he came to her rescue. With his professional demeanor back in place, he said, "It's getting late." He turned and walked to the door. "I'll leave you to get ready." The latch clicked shut behind him, and she listened to his footsteps as he moved down the hall, taking her heart and her soul along with him.

A short while later, they found themselves outside Mike's Tavern, not too far from Candy Cane, as a matter of fact. As the police quarantined the area, people spilled from the tavern and milled about, trying to get a glimpse of the action behind the taped-off area.

Sunray's heart squeezed when she caught sight of a young man on the ground, blood oozing from his neck as officials made a chalk outline. Kane studied the victim and then let his glance move over the crowd, discerning each and every person fluttering about.

With the scent of Vall still lingering in the night air, Sunray turned, prepared to follow the smell. But when she twisted around, she smacked right into a wall of muscles that nearly knocked her off her feet. Thick hands slipped around her waist to steady her, and when she identified who those hands belonged to, she immediately doubled the shield she had around her thoughts.

"Whoa there, little lady," Jaret said, tightening his hold on her waist.

She extricated herself from his strong grip. "Excuse me," she said. "My fault."

He didn't let her go. Instead he gripped her elbow and hauled her closer. Much to her discomfort, he continued to invade her personal space. Dark hair fell over his forehead as he dipped his head and stared into her eyes, studying her features.

"Do I know you?" he asked.

Keeping herself calm, she tamed a few temperamental curls and met his gaze unflinchingly. "No. I'd remember."

"Are you sure?" He breathed deeply, his nostrils flaring, and she could practically feel him surfing around inside her head. He frowned when he came up with nothing. "You seem very familiar."

Just then, Kane stepped up to her, and Jaret released his grip on her arm. "Kane," he said with a curt nod, and turned his attention to the case. He gestured toward the body. "Is this the work of your guy?"

"Appears so."

Leaving them to talk, Sunray slipped away, fully aware of Jaret's eyes on her as she disappeared into the crowd. She positioned herself out of his line of sight, but not far enough that she couldn't hear them.

Jaret folded his arms across his broad chest and stared at Kane. Then he leaned in slightly, inhaled, and gave a slow shake of his head. "Jesus, she's with you. I can smell her all over you."

"Yeah, what's your point?"

"Since when do you bring a date to a crime scene?"

Explosive tension coiled around them, and she could practically hear Kane's teeth clench. "Not that it's any of your fucking business, but we were together when the call came in."

Jaret inched closer, crowding Kane. "Actually, since when did you get a soft spot for any girl?" He scoffed, and slapped his palm to his forehead. "Now it makes perfect sense." He gestured behind him with his head, as though knowing exactly where she was standing in the crowd. "You've spent so much time whoring with your girl over there that you've gone soft and lost your edge."

Sunray wasn't sure who swung first, but she could guess that it was Kane. They barely got in a couple of punches each before a swarm of officers surrounded them, hauling them off one another.

A large man with a take-charge attitude pushed through the crowd. He had an authority about him, and as he jerked his thumb at the men, she could only assume it was their captain. "You two keep this up and you're both out of here. Got it?"

"Got it," they said in unison.

Jaret's shrewd glance went from Kane to where Sunray stood, back to Kane. He leaned in and spoke softly, his words meant for Kane's ears only. "If you're up to something, Kane, I'll find out."

"Good luck with that," Kane shot back, and made his way

to his truck. When Sunray slipped into the passenger's seat, he peeled out of the parking lot.

"We need to find him." He pounded the steering wheel. "Fuck, this has to stop."

"We will," she assured him, suddenly not so sure herself as she took in the dab of blood near his mouth.

"Is he still in the area?" Kane wiped his face with the back of his hand. "Can you sense him?"

"I did at first, but not anymore."

With a twist of the steering wheel, Kane maneuvered his truck into traffic. "Let's drive a bit, to see if you can pick up his trail."

They drove around the south side for hours, and it was nearing nine when both Kane and Sunray decided that Vall's track had gone cold.

"You hungry?" he asked.

"Famished."

"Let's get something to eat. I know this great spot."

She smirked and tried to lighten his mood. "Let me guess: Rosie's café."

"Not quite."

Kane led them out of downtown and into suburbia. He pulled his truck up to a nice family diner. "They have great pie here. Do you like pie, Sunray?"

She nodded. "I like everything." As she hopped out of the truck, she stopped dead in her tracks. Kane came around to her side.

"What?"

"I thought I saw something."

Kane slipped his hand inside his coat and spun around. "Where?"

She peered into the dark, cold night. "Something on the side of the building. A flash of brown against the white snow."

Together they cautiously made their way around the restaurant, Kane's fingers tightening around his gun. A chill seeped into their bones as they spent a good long time looking and listening. They followed the tracks until the snow thinned and trailing became impossible. Clear that they'd lost him, they began backtracking, Kane's appetite long gone as he thought about who lived nearby in the quiet, rather safe neighborhood.

"You still feel like that pie?" he asked.

She pressed her hand to her stomach. "Not really."

They made their way back to the truck, and Kane glanced around. "Why would he be here? In suburbia? This isn't his usual stomping ground."

"Like I said, Kane, he likes them young and innocent."

His eyes darkened. "Get in the truck."

Sunray shimmied in beside him and couldn't help but notice that he seemed nervous about something. More agitated than usual. Had the fight with Jaret hit a nerve, or was it something else entirely?

They drove in silence for a while before he asked, "Anything?"

"No. He's long gone."

Kane blew a sigh of relief, and she noticed that he'd slowed his truck down outside a homey, two-story house at the end of a nice, quiet cul-de-sac. He gazed with longing as he panned over the windows and the people milling about inside.

"Kane, who lives there?"

He shook his head. "No one."

"Like hell." She reached for the door handle.

He leaned across the cab, and his palm closed over hers. "Sunray, don't."

She squeezed his hand. "You know, Kane, I'd kill to be with my family. I'd kill to see my mother again."

Expression uncertain, he unconsciously brushed his finger over the deep scar above his eye and said, "I wouldn't know what to say; we haven't spoken in a few years."

"And you haven't really been living for years."

His eyes were both pleading and sad when he said, "I can't drag them into my life."

"What good is this life if you don't have anyone to share it with, Kane? The good times and the bad." She pointed a finger toward the house. "Your family is in there, and I just bet they love you and miss you as much as you love and miss them." Distraught, Sunray rested her head against the seat. "God, I miss my brethren so much it hurts. Honestly, I'd do anything to see them again, but I can't go back. But you, Kane, your family is right there." She tapped her finger on the window. "Right there. And you're purposely shutting them out of your life."

Astute officer that he was, he asked, "Where, exactly, are your brethren, and why can't you go back?"

Frustrated from trying to get through to him, and aware that she'd said too much, she climbed from the cab, letting the cool wind soothe her emotions. "You'll thank me for this."

"Sunray, don't," he yelled as he jumped from the truck and raced around her side to stop her. But he was too late. She'd already reached the front door and rung the bell.

A moment later, a pretty woman in her late thirties answered. She blinked her big brown eyes and asked politely, "Can I help you?"

Sunray said nothing; she just waited. The woman's short chestnut hair swung around her jawline, and dark eyes widened as her glance went from Sunray to Kane.

"Kane," she squealed, her palms going to her cheeks in astonishment.

For a long moment, they stood there staring at each other in shocked silence; then Kane broke the uncomfortable moment. In the softest voice, he said, "It's nice to see you, Cara." He put his arm around Sunray's shoulder, and the comforting gesture warmed her from the inside out. "This is Sunray."

Smiling, Sunray shook Cara's hand and looked past her shoulder. Behind Cara, a man who Sunray presumed was the woman's husband came sauntering down the hall to see what the commotion was all about.

He folded up the wet cuffs of his sleeves and asked, "Cara, is everything okay?"

"Matt, Kane is here," she said. "And this is Sunray."

"Well, invite them in then." Feigning cold, Matt rubbed his arms. "It's damn freezing outside."

Grinning, Cara hooked her arm around Sunray's and ushered her inside. "Goodness, where are my manners," she said, flustered.

"We didn't mean to take you by surprise," Sunray explained as she studied the striking similarities between the siblings. "And I know it's late, but we just happened to be in the neighborhood."

"Nonsense." Cara waved her hand, and it occurred to her just how kind and welcoming the woman was and what a wonderful sister-in-law she'd make. Oh, boy. She shouldn't be thinking about such things—things she could never have and knew better than to long for.

"Kane is welcome anytime. He knows that." She turned to him, pinched her brows together, and questioned, "You do know that, right?"

"I know that," he said in a tone that alerted Sunray to his discomfort. She slipped her hand into his and squeezed, a silent, reassuring message.

Cara guided them into her family room, gestured toward the sofa, and then turned to her husband. "Matt, can you please put on the coffee?"

Kane sat on the plush brown sofa, and Sunray nestled close to offer him her support. He moved restlessly beside her, and she knew this was hard on him. But family was everything, and just because he was a hunter, surely to God that didn't mean he had to shut everyone he loved out of his life.

She watched something pass over Kane's eyes as he glanced around the cozy, toy-filled room; she saw just how much he really wanted this. All of this. And dammit, he deserved it.

Kane tensed and straightened in his seat as a boy about six years of age, freshly bathed and dressed in a pair of pajamas, came flying into the room, making noises and holding a model airplane above his head. He zigzagged around the furniture, then abruptly froze when he spotted Kane.

"Uncle Kane," he said.

Fingers linked together and muscles tight, Kane said, "Hi, Ben."

Ben crinkled his cute freckle-laced nose. "What are you doing here?"

"Ben, mind your manners," Cara piped in.

"It's okay." Kane held his hand up in a gesture meant to reassure his sister that he had everything under control, even though Sunray suspected he didn't. "I just thought I'd come by to say hi."

"But you never come by to say hi."

From the mouths of babes.

Sunray glanced at Cara and could tell she was uncomfortable with her son's blatant honesty.

"Maybe I need to change that," Kane offered with a smile, and Sunray could see something inside him shift as he visually relaxed.

Ben eyed Sunray. "Is that your girlfriend?" Before Kane could answer, Ben probed, "Are you going to marry her?"

"This is Sunray," Kane explained.

"That's a funny name. Can I go to the wedding? Will that make her my uncle too?"

"That's an awful lot of questions, Ben," Kane hedged, chuckling.

"If you marry her, you'll have to kiss her, and kissing is gross."

"Bedtime, little man," Cara said, a light blush moving up her neck to her cheeks.

With that, Ben made a face and said, "Timmy's getting a new tooth."

"Is he, now?"

"Yeah, he cries a lot through the night, but Mom says I'm the big brother, so I have to be patient and take care of him, the way Aunt Linda always used to take care of you and mommy." He rolled his eyes. "Family's gotta take care of each other, you know."

"Aunt Linda?" Sunray asked.

"My oldest sister," Kane explained without taking his eyes off Ben.

Cara clapped her hands. "Okay, Mr. Benjamin Armstrong. Off to bed."

It suddenly occurred to Sunray that she didn't even know Kane's last name.

"Night, Uncle Kane and Uncle Sunray." Once again putting his plane above his head, Ben flew down the hallway, disappearing as quickly as he'd appeared.

Matt stuck his head around the corner, and the fresh scent of coffee wafted before everyone's nostrils. "You all get caught up. I'll tuck him in and be right back with the coffee."

When Ben left the room, Kane turned to Cara. "I'm surprised he remembers me."

She gave him a warm smile and pointed to the array of family pictures on the cranberry-colored walls. "I'd never let him forget you."

"He's adorable," Sunray said. "And quite the character."

"I call him Little Kane."

"You do? Why?" Sunray asked, eager to hear more about Kane's childhood antics.

"Because he's a handful, like Kane was when he was young. Always curious, and always into everything," Cara said with a grin.

Kane rolled his eyes. "Just promise me you won't get out the old photo albums."

Cara winked at her brother. "I don't think that's a promise I can keep." Kane let out a low groan, and Cara laughed. She turned to Sunray and questioned, "Do you have children, Sunray?"

"No."

"Are you planning to?"

When Sunray hesitated, embarrassment spread over Cara's face, and she rushed out, "Oh, I'm sorry. I didn't mean to pry."

A whimper came from the baby monitor on the windowsill. Seemingly thankful for the distraction, Cara grinned and stood. "Never a moment's peace."

A short while later, she came back with Timmy in her arms and a bottle of milk in her hand. She threw a blanket over her shoulder and cradled the baby as he greedily drank from the bottle.

As she fed her child, Kane watched on, smiling as he met his nephew for the first time. Cara led the conversation as her sweet baby gulped milk. With all the questions she was firing Kane's way, it was easy to tell how much Cara had missed her brother.

"Mooommmmmyyy." Ben's loud wail came from down the hall.

"Apparently, Ben needs his mommy." Cara stood and handed the baby to Sunray. "Do you mind?"

Sunray's heart twisted as she gathered little Timmy into her arms and plopped the bottle back into his tiny, puckered mouth. She inhaled the sweet scent of baby powder. As his big brown eyes stared up at her, she couldn't help but smile.

"You look just like your uncle," she said, and rubbed the backs of her fingers over his soft cheeks. "So sweet. I wonder if you'll grow up to be just like him."

When she glanced up at Kane, he looked on in horror. "What . . . what are you doing?" A muscle along his jaw clenched, and as his gaze moved over her face, her stomach sank. Good God, what did he think she was doing? Preparing to tear into the baby like a hungry jackal? A ravenous werewolf?

Disgusted by his reactions, she handed the baby over to him. Cripes, here she thought he was beginning to trust her, especially after everything they'd been through, but she must have misread his intentions when he'd handed over her gun.

Kane looked at the baby in his arms, and she didn't miss the vulnerability in his eyes. "What do I do?"

Despite her anger, warmth moved through her. There was just something about a big, powerful man holding a baby that tugged on the heartstrings. She helped him adjust the child, and showed him how to position the bottle to avoid air bubbles.

Kane angled his head, and she caught his crooked grin. "He does kind of look like me."

A lump lodged in her throat as she took it all in. Oh, God, how she wanted this. All of this. With Kane.

Before she could dwell on those feelings, both Cara and Matt returned with a tray of coffee. Cara smiled when she saw Timmy in Kane's arms, and as he became more comfortable with the child, Kane didn't seem in any hurry to relinquish him.

The four of them talked for a bit over their steaming mugs of java. They kept to safe subjects like the weather, the price of oil, and the kids. A short while later, when Cara yawned, Sunray tapped Kane's leg.

"It's late, and Cara needs her sleep if she wants to keep up with Ben and Timmy."

When Kane stood, Matt took the baby from his arms; then they all walked to the front entrance together. Kane's hand closed over Sunray's, warm and strong. When she touched him in return, just to feel connected, he gave her a look that conveyed his jangled emotions.

Cara leaned in and gave Sunray a hug. "I don't know how you did it, but thanks for bringing him here."

After saying their good-byes, there was a heavy silence as Kane and Sunray walked back to the truck. When they got inside, she turned to him and questioned in a soft voice, "What were you thinking back there, Kane? Why were you looking at me like that?"

"Like what?"

"Like I was going to eat little Timmy. Haven't we gotten past this?"

He took a breath and let it out slowly. "I didn't think you were going to eat him, Sunray."

"Well, please enlighten me, then. What, exactly, were you thinking?"

"I don't know." He rolled one shoulder. "Just seeing you holding him, feeding him, and nurturing him . . ." His voice hitched and he stopped for a second before adding, "It made me feel—I don't know—it just made me *feel*, okay?"

His mouth tightened, and the pain and other emotions etched on his troubled face made her throat constrict. "Kane, it's okay to feel."

"Sunray?" His voice deepened and took on a serious edge.

Her stomach rolled. "Yeah?"

"My older sister, Linda, has a teenage daughter."

Sunray sucked in a gasp. "Why didn't you tell me this be-fore?"

His eyes met hers. "I . . . I guess because I didn't trust you before."

Her heart skipped a beat, hardly able to believe what she was hearing. "You trust me now?"

"Yeah, I do."

Love rushed through her veins. Her hand touched his face, and everything inside her reached out to him. "Kane."

"If Vall knows who I am, he knows who my family is. That's probably why we sensed him in this neighborhood. He's definitely toying with us." He raked his hands through his hair, and his angst-filled voice shook when he said, "This is why I've distanced myself for the last few years. I didn't want to lead a rogue to my family."

Guilt swamped her. "Jesus, this is all my fault."

He gave a quick shake of his head, and she noted the dark circles shadowing his tired eyes. "You were only doing what you thought was best for me. None of this is your fault."

"Yes, it is. Vall is after me, and I brought him into your world, your life."

"No. I was already after him. You're not owning this, Sun-ray. We're in this together."

Still feeling responsible, she vowed, "I won't let him hurt her, Kane. I swear to you, I'll kill him first."

He leaned in to her, his voice low, his words soft. "Sunray, he's stronger than you, and stronger than me, but no way in hell is he stronger than the two of us together."

She snuggled close, in search of comfort. "Yeah, we make quite a team, you and me," she said, using his earlier words.

"Let's go home," he whispered, and Sunray's heart lurched with his use of the word *home*. Unfortunately for her, a home—a real home like Cara's—was something just beyond her reach.

Chapter Thirteen

With exhaustion pulling at him hard, Kane flicked on his kitchen light, shrugged off his coat, and hung it on the rack just inside the door. He stifled a yawn, stretched his arms out, and said, "It's been one hell of a night."

Sunray shed her jacket and put it on the rack next to his.

"You got that right," she agreed, and leaned against the wall to remove her boots.

Kane drove his hands into his pockets and watched the seductive way her hair fell over her breasts as she paired her boots and placed them under the rack. "I'm beat."

"Me too." Sunray strolled across the floor, reached into the cupboard, and pulled out a glass. "Drink?" she asked, as she opened the fridge and pulled out the orange juice.

Just watching her move through his kitchen, all domestic-like, while she poured herself a drink made him feel weird inside.

"Kane, would you like a drink?" she asked again when he didn't answer.

"No, I'm good."

As she eyed him, warmth flooded his system.

"Are you okay?"

"Tired," he reminded her.

"Well, go get some sleep, then." With that, she turned her back to him and poured a glass of juice. She gave the near-empty container a shake before putting it back in the fridge, and tossed her words over her shoulder. "We need to pick up more juice tomorrow."

"Sunray . . ."

With the glass poised at her lips, she turned to face him. "Yeah?"

His eyes went to her mouth and he stepped close, invading her personal space. He reached for the hem of her sweater, ran the fabric between his fingers, and pitched his voice low. "I want you in my bed tonight," he said with a quiet certainty.

Surprise registered in her eyes. She lowered the glass, and he could almost hear her mind race, sorting through the turn of events as a tremble raced through her body.

"I was just—"

He leaned in and kissed her, so soft and so tender he could feel the breath rush from her lungs. "I need you with me tonight." His voice sounded a little unstable, a little shaky, even to himself. "In my bed. Now," he confessed, his lips still hovering over hers as he gathered her hand into his. "Will you sleep with me, kitten?"

With the distant way he'd been acting, he honestly had no idea if she'd agree. But it was difficult to put into words how much he needed her with him tonight, to make sweet, passionate love to every inch of her body, to feel skin on skin as they slipped between the sheets, and to just hold her in his arms as they drifted off sleep.

Juice forgotten, she gave a slow but sure nod and followed him to the bedroom. A warm, comfortable silence fell over them as Kane shed his clothes and helped her remove hers.

Once she was naked, he stood back to drink in the beautiful sight of her. The way she stood there, looking so vulnerable, fragile, and emotionally damaged, had him aching to take her into his arms and kiss away all her worries.

She held her hand out to him. "Kane . . ."

As she reached for him, his heart tightened. He stepped in to her and swept his lips over hers, aching to touch her, for her to touch him.

He inched her back until she was pressed against the wall. Gripping both her wrists in one hand, he lifted them over her head, opening her body to him.

"Let me make love to you, Sunray. The way you deserve." When she continued to stare up at him with those big, expressive eyes of hers, he smoothed his thumb over her lush mouth and continued. "Would you let me do that, sweetheart?"

Her body spasmed with pleasure and it fueled the flames inside him. "Yes, please. I want you to do that more than anything." The desire in her eyes touched his soul, and her breathy voice caressed him all over.

He soaked in her warmth before dropping to his knees. He buried his face in her stomach, slipped his hands around to cradle her backside, and just held her to him for a long moment.

Her body fairly vibrated as she pushed her fingers through his hair and anchored him to her abdomen. Kane inhaled her scent and growled deep.

With his insides churning, he murmured against her stomach, "I love how much you want me."

She whimpered. "You have no idea how much I want you, Kane." Her voice shook, a melee of emotions rushing through her blood.

He slipped a finger between her legs and dipped inside her drenched pussy. When she drew a deep, shuddering breath, he tipped his head and shot her a grin. "Yes, I do."

A smile touched her mouth, and when she bucked against him, he withdrew his finger. "You're an evil man," she muttered, and threw her head back in sexual frustration.

He let out a low laugh. "No need to rush things, baby. We have all night. And there are so many things I want to do to you." He grazed his lips over one nipple before pulling it into his mouth. His cock throbbed and grew another inch as it clamored for her attention.

She moaned and arched into his touch. "Kane?"

"Yeah, kitten?"

"What's your last name?"

He glanced up, surprised by her question. "What?"

The look in her eyes had him softening like his down-filled pillow. He had to admit, as a hunter, he was prepared for just about anything in life. But as a man, he wasn't prepared for this at all, especially the love shining in her eyes and the way it stirred things deep inside him, things he'd kept buried.

"I don't know your last name," she explained. "And I want to know everything about my Ray in this lifetime."

He drew a steadying breath. "It's Reynolds," he said as her love wrapped around his heart and weakened his knees. "Kane Reynolds."

"Reynolds," she echoed. "That's a good, strong name." She said his name again, as though tasting it on the tip of her tongue as her fingers combed through his hair and guided his mouth back to her perfect pink nipple, boldly letting him know what she wanted.

He drew her breast into his mouth and laved it with his tongue, savoring the way it swelled and tightened beneath his ministrations. His hands slowly moved over her silky, soft body, taking his time to properly introduce himself to her this time.

He traced the pattern of her curves and felt the shiver that stole over her. God, he loved the effect he had on her.

He tapped her legs, and she widened them. When her pussy lips parted, he murmured, "Now let me show you how much I want you."

Kane wet his dry lips, lowered his head, and made a slow

pass over her dripping cunt. As he basked in the sweet taste of her cream, his entire body broke out in a sweat. He buried his face in deeper and swirled his tongue through her heat, until small spasms began in her body. But he wasn't prepared to bring her over yet. He wanted to play with her first.

He stroked her swollen clit lightly, and a tortured moan sounded in her throat.

"What is it, Sunray?" he asked, a teasing grin on his lips. "Are you in pain?"

"Like I said: evil," she murmured breathlessly.

Chuckling, he pushed a finger inside her. "Is this what you want?"

"God, yesss . . ."

Feeling ravenous as her taste lingered on his tongue, Kane bit down on his bottom lip as she dripped over his finger. He slowly began to ease his finger in and out, and her muscles pulsated in response.

"More," she purred.

He pushed another finger inside as his mind raced with all the things he wanted to do to her. All the ways he wanted to mark her as his. "Is this what you want?"

"You know it is." She bucked against him with wild abandon. "Harder."

With easy movements, he pumped his thick fingers in and out of her, ever determined to build her climax slowly, so that once he took her over the edge, she'd never, ever forget the moment.

Panting and wild with need, she pushed against him and ground her cunt into his face, nearly knocking him backward. He flicked his tongue out and lapped at her engorged clit.

"Easy, kitten," he whispered, and put his hand on her stomach to anchor her to the wall. Her body rippled and his groin tightened as he took control of her pleasure.

She watched him work her body with a riveted gaze. "Kane . . . please . . ."

"Are you aching, sweetheart?"

Her eyes flared hot when they met his. "Yes," she whimpered.

Her pussy muscles gripped him harder, and urgent need colored his voice when he promised, "Just so you know, once I give you what you want, kitten, I plan on taking what I need." He pushed his fingers deeper and harder, and she grew slicker, creamier, with each determined stroke.

She whimpered and sagged against the wall. He swirled his tongue over her clit and drew it between his teeth. Desire thrummed through his veins and he damn near went off like a supernova just from touching her.

With his libido in an uproar, he worked to marshal his raging lust for the time being. He wanted to lavish her body with lots of attention and make this exceptionally good for her.

Her legs quivered and he pushed against her, working his fingers in deeper and lightly circling the sensitive bundle of nerves. Her aroused scent filled the air and teased and tormented his senses.

"I love how you touch me," she murmured, her sex clenching and alerting him to her impending climax.

He tapped her clit and rolled his index finger over her G-spot, giving her what she needed.

Her body shook from head to toe, and her sex muscles squeezed his fingers so hard, he damn near shot off himself.

He eased in and out of her as she concentrated on the points of pleasure and rode out her climax.

"Now let me show you what I need." He stood, gripped her hips roughly, and spun her around until her back was pressed against his chest. He ground his cock against her sweet ass and slid one hand over her breasts, going lower until he reached her wet cunt. He dipped inside and her breath caught on a gasp. He wet his finger and brought it to her ass to cover her tight opening with cream. She made a sexy noise and shifted.

"I want to be inside you. Everywhere."

"God, Kane, yes."

He walked her to the bed, placed a pillow near the edge, and gently nudged her downward until her breasts were pressed into his mattress and her ass was tipped up and wide open for his viewing pleasure.

As he took in the erotic sight of her, his body tightened and his muscles throbbed with need. "You're mine." He widened her ass cheeks and toyed with her opening. "Say it, Sunray," he demanded. "Say you're mine."

"I'm yours, Kane. I've always been yours. No one will ever be my master but you."

Heat rocketed through him, and he dipped into her cream again. As he lubricated her puckered ass, he gently probed to test her opening. His cock ached, and he could barely think straight as her slick heat tightened around his finger. Fuck, he needed to be inside her so much, he felt dizzy. As she pushed against him, he carefully eased his finger past her ringed passage, stretching and widening her in preparation for his substantial girth.

Once she was ready, he positioned his cock at her opening, and he felt her body soften and draw him in. "Oh, God, girl. You're so tight."

He sank deeper, and she moaned, encouraging him to feed her his entire length. A slow burn worked its way through his body as he took his time to enter her completely. Once inside, he drew a fueling breath as his passion-rattled brain tried to catch up.

When her ass muscles squeezed his cock, he pulled out and drove into her again, deep, hungry stabs that pushed him beyond sanity. Moving restlessly, she bucked her hips, meeting and welcoming each urgent thrust, and together they established a rhythm.

Seeking an even deeper intimacy, he gripped her hips hard and slammed into her, unable to get enough of her. He briefly closed his eyes and savored the sensations. Christ, he knew he was acting like some wild animal marking its territory, but he couldn't help it. She was his, goddammit.

His.

Her soft moan pulled him back. "Kane, please, I need . . ."

He leaned over her and slipped a hand beneath her body to toy with her clit, and in that instant, her cream exploded over his hand and her ass tightened.

Kane threw his head back and let go, releasing every ounce of himself inside her and giving her a piece of himself that he'd never given another.

He remained on top of her, sweat merging their bodies as one. A short while later, as his heart settled back into a steady rhythm, he withdrew, leaving his mark on her in so many ways.

He pulled her to her feet, gathered her into his arms, and hugged her to him.

"Mmm, so nice," she murmured.

"Very nice," he said, and tapped her ass cheeks. "Let's get cleaned up."

Kane led her to the shower, and they both climbed into the hot, steamy spray. He soaped down her body, taking care to clean every inch of her skin before she turned the soap on him.

Sated and completely drained, they hopped out of the shower, towel-dried their bodies, and prepared themselves for bed.

A warm, comfortable quiet fell over them as he captured her hand in his and led her back down the hall to his room. Needing to keep her close, he gathered her into his arms and placed her between his warm flannel sheets.

Sunray snuggled against him and rested her head on his chest, and he pulled her closer to enjoy the easy intimacy between them—an intimacy that went well beyond sex.

Honestly, he had had no idea how wonderful it was just to snuggle in bed with someone—of course, he couldn't imagine it would be as wonderful with anyone other than Sunray. She'd opened his eyes to so much tonight, making him realize just how much he was missing out on. And the truth was, until he'd met her, he wasn't living at all. He was merely surviving. He brushed his lips over her hair and kissed the top of her head, reveling in the feel of her next to him.

"Sunray."

"Mmm?" Her voice was sleepy.

"You never did answer Cara's question."

"Question?"

"Yeah. Do you want kids of your own?"

He felt her tighten against him, and he brushed his fingers over her arms in a bid to relax her.

"Have you forgotten that I'm a lycan?"

He paused for a second, then said, "No."

"Then you know I can only mate and have babies with other lycans, right?"

"Yeah, but that still doesn't answer my question."

She angled her head to see him, and the longing in her eyes tore at his heart. "Yes, Kane. I do want babies. Lots of babies. But it's not in my future. I don't live with my brethren, and as you know, the man I love"—she stopped to poke him in the chest—"the only man I want to have babies with is human."

His throat tightened as he brushed his fingers over her warm cheeks. He couldn't believe how close he felt to her at that moment, even closer than when they were having sex, when he was buried deep inside her.

"So if I was a lycan, you'd have babies with me?" he managed around the lump in his throat.

As she regarded him warily, emotional chaos erupted inside him. "Yes, Kane," she answered, her eyes so full of want, it fed the incessant ache inside him. "But you're not, and you never will be. So the point is moot." She pressed a soft kiss to his mouth and whispered, "I think you're overtired. You need sleep." With that, she curled up next to him and shut her eyes.

Warmth rushed to his heart as her heat and love enveloped him. A moment later, his eyes slipped shut, and as he drifted off, he wondered exactly when it was that he'd opened up his heart to her. But how could they be together, and how could he give her the family that she so desperately wanted? After all, he was still a hunter and she was still a lycan.

His soft moans pulled her awake. Sunray blinked her eyes open and took in the unfamiliar surroundings. As she tried to gather her bearings, the deep, tortured moan came again. She looked at the man sprawled out on the mattress beside her, and reality came rushing back as she read his distress. *Kane!* Oh, God, he was having another nightmare. She gave him a light shake.

"Kane, wake up."

His head thrashed to the side and one hand went to his neck. Oh, Jesus, he was reliving the night Vall had murdered him.

But had those memories sorted themselves out or were they still a jumbled mess? Fear chilled her blood and brought on a shiver. Would he awaken and still think it was she who'd killed him? If so, how would he react when he found her leaning over him? Would dream and reality intertwine? She began to inch back, but when his lids flew open, she froze, her breath catching in the back of her throat as pain flitted across his face.

Panting, his brown eyes narrowed in on her and he patted his hand over his neck as though checking for puncture wounds. His other hand went to the nightstand, to where he kept his gun.

Sunray gripped the edge of the blanket and pulled it to her neck. "Kane, it was just a dream." She spoke softly, not wanting to startle him. "You're safe in your room with me, Sunray."

His heart pounded against his chest, and she could hear the furious pulse of his blood. Perspiration matted his hair to his forehead. She resisted the urge to brush it back and soothe away his harsh nightmare.

He grabbed a fistful of his hair and with a great deal of tenderness on his face, he questioned her in a soft voice: "Why didn't you tell me?"

Her throat tightened. "Tell you what?"

"Why didn't you tell me the details about the night Vall attacked us?"

She touched his arm gently. "I didn't want you to think I'd somehow planted those memories. Your brain just needed time to sort things out, to come to terms with everything that had happened."

"Vall killed me," he stated.

Sunray lowered her eyes to shadow her emotions as those painful memories tore through her. "Yes, he did."

He pressed the butt of his palm to his forehead and tossed his head from side to side in disbelief. God, he looked so shaken, so lost.

"Holy Christ, Sunray. Everything you've said. Everything you told me. It was true. All true."

Sunray put her hand over his chest to calm him. "I know it's a lot to deal with, Kane."

His throat worked as he swallowed, and he slipped his hand around her head and drew her close. His thick, dark lashes blinked over solemn eyes. "Sunray—God, Sunray—I'm so sorry I wasn't able to protect you." The anguish in his voice tore at her. He pounded his fist against the mattress. "Fuck. I should have been able to protect you."

"Kane, we were young and innocent and didn't know what we were up against. And like you said before, neither one of us can take Vall out alone, but together—"

"What did he do to you after he killed me?"

She gathered him into her arms, held him tight, and lowered her voice. "He's been trying to make me his, make me *willingly* submit to him for the past one hundred years."

"But—"

"Shhh . . ." she whispered, giving him the time he needed to sort things out.

As her hands skimmed his sinewy muscles, he cupped her face, pushed back her hair, and stared deep into her eyes. A moment later, his lips took possession of hers and he whispered into her mouth, "I can't believe you've never stopped loving me."

His kiss was so full of emotion and tenderness. The soft warmth of his voice pulled her into a cocoon of need. "I'll never stop loving you," she reaffirmed.

Kane moved over her and pressed his body along her length. Breathing labored, his brow knit and his fingers bit into her hips. "Why did Vall want you so badly? You were mine, not his." His hands wrapped around her possessively, as though at any minute Vall would pounce and take her from him again.

"I still am yours, Kane."

She felt the swell of emotions inside him. "Thank you for never giving up on me." There was a deep timbre to his voice that warmed her from the inside out.

Her lips found his and she kissed him long and deep, her heart overflowing with the love she felt for him.

Kane inched back, his expression questioning. "What is it, Sunray? What is it Vall wants from you, and why is he toying with us now, after all these years? Hasn't he done enough damage to the both of us?"

Her thoughts raced to Serene, and her suspicions that Vall was building an army to shift the power in his favor. Kane must have read her unease.

He pitched his voice low. "What is it you're not telling me?"

"Kane, don't . . ."

A mixture of sadness and hurt passed over his eyes. "I don't understand. Don't you trust me yet?"

Even though he was intense and troubled and damaged, and even though he was a lycan hunter, she trusted him with her life. She cupped his cheeks. "Of course I do."

But she couldn't risk telling him. What if one of the Darkland cousins managed to sort around inside his thoughts and discover her secret town through him? It was just too dangerous.

"I can't help you if you don't tell me."

Sunray slid her hands down his back and cupped his buttocks. She widened her legs, and when his cock breached her opening, his gaze panned her face. In an instant, his mood shifted, and his body buzzed to life.

"Sunray, kitten, what are you doing? I can't think when you open yourself to me like this."

"Good, because it's time to feel, not think. I want you to share yourself with me."

His body quaked with want as he eased inside her, gently, slowly, offering her only one inch at a time.

She moaned. "I don't know how long we have together, Kane, but I plan to enjoy every minute of it."

Perplexed, he jerked his head back and questioned in a soft voice, "What are you talking about, Sunray?"

Did he really need her to state the obvious at a time like

this? That no matter what they felt for each other, they were still on opposite sides of the tracks. Instead of answering, she guided him away from the subject.

"I want you inside me, Kane. I want you to unleash yourself on me."

She bucked forward, driving his cock all the way up inside her and welcoming him home. The turmoil and emotions in his eyes as she gave herself over to him turned her inside out. As he raced his hands over her body, her senses exploded and all worries were temporarily forgotten.

"Take me," she whispered. And with that, Kane gripped her hips and began pounding into her. Her cries of ecstasy merged with his as together they both gave themselves over to their needs.

Lost in each other, Kane made sweet, passionate love to her until exhaustion pulled at them both, until night merged with day and lust bled into love.

Chapter Fourteen

The sound of his cell phone ringing jerked him awake. Feeling foggy-brained from numerous rounds of lovemaking and a night of little sleep, Kane reached over the side of his bed in search of his pants. He poked around on the floor until he found the bundle of clothes left forgotten in a heap from the previous evening.

He opened one eye, and a quick glance at the clock told him it was midmorning, which made him wonder who'd be calling him this early. With unease weaving its way through his veins, he rifled through the front pocket, grabbed his cell, and flipped it open.

"Hello."

"You'd better get your ass out of bed and get down to Cobblestones Lounge," Cavanaugh rushed out.

The sound of his captain's voice snapped the fog from his

brain and had him sitting up urgently. Kane rubbed his chin and shot a glance to his window. He winced and turned away when the midmorning sun seeped through his open curtain and caught his eye. Kane focused his thoughts, and could hear a commotion in the background. His stomach knotted.

"What's up?" he asked.

"It's a goddamn mess down here."

As visions of shredded bodies and blood-spattered alleyways raced through his mind, he cursed. He sank back down onto his pillow. "Fuck."

"Your rogue left a message for you."

Just then, Sunray rolled into him and gave a moan in her sleep, loud enough for his captain to hear it on the other end of the line.

"Do you have someone there with you?"

"This message?" Kane turned the conversation back to the case. "What did it say?"

Instead of answering, Cavanaugh let out a long, slow sigh and asked, "What's going on with you lately, Kane?"

"Nothing." Kane raked his fingers through his hair, not in the mood for one of the captain's lectures on keeping a clear head. "Why?"

"You're off your game. And Jaret mentioned—"

"Fuck Jaret."

"Kane," Cavanaugh's voice grated in warning. "What's with you two anyway?"

Jesus, where did he even begin? "I don't trust him or his cousin."

"Trust them or not, I don't care. If you don't catch this rogue by nightfall, I'll be putting the Darkland cousins on the case," he assured him. "So get the goddamn job done, Kane. Tonight." With that nonnegotiable piece of advice, the captain hung up.

A burst of anger coiled through Kane as he flipped the phone shut and turned to Sunray, who was staring up at the ceiling, her pewter eyes wide.

He pulled her in tight, dropped a soft kiss onto her forehead, and explained, "We have to—"

She tilted her chin, bringing them face-to-face. "I heard."

A look he didn't understand crossed her face, and he suspected she'd heard everything, including the captain's warning about pulling him off the case. Kane couldn't let that happen. Wouldn't let that happen. He had a score to settle with Vall. And he damned well planned on settling it tonight. He owed it to Sunray to finish this once and for all. And he owed it to himself.

But after this case, maybe he didn't want to do this job anymore. Maybe he was tired of having to live alone, hunt alone, and, dammit, just plain tired of being alone. Maybe what he really wanted was what his sister had. A family. People who loved him. People he loved.

Warmth flooded his heart when he recalled an exuberant

Ben flying around the living room, and the way little Timmy had stared up at him with those big, curious eyes as he greedily drank from his bottle.

As emotions clogged Kane's throat, he lightly tapped Sunray's arm. "Let's move."

She stretched out her limbs and climbed from the bed.

"Captain said Vall left me a message," he said.

Poised on the edge of the mattress, she looked over her shoulder at him. Her long hair cascaded down her back as she narrowed her eyes. "What kind of message?"

"I don't know. But look, Cavanaugh said it's pretty messy down there. So you might want to stay—"

She stood, and as the sunlight poured over her naked body, longing ripped through him. She looked so damn beautiful and inviting, he lost his train of thought.

"You want me to stay here?" she questioned, hands going to her curvy hips.

He shook his head. Didn't she understand that he needed her with him at all times, needed the connection more than he needed to breathe? But he also needed her to understand what she was about to see. "No, I want you with me, Sunray. But you might want to stay in the truck for this one. I think you've seen enough carnage for a lifetime."

She gave him a grateful smile, and her voice softened. "I think I need to see the message, Kane. You never know. It might be for me."

He had to admit she did have a point, and she knew Vall a

hell of a lot better than he did. Nodding in agreement, he conceded and said, "Then let's get to it."

A short while later, Kane pulled his truck into the Cobblestones parking lot. There was a flurry of activity at the back side of the building. He turned to Sunray and took in her big blue eyes, her true identity camouflaged behind contacts. "You up for this?"

"Yeah."

"No matter what you see, keep your thoughts clear. I'm sure the Darkland cousins aren't too far off." He reached across the cab and pulled her zipper to her neck to protect her from the outside elements.

"Got it."

Kane pulled his hood up against the wind and circled the cab to meet Sunray. Together they walked to the side of the building, and Sunray lost herself in the throng of people as Kane pushed his way through the crowd.

He cringed and bit back a groan as he took in the mutilated body and blood-soaked snow. His captain came up beside him, arms across his chest as he gestured toward the message. "What the hell is that supposed to mean?"

"Here, kitty, kitty." Kane read the blood-sprayed message aloud and frowned. He took a moment to search his memories, but was still unable to grasp the meaning. Determined to find an explanation, he made a move to search out Sunray.

"It means tonight is the night. He's coming for me."

Kane spun around to see Sunray standing behind him. Her face was pale, her eyes were suddenly tired, drained, and as she visually tightened, her tension wrapped around him like a deadly serpent. Kane slipped his arm around her to offer his comfort, warmth, and support.

She blinked up at him, and the vulnerability in her expression spoke volumes; she felt personally responsible for the recent bloodshed and loss of lives. Anger rose sure and swift, and Kane clenched his jaw, determined to put an end to this.

"Who the hell is this?" his captain asked as his inquisitive gaze panned Sunray.

"That's what we'd like to know," Jaret said, as he and Toby stepped up beside them all.

Kane turned, offering his back to the Darkland boys as he focused on his captain. "She's my snitch," he offered. "She knows the rogue."

The captain was quiet for a long moment; then, with a raised brow, he questioned, "Kane, you sure you know what you're doing?"

Did he know what he was doing? Christ, no! How could he possibly know what he was doing? He was in love with a lycan. And even though he trusted her, he never forgot that she was still keeping secrets from him.

Oh no. Besides breaking all the rules, he had no fucking idea what he was doing.

"Yeah. I've got everything under control," he assured the captain in an attempt to put his mind at ease.

Impulsive

Cavanaugh's silver brows furrowed together. "You can end this tonight, then?"

Kane opened his mouth, but Sunray leaned in to him and spoke up. "Yes, we can end this tonight."

"Then get to it."

Kane and Sunray turned to leave, but Jaret stepped in front of them to block their path.

"Not now, Jaret," Kane warned, tension hanging heavily around them.

"When you fuck up tonight, Kane, Vall is mine. Then I'll end this once and for all. And your reign as the captain's golden boy will be over." He smirked and nodded toward Sunray. His lecherous gaze raced over her. "By the way, does the girl come with the case?"

Kane stiffened, and Sunray's fingers brushed over his in a calming gesture. "He's not worth it. Let's go."

As they pushed past Jaret, Toby shot out, "There's something not right about her, Kane."

Kane scoffed and forced a quick laugh. "And what might that be—that she's in my bed and not yours?"

When Jaret cursed something incomprehensible under his breath, Sunray grinned and arched a brow. "Couldn't help yourself?"

"Nope."

They climbed into the truck, and she turned to him. Her eyes were serious. "'Here, kitty, kitty' was your signal, Kane. It was your way of letting me know you were coming for me."

Kane scraped his fingers over his chin. "So now it's Vall's way of letting us know *he's* coming for you."

As she regarded him with wide eyes, she pulled her bottom lip between her teeth, and her quick flash of panic didn't go unnoticed. "Exactly."

"Christ, Sunray, how many nights had Vall watched us before he killed me and turned you? He sure seemed to know our routine and pattern pretty well, don't you think?"

Kane pounded his fist on the steering wheel, and his mind sifted through all the events as he did a rundown of Vall's most recent hits. First it was the Candy Cane, then Mike's Tavern, and now Cobblestones. He got his bearings and turned to her. "Where, exactly, is the old abandoned building that we used to go to?"

She pointed a finger. "Not too far from here."

Kane stared out his window and sucked in a breath. "He's leading us there."

"Yeah, he's baiting us," she agreed. Apprehension moved over her eyes. "I guess he wants to finally put an end to this in the exact same spot where it all began a hundred years ago."

Kane flashed his gun. "Then let's go put an end to this right now, Sunray."

Shaky fingers grabbed his arm, and her voice wavered. "I can't watch you die again, Kane."

Kane put his hand over hers and gave a reassuring squeeze. "You won't."

"Kane—"

"As long as we know what we're up against and we're working together, we can do this." She nodded, but he could still see the unease in her eyes. "Now show me how to get to the building."

They parked their car near the tracks, and Sunray glanced around. She hadn't been back to the old abandoned building since Vall had attacked her, and so much had changed over the past century. Gone were the trees and densely packed foliage; instead, strategically lined rows of huge orange self-storage facilities ate up the area.

She blinked, looking for something familiar. Her gaze shifted from one row of buildings to the next. "It's so different," she murmured. "Vall could be hiding in any one of those structures."

Kane pulled his gun from his holster. "Then we'll have to check them all."

As her gaze panned the area, her mind revisited that dreadful night Vall had killed Ray, and her entire body shook violently. The thought of another face-off with Vall, in the exact spot where he'd stolen her life so many years ago, had her wolf stirring, growling, itching to unleash its pent-up rage.

Tamping down the animal inside her for now, she pulled open her door. The midafternoon sun warmed her face as she climbed from the truck, and when her feet hit the ground, the ice and snow crunched beneath her boots. She winced as the sound carried on the breeze. If Vall was anywhere in the vicinity, he'd undoubtedly hear their approach. Vall was a creature of habit, and she knew him well enough to know that he probably wouldn't expect them until nightfall, when they usually hunted. But he was a powerful enemy, adept at identifying approaching danger.

Her gaze skirted the area, and as memories rushed back, the air turned heavy, like it was pressing down on her chest and suffocating her. She put her hand to her throat, finding it most difficult to draw in air. A fine shiver worked its way through her veins, and she knew it wasn't from the cold winter wind.

Kane gathered her hand in his and questioned, "Are you okay?" His soft whisper covered her like a blanket of warmth and gave her the courage she needed to continue.

She nodded and stared straight ahead. Always ready to pounce in the face of danger, her wolf crouched low. A quiet fell over them as Sunray sniffed the still air, pulling every ribbon of scent into her sinuses in an attempt to help her decipher Vall's locale.

"Is he here?" Kane asked.

"I can't tell." She reached inside her coat pocket and closed her hand over the gun for reassurance.

They cautiously moved along the snow-dusted walkway. Kane examined the outside of each storage facility for recent activity, while Sunray used her heightened senses to detect signs of Vall.

As Sunray fine-tuned her hearing, a noise on the other side

of the tracks caught her attention. She caught a flash of black before it disappeared from her line of sight. Inhaling, she continued to scan, and her stomach knotted as a very familiar scent rolled over her. What the hell?

She exhaled slowly. "We're not alone."

Kane turned and followed the direction of her gaze. "Human or wolf?"

"Witch."

"Witch? What witch? What are you talking about?"

"I can't—"

"Sunray, Jesus . . ."

"Look, Kane, what I can tell you is this: I watched Vall die once about six months ago. The only thing that can bring him back is the magic of a powerful Earth witch. And if that's who I think it is out there . . ."

"Then we're in a shitload of trouble?"

"Yeah, and we just have to make sure she doesn't get anywhere near Vall after you pump him full of silver."

Cautious of Harmony trailing them, Sunray crept forward as Kane kept pace beside her. Two more steps led them to the next set of storage containers. Sunray stilled and starched her spine, the fine hairs on her nape rising, and her wolf growled low. Kane turned to her, and she pointed a finger to the shed a few doors down.

"Is he in there?"

"I think so. I just hope it's not going to be an ambush," she whispered. "Should we call for backup?"

"If we do, they'll be sure to take you out with him." Kane pressed his back to the wall and shimmied forward. He gestured toward the small gap between the garage door and the cement pad. "We have to do this ourselves."

"What's our plan?"

"We shoot anything and everything that moves."

It was a good plan. Their only plan under the circumstances, really. But if things went badly, Sunray knew she'd do whatever it took to protect the man she loved.

Signaling his intent, he dropped onto the cold ground and peered under the steel door. The action was far too familiar to Sunray. She tightened, half expecting a big paw to reach out and grab him, the way Vall had done so many years ago.

A moment later, he climbed to his feet and brushed the snow from his jeans. "I don't see anything."

"Around back." They cautiously made their way around the back of the facility and came across a steel access door. Sunray pulled a pin from her hair and made short work of the lock.

Once she released the bolt, Kane positioned her behind him. With his gun aimed, he kicked the door open and peered into the black, prepared to fire at the slightest of movements.

Sunray slipped in beside him, gun now in hand, and glanced around, knowing they had indeed just entered Vall's den. Boxes, blankets, sofas, and food wrappers were strewn about the room. The scent of wet dog hit her hard, and it was easy to tell that Vall and his minions had been camping out here.

With no sign of Vall, she felt along the wall just inside the door and powered on the lights for Kane's benefit. As the over-head fluorescent bulbs slowly blinked on, a wolf came out of nowhere and lunged at them. Before Kane could get a shot off, the attack sent him flying backward. He hit the wall with a thud, his gun scuttling across the floor.

The wolf sat back on its haunches, purposely positioning itself behind Kane so Sunray couldn't get off a shot.

A movement in the corner caught Sunray's eye, and her wolf howled.

"Kill him, Sunray," Kane bit out.

"I can't." Jesus, if she shot Vall, his minion would immediately finish off Kane. There was only one way to handle this.

In his human form, Vall stepped out from behind a packing box. "Sunray, my little cub. So nice to see you." He looked at the gun, and a sly smirk crossed his face. "Put the gun down," he ordered in a soft tone. "You know you don't want to shoot me. We have so many plans to fulfill." He chuckled easily and angled his head and glared at Kane. "Ray," he greeted and made a *tsk*ing sound. "Some people don't know when to stay dead."

Chapter Fifteen

Kane suddenly froze, and when Sunray said nothing in response to Vall's order, his body stirred and a warning bell echoed in his mind. Kane turned to her and watched her eyes sweep the room, taking it all in, and then her glance turned on him as she lowered her gun. Something about the way she was looking at him nearly stopped his heart.

"What?" he asked. "What's going on, Sunray?"

Sunray held her hand up. "Easy, Kane."

"Don't tell me to take it easy, Sunray." His head began spinning as he pressed harder against the wall in a defensive move. Just then, he spotted two wolves step out from behind the sofa, and move in front of Vall to protect him. They could easily jump and block a direct shot if Kane somehow managed to reach his gun. Jesus Christ, Sunray couldn't be in on this. She just couldn't be.

But what about all the secrets? And how she mentioned that we had such little time together? Was she working with Vall? Baiting me?

And why the hell doesn't she just shoot me?

Fuck!

Had he made a mistake in trusting her? Had love merely congested his ability to think rationally?

"Come here, little cub," Vall murmured, as his minions stalked closer to Kane.

Without preamble, Sunray lowered her head in a submissive stance and moved toward him. His smile widened as he crooked a finger and beckoned her closer. "Do you have any idea how much I've missed you?"

"Sunray?" Kane asked, his voice as shaky as his hands. "Talk to me."

Vall chuckled and ignored Kane, no more threatened by him than by a harmless fruit fly. "On your knees before me, Sunray."

When Sunray sank to her knees, Kane's heart sank right along with her, and the bottom dropped out of his world. How could this be happening?

As his mind reeled and his blood pulsed hot, Sunray glanced over her shoulder at him and blinked. In that instant, he recognized that look, the silent message she was sending him. As he sorted through the information, he fought the urge to let loose a breath of relief, hating that for one minute he'd actually questioned her loyalty to him. Sunray was playing along with Vall for a reason, which meant that he had to take her signals and play along, too.

Vall must have noted the exchange. He hardened his voice and said, "Let's not do this the hard way this time."

Sunray turned back to Vall and glanced up at him. "It's always going to be the hard way with you, Vall."

"Ah, so young and rebellious." Wearing a bored expression, Vall signaled his minions to close in on Kane. "The only one you're going to make this hard for is Ray."

As Kane took in the power struggle, he watched Sunray tense as the stakes were raised. "When we met in the woods, you said with the right motivation I'd willingly submit to you." She nodded toward Kane. "Was this what you were talking about?"

"Partly."

"Let me guess. The army you're building has something to do with it too."

"You're very astute, little one."

"What's the army for, Vall?"

"Insurance."

"Insurance for what?"

"So that you come back to Serene with me."

Serene? Where the hell is Serene?

"If you don't agree to come back"—he waved his hand toward the three lycans trapping Kane against the wall—"not only will those three finish Ray once and for all, but they'll also happily join the rest of my brand-new pack and help me destroy and replace your brethren in Serene."

Sunray's eyes widened; her hand went to her stomach. "Drake will stop you."

Drake?

Ignoring her, Vall asked, "Do you want that on your head, my little cub?"

Sunray scratched at her arm, and Kane suspected she was purposely holding back her wolf.

"You wouldn't," she said.

"Sunray, you always did have a soft spot for others. Now be a good little cub and obey your alpha's rules. I want you to give yourself to me"—he paused to shoot Kane a lecherous glare—"in front of him, so he'll finally understand you're mine, not his."

"One question, Vall. Why? Why me?"

Vall laughed out loud. "You really don't know, do you?" When she shook her head, he went on to explain, "Eight hundred years ago, you were mine, Sunray. We were lovers. But you were killed, and I was turned when the lycan species was trying to grow its pack and bring in virile males."

Kane's glance went from Vall to the wolves inching closer, back to Vall again, hardly able to believe what he was hearing. By the incredulous look on Sunray's face, he hazarded a guess that she was just as shocked as he was.

"It took forever for you to come back to me, and when you finally did, a little over a hundred years ago, I waited for you to start remembering me, to start having dreams about us."

"But you turned me before that happened," she stated. "Why?"

Vall snarled and gestured toward Kane. "Because you were

falling in love with Ray. I saw the way you looked at him. It sickened me."

He jabbed his thumb into his chest. "I want you to look at me like that. And only me."

Sunray slowly turned her head and cast Kane a glance. As they exchanged a long, lingering look, Vall roared with fury.

"Stop." His voice reverberated off the metal walls as he ripped his shirt from his body. "From here on out, you will only ever look at me like that."

"Tell me, Vall: Were you as callous with me then as you are in this lifetime?"

He gave an insidious smirk. "You were always a little strong-headed."

"Then maybe that's why I never had the dreams. Maybe my subconscious blocked you out." She gave a humorless laugh. "And somehow I doubt that I was ever really in love with you."

Vall growled, and as anger overtook him, his face began to elongate.

"Maybe deep in my subconscious, I always knew you weren't good enough for me. You could never be the man Ray was, or Kane is today."

It occurred to Kane that she was deliberately trying to provoke Vall. And if there was one thing Kane had always been taught, it was that you fought with intellect, not emotions.

"You *will* submit to me, Sunray, willingly. And you will return to Serene as my mate. Or your entire brethren will be terminated." He ripped the rest of his clothes from his body, dropped to the floor, and crouched down on all fours, ready to pounce.

Kane made a noise to gain Vall's attention. Vall snarled and turned to him. "Oh, she might be forced to submit to you, Vall, but she'll always willingly submit to me," he said, adding fuel to the rage inside Vall and giving Sunray time to shed her clothes and shift.

Furious, Vall lunged toward Sunray just as she took on her wolf form, temporarily distracting the three lycans that had Kane pinned. Kane took that opportunity to dive for his gun. He rolled across the floor and peeled off a few shots.

The three wolves yelped and fell to the ground. As they morphed back to young human females, Kane repositioned himself and waited for a clear shot. Sunray and Vall fought and rolled toward the open door. The afternoon light lit the tangled mess of claws and fur.

Sunray caught Vall with her legs and sent him flying backward. He hit the steel wall with a thump, and was temporarily stunned. With little time to spare before Vall pulled himself together, she gained purchase, morphed back to her human form, and scrambled across the floor. She grabbed her gun and climbed to her feet. Vall snarled and pounced, but before he could reach her, she pulled the trigger.

The sound of gunfire pierced Kane's ears and rang off the walls as Vall fell to the floor, his body morphing back to human form. Sunray moved closer and stood over him. Breathless, she said, "Some people don't know when to stay dead." With that, she turned back to face Kane.

Heart racing, Kane lifted his gun and took aim, his pistol centered on her forehead. Shock spread across Sunray's face as she gasped and gripped her chest, her other hand tightening on her gun.

Kane held out his hand. "Easy, Sunray."

Taking him by surprise, she widened her arms and let her gun fall. It clattered against the cement and she kicked it away.

A strange look came over her face, and love shone in her eyes as they met his. "So it seems you're going to keep your promise, Kane. Then go ahead. Do what you have to do. I have no plans to kill you. I never did."

"Drop."

She blinked and he yelled it again. "Drop."

Sunray dove to the ground just as the lycan lurking in the doorway was about to lunge. Kane took aim and caught it in the shoulder.

With her tongue thick from fright and her heart racing, Sunray crouched on the ground and tried to remember how to breathe as Kane terminated the wolf behind her and spared her life. Again. A moment later, he quickly crossed the cement floor, gathering her clothes along the way, and gently helped her to her feet.

His warm, compassionate gaze raked over her with tender concern as he checked her body for injuries. "Get dressed," he said in the softest voice, and briskly ran his hands over her arms to take away her chills. "I have to call this in; then I'll get you out of here."

She swallowed, and there was nothing she could do to keep the tremble from her voice when she warned, "We have to stay here, to make sure Harmony doesn't get near Vall until your men show up."

Sunray dressed as Kane pulled out his cell phone and punched in the captain's number. She listened as he gave the directions to Vall's den, and warned the captain that other lycans would be in the vicinity.

As soon as he finished the call, he gathered Sunray into his arms and just held her against his chest, shielding her from the carnage around them while he pressed his mouth to her head.

"At least now that we know where the den is, we'll be able to find and terminate the rest of the pack."

Sunray flinched, hating that so many innocent lives had been forever lost. She also knew the PTF officers had no choice but to annihilate them all.

Voice bleak and tears threatening to overwhelm her, she said, "They're all so young, Kane. Just little girls, not monsters. They don't deserve any of this."

"I know, baby. I know." He pulled her impossibly tighter. "You've taught me so much."

She remained in his warm embrace, listening to his rapid heartbeat and the rush of blood through his veins, wondering when he was going to question her on Serene or Drake or all the little secrets she'd been keeping from him.

But right now she didn't want to think about that. She only wanted to think about how damn good it felt to be held by him. How protective he was of her, and for the first time in a long time, how safe she felt in a man's arms.

At the sound of distant sirens closing in on them, Kane inched back, brushed a soft kiss over her lips, and led her outside. She blinked against the blinding sun reflecting off a nearby snowbank. When they reached his truck, he pulled open the door and ushered her inside the cab.

"Wait here," he said.

Sunray wrapped her arms around herself to ward off the cold as she watched the action from inside the safety of the vehicle, her glance continually scanning the perimeter for any signs of Harmony. Jesus, what the hell was Harmony up to, and why was she helping Vall? Damned if she didn't have every intention of finding out. Her stomach tightened just thinking about the power those two could summon if they forged an allegiance.

Her mind raced, sorting through the turbulent events and strategizing her next course of action, while Kane went to talk to his captain.

A few minutes later, he climbed in beside her and reached out to squeeze her hand. "You okay?"

She conjured a smile. "You scared the shit out of me back there." The same way she'd scared the shit out of him back at Candy Cane when she morphed to protect them both, she supposed.

He smiled. "Sorry about that." Then he chuckled easily and tried to lighten the mood by saying, "I guess we're even, then."

When Sunray yawned, he put the keys into the ignition and said, "Let's get you home."

Once again her heart turned over in her chest at his use of the word *home*.

Chapter Sixteen

Kane parked his car in the garage, shut out the cold winter wind behind them, and led Sunray in through the kitchen entrance. Despite the warmth inside Kane's truck and inside his comfy bungalow, Sunray couldn't seem to keep her body from shivering.

Feeling both emotionally and physically drained, she hugged herself and rubbed her hands up and down her arms, but still couldn't stave off more violent tremors.

Once inside the kitchen, Kane flicked on the light and turned to her. He opened his mouth like he was about to question her, but when his turbulent gaze landed on her face, his eyes softened and he reached for her.

Attentive and considerate, he said, "Let's get you warmed up."

Her heart pounded as her love and desire for him moved

through her. Kane helped her off with her winter wear and led her to the bathroom, where he drew her a warm bath. God, he was so sweet and caring, it had her aching to kiss him, to touch him, to feel him inside her. She closed her eyes against the flood of love as she eased herself into the luxurious, steaming tub.

As Kane disappeared around the corner and made his way to the kitchen to put on a pot of tea, Sunray relaxed against the porcelain. She waved the water over her trembling body, but the chill was too deep inside her soul for the hot water to thaw it.

Kane came back with her tea and as she sipped it, he took a seat on the edge of the tub. "Thanks," she murmured, so grateful to have him at her side.

He glanced at her, the concern in his eyes evident. "It's all over, Sunray."

She couldn't tell if he was trying to convince her or himself. "It's over," she agreed, putting his mind at ease.

Sunray blew a wispy bang from her forehead and took a moment to consider everything that had happened over the last week. She could only imagine the havoc Vall had wreaked on her beloved town since she'd left. And now with Harmony on the loose, she knew it was far from over. She also knew she couldn't sit back and do nothing, even if that meant she had to return and face the firing squad. She had to at least try to help mend the relationships and put the pieces of her home back together.

If only she could tell Kane that. If only she could share that side of herself with him. It pained her to keep secrets from him.

Kane grabbed a cloth and brushed it over her body in a soothing gesture. She could tell he wanted to talk, but she also suspected he was waiting for the right time.

Once she finished her tea, she climbed from the tub and Kane towel-dried her. He gathered her hand in his, led her to his room, and tucked her beneath his flannel sheets.

Before he climbed in beside her, he asked, "Do you need anything?"

She reached for him. "Only you."

Kane removed his clothes, slipped between the sheets, and snuggled close, her body absorbing his warmth and comforting presence. When his hewn muscles relaxed against her, she drew in his enticing scent and let it weave its way through her. As she found solace in his arms, his gentle fingers brushed her hair from her forehead and lightly massaged her stiff shoulders.

She melted against him as her mind sorted through everything that had happened to her since she'd caught his distinctive aroma on Jaclyn's coat. And what about everything that had happened to him since he'd met her? She couldn't deny that she'd made a mess of his structured life and his job was now in jeopardy, not to mention his relationship with his fellow officers. She could only imagine what would happen if they discovered she was a lycan.

The last thing she wanted to do was get him kicked out of the precinct. His expertise was needed on the dangerous Chicago streets. Kane was a great man and an exceptional hunter who deserved to keep his job. He also deserved to have a family to come home to at the end of the day. That last thought had her mind revisiting their trip to his sister's and the warmth she spotted in Kane's eyes as they made love afterward.

"Kane."

"Yeah, baby?"

"You asked me if I wanted kids, but you never told me if you did."

He gave an easy shrug. "I never used to think about that."

He trailed the pad of his index finger over her arm, and she shivered in response. "But you do now."

"Yeah, I do now." Intense brown eyes met hers question-ingly as he wrapped his arms around her.

"So you'd like to have kids, then?"

"Yeah, baby, I would."

Sunray traced her finger over his chest and nudged him, encouraging him to go on. "You'd like to have a family?"

"You were right, you know." His voice came out low and gruff as his arms drew her in tighter. "When you said I wasn't living, I was only surviving, you were right."

Sunray smiled at him. It gave her a measure of comfort to know that he was going to be okay, that she'd opened his eyes and showed him what he could have. She touched his cheek, and as though soothed by her touch, he leaned into her hand. God, she loved him so much it hurt, which was why she had to leave him. To flee Chicago and never set eyes on him again.

Kane deserved a normal life. A life with a mortal wife, chil-dren, and a bungalow nestled behind a nice white picket fence.

Her heart dropped into her stomach with the knowledge that he could have those things—just not with her.

The truth was, her life was in Serene, and Kane's life was here in Chicago. His family and his precinct needed him. What he didn't need was to harbor a lycan who needed and loved him.

Kane shifted and climbed over her. "By the way, I never did thank you properly."

She blinked up at him. "For what?"

"When you knocked on my sister's door, you told me I was going to thank you."

His lips found hers and she knew she should just run, but she couldn't, not yet. She needed to be with him again.

Just one more time.

"Define *properly*," she murmured into his mouth.

Kane chuckled and parted her legs. He slipped a finger between her thighs to test her readiness, and when he found her wet and wanting, he growled in pleasure. She didn't miss the emotion in his voice when he said, "God, girl, I love how you want me."

She lifted her hips and he entered her, pushing his magnificent cock all the way inside. Her arms snaked around him and she held him tight as her lips met his for a deep, soul-searching kiss. She blocked her mind to everything except this minute and this man, knowing she'd need these warm memories to draw on later.

"Love me the way only you know how, Kane."

Her words brought dark passion to his eyes and he began rocking into her, filling her body and her heart with each glorious thrust. She surrendered to the pleasure as they each gave themselves to one another. This time, their lovemaking was less hurried, less urgent, but so damn intimate and potent Sunray felt like she was going to shatter into a million pieces. It was all she could do to keep herself together.

He brushed her hair from her face and his touch went right through her, immediately bringing on her orgasm. His cock stroked deep, and she gave a broken gasp and scraped her nails over his skin with each powerful clench. As her liquid desire singed his cock, his mouth crashed down on hers. He poured himself into her.

A long while later, Kane released a sigh, slid beside her, and pulled her close. He stroked a tender caress over her flesh, and she shivered in response.

"Tomorrow, Sunray," he murmured, his voice sated, sleepy. "Tomorrow we'll talk."

She ran her fingers across his mouth and lightly kissed him as a surge of love stole over her. "Tomorrow, Kane," she assured him as she watched his breathing regulate. A moment later, he drifted into a deep, restful sleep.

"Dream well," she murmured.

Her gaze panned over his features, taking in his rumpled hair, the scar over his eye, the shadow on his strong chin, and his beautiful mouth.

As she committed his features to memory, she dragged herself away, both physically and emotionally, and tried to come to terms with what her future held.

And what it didn't.

Her throat clenched and tears pricked her eyes as a myriad of emotions pressed against her chest. Frowning, she drew a centering breath, slipped from the bed, pulled on her clothes, and tiptoed to the door.

Feeling like her heart had been ripped from her chest, she shot him one last, longing glance.

"Good-bye, Ray," she whispered under her breath.

Chapter Seventeen

After leaving Kane, Sunray had made her way home and called Jaclyn and Slyck, who were less than pleased that she hadn't asked for their help where Vall was concerned, or filled them in on her relationship with Kane. But they also understood her reasons for leaving Chicago and her need and desire to return to her former home.

Now here she was, sitting in her car just outside Serene's protective walls, looking at the quaint village from afar, a confusing mixture of elation and sadness closing in on her.

As the midday sun shone down on her vehicle, she gathered her bravado and pulled off the road. She climbed from the vehicle, stretched out her legs, and drew a fueling breath. It was time to face her friends and family head-on and deal with whatever punishment came with her escape.

With her heart pounding, she walked the icy, cracked and

pitted road until she came to the security booth. Inside sat Jake, a demon with the MO of a rough-and-ready cowboy, one of the strange personae he'd taken on over his lifetime. With no idea how the demon would react to her presence, she cautiously approached.

"Good afternoon, Jake."

He angled his head, his amber gaze narrowing as his leather hat shaded the winter sun from his eyes. Then, suddenly, his lids flew open and he abruptly froze as recognition hit. A heartbeat later, Jake's hand disappeared from the counter, and without his eyes ever leaving hers, he began fumbling around. Sunray's body tensed, fully expecting him to draw a weapon. After all, rogues were terminated on the spot.

Sunray shifted her body and held up her arms, palms out. "Easy there, Jake."

"Sunray," he said, and much to her surprise, the armored gate began opening for her. "Welcome home."

Her glance went from Jake to the widening gate, back to Jake again, shocked that he'd so readily welcomed her home. She let out a relieved breath, and with careful concentration her gaze panned the wide expanse of stores and houses that slumbered in the picturesque village just beyond the security entrance.

She placed her hand over her forehead and shaded the sun from her eyes. "How are things?" she questioned as she slowly moved past the security gate and took in the people milling about. With its one main street, small bank, grocery store, candy store, and schoolhouse, to an outsider, Serene looked like any other small rural town.

Panic apparent in his expression, Jake shot a guarded glance around and lowered his voice, and it occurred to her that he was afraid. "Is Vall with you?"

What the hell had Vall done to this place? "Vall's dead," she assured him. "I killed him."

Relief washed over his face. "It's good to have you home, Sunray."

She redirected her thoughts, wanting to get to the bottom of things right away. "We need to call—" Her voice fell off when she spotted Drake, the Panther Overseer, approaching. She scanned the snowy sidewalk, noting how everyone had stilled and all eyes were trained on her.

As the gate shut behind her, Drake quickly closed the distance between them and stepped up to her. His eyes moved over her face, appraising her. "Drake, I—" she began, but Drake stopped her.

He placed his hand on her shoulder in a calming gesture. "Slyck and Jaclyn filled me in on everything."

Sunray's eyes widened and her heart swelled. "They did?" She loved how her panther friends were always looking out for her.

Drake pulled her into his arms and whispered, "Welcome home, Sunray. You're needed here."

She gave him a doubtful expression. "Won't security, or even my pack, label me a rogue and demand punishment?"

"After what Vall put us all through, they'll be happy to know that you killed him and are here to help make things right."

"Really?" Jesus, she honestly had no idea it could be this easy. The least she expected was to be placed before the disciplinary board before being allowed back into society.

Solemn eyes met hers. "Sunray, trust me, they know it was Vall who forced you out of town in the first place. Everyone here knows how badly he treated you, and that he was trying to shift the power to his own advantage. Even his own people were afraid of him after he challenged and killed Cairan to reclaim his old position."

Stepping away from the circle of his arms, Sunray glanced around as members of her brethren tentatively approached. Her body tightened with unease, but when they greeted her with open arms, a relieved rush of air left her lungs in a whoosh.

She was home.

Oh, God, she was finally home.

And home was where the heart was.

Well, at least that was how the saying went. Because the truth was, a big chunk of her heart would always be in Chicago, with Kane.

Behind her brethren she spotted Harmony. When their gazes collided, the coven guide rushed inside the café, a note of desperation on her face.

Sunray turned to Drake and linked her fingers together. "We need to call a council meeting. Harmony is involved."

"So Slyck was right. She was working with Vall to shift the

power in the community, and resurrected him so they could continue with their plans. I suspected as much, but had no proof."

"Vall told me himself that she resurrected him. That should be proof enough."

Drake nodded and smiled. "It's time to put this place back in order." He reached a hand out to her. "Now let's get you settled."

Chapter Eighteen

Kane glanced at the map and then back at the snow-sprinkled, cracked and pitted road. Surely he must have gotten lost, because no way in hell could a town exist this far off the beaten path. He was in the middle of nowhere, for Christ's sake.

He played with the radio dial, but when all he could get was static, he gave up and switched it off. He gripped the steering wheel tighter, certain he was going down the garden path to nowhere. Just when he was about to turn around, a big armored gate materialized before him. *What the hell?*

His mind raced. Was this the pack's den?

He eased his truck off the road, secured his gun to his holster, and climbed from the vehicle. He pulled on his parka, and without bothering to zip it, he cautiously approached the security booth. When amber eyes—the eyes of a demon—turned on him, Kane's head jerked back with a start.

What the fuck?

Demons and lycans together in one town? Of course, after everything he'd been through, he'd believe in just about anything.

"Can I help you?" the man asked in a Southern drawl that sounded ridiculously out of place coming from a demon.

"I'm looking for Sunray. Sunray Matthews."

The man stared at him for a long moment, his amber eyes cutting through him like deadly daggers, and despite the cool temperatures, Kane's palms began to sweat. He shoved his hands into his pockets and rocked on his feet. Jesus, what had he gotten himself into?

The guard picked up a phone and made a call, but he kept his voice too low for Kane to hear. As the guard spoke, Kane looked past the gate at the quaint town and all the people outside. A cluster of dark-haired women all dressed in dark clothes with amulets around their necks walked down the street. His mind raced to the witch who'd been following them back in Chicago.

Demons, lycans, and witches all living together?

Hell, there was a whole lot more to this town than met the eyes. Which was, undoubtedly, why Sunray had kept it a secret. To protect her family, her brethren. Honestly, he couldn't say he blamed her. After all, the last thing she wanted to do was lead a hunter to her home.

He glanced at the department store, and spotted Sunray exiting the building.

His heart began to race, and he had to lock his knees to keep them from collapsing. As if she sensed his presence, she slowly turned in his direction. From across the road their eyes met and locked, and he watched her suck in the cool winter air.

His presence seemed to have garnered quite a bit of attention, as those surrounding Sunray all turned to face him, their silver eyes staring him down.

Dressed in jeans, boots, and her blue down coat, zippered to her breastbone, she began to move toward him. The guard spoke, but Kane couldn't concentrate on anything other than Sunray as she approached.

She stepped up to the gate and grabbed the metal bars. "Kane, how?" Her voice sounded tight, apprehensive, but he didn't miss the turbulent emotions in her eyes when they probed his.

"When you were fighting with Vall, you made mention of Serene," he answered. "It took me a while, but I eventually figured it out." He glanced at the demon, pitched his voice low, and said, "But I think there's still a lot you need to fill me in on."

"Why?" She sounded entirely breathless. "Why are you here?"

Exasperated, he said, "Jesus, Sunray, did you really think I was going to let you run out on me like that?"

She swallowed and took note of his gun. He felt the tension rising in her and knew what she was thinking. She'd led a hunter to her beloved town, and the day could only end in bloodshed. His blood, seeing as how he was completely outnumbered.

"What are you doing here, Kane?" she rushed out. "It's not safe for you to be here."

He opened his heart and laid his emotions on his sleeve. "I'm here for you, Sunray."

She shook her head, and confusion clouded her eyes. "You don't understand." She gestured to the crowd forming behind her. "Everyone in here knows what you are. If Jake opens this gate, I won't be able to stop them from—"

"Then open the gate, Sunray."

His words stopped her cold. "Are you insane?"

"No, I'm in love."

Sadness passed over her eyes, and she spoke in whispered words. "Kane, look around you." She rattled the metal bars. "Don't you get it? You're a hunter. I'm a lycan. And once again, we're on opposite sides of the track." She blinked as tears filled her eyes. "It's just not meant to be." She lowered her head and said, "You can still have a good life, Kane. A normal life. One with a wife and kids . . ."

"Is that why you left me? You thought that that was what I wanted?"

"I wanted to give you a chance."

He shook his head slowly and gave her a look that suggested she didn't know him very well at all, when, in fact, she knew everything about him. "I made a promise to you a very long time ago, *Sunni*. And I'm here to fulfill it."

Her eyes widened, then she blinked rapidly. "Oh, God, Kane."

Fueled by need, he spread his arms. "I want to be with you. Forever. And there is only one way for us to make that happen."

He'd spent a lifetime believing lycans were ferocious creatures with selfish interests, but Sunray had opened his eyes to so much and helped him let go of old beliefs.

"Surely you're not asking me to—"

"I want you to turn me, Sunni."

She gasped. "What about your job, your family?"

"I can still keep contact with my parents and sisters. I went to see them all before I came here." He put his hand over his heart. "And it was good, Sunray. Really good to see them all. I told them I'd be working out of state and that we'd keep in touch by phone, computer, and even webcam." He conjured a smile. "I can still see my nieces and nephews grow up." He gave her a moment to take it all in before he lowered his voice and added, "But you're my family. You've always been my family."

"And your job?"

As much as he hated to say it, he said it anyway. "The Darkland cousins are quite capable of taking over where I left off." He took in the array of silver eyes staring at him. Her brethren used their bodies to circle and protect Sunray. "Now that Vall's gone, are you alpha here, Sunni?" When she nodded, he continued, "That's a pretty big job to take on by yourself."

She planted her hands on her hips. "I can handle it."

He grinned. "Oh, believe me, I know you can. But I also know we make a good team, you and me."

A long pause, and then, "Do you understand what you're asking?"

He looked past her shoulders at the people pacing restlessly. Suspicious eyes were turned on him, ready to strike if he made one threatening gesture, or if Sunray gave the command.

When he reached through the gate to touch her, a low growl came from behind her. Ignoring it, because he needed the intimate contact, he pressed on. "What I understand is that I love you and want to be with you. I want to hold you, kiss you, and love you, Sunni. The way only I know how. From now until eternity." He rooted his feet. "And I'm not going anywhere until you agree." With that, he pulled her zipper to her neck to protect her from the elements, and warmth passed over her eyes.

She clutched her stomach, and he could feel her love reaching out to him. Her voice hitched. "Oh, God, Kane. Are you serious?"

He smiled at her. "Yes, I'm very serious. And Sunni . . ."

She blinked up at him, and the furtive brush of her hand over his let him know she was welcoming him home. "Yeah?"

"You can call me Ray."

Epilogue

Serene: Present Day
April 15, Full Moon

With the wind in his face, Kane ran, dodging trees and brush and enjoying the cool ground beneath his feet. Up ahead, Sunray taunted him, lifting her tail and baiting him with her scent. But she was so fast, too fast for a new cub like him. He'd morphed only three times so far and was still trying to get used to working four limbs without stumbling. But thanks to Sunray, who had been guiding him and teaching him how to control his wolf and use it as a strength instead of a weakness, he was progressing quite nicely.

Even though she was now his alpha—and he kind of liked it when she took charge—they were still a team, both working together to help put Serene back in order. Harmony had been removed from the council, and Lily, another powerful witch, had taken her place. Harmony's punishment was left in the hands of the demon guide, Devon, who was chief of discipline.

Having a pack in a town full of secrets was a lot for Kane to take in, a lot of adjustments for a hunter who had lived a solitary lifestyle, but as long as he had Sunray with him, he could handle anything thrown at him.

Sunray slowed her pace, letting him catch up, and he growled with longing, his cock growing hard as her aroused scent curled around him.

She dropped on the ground before him and extended her paws, offering herself up to him so nicely. With her ass tipped up, the position provided easy access to her warm, sweet sex.

Growling, Kane went up on his haunches and came down on top of her. Their cries of pleasure merged as he pushed into her in one hard thrust. Jesus, he couldn't believe how incredible it felt to take her in primal form. Her tight sex muscles closed around him, and he powered his hips forward.

A few other females sidled up, rubbing their muzzles against him and waiting their turn as he marked their alpha. As brethren, it was natural for all the animals to mate, and Kane couldn't deny that he enjoyed the love and intimacy between them all. But his heart belonged to Sunray, and only to Sunray.

He drove into her hard and deep until her cream poured over his shaft. She let out a deep howl, and he depleted himself inside her. Sated, he climbed off and she rolled onto her back, contentment written all over her muzzle. Kane sat over her, his heart filling with love as she playfully pawed at him. He brushed his paw over her growing stomach and smiled.

"So, what do you think—boy or girl?"

"How about a dozen of each?"

Chuckling, and still not used to being able to communicate in this primal form, he dropped down beside her. "Jesus, I don't know if I have the stamina for that."

Sunray laughed. "Oh yeah, you have enough stamina to go around." She gestured with a nod to all the female lycans circling them. "Just ask any of them."

Kane got serious for a moment. "You know I love only you, don't you?"

"After everything you've done to be with me, I'd be crazy not to know."

Kane nuzzled her neck. "Does it bother you when I fuck them?"

She licked his face, long, sensuous strokes that had his cock hardening again. "Actually, it kind of excites me."

He shook his head, and with renewed interest, he began to climb over her. "You really are a bad girl, aren't you?"

Suddenly, Sunray's eyes widened and her nostrils flared. She flipped over onto her stomach and crouched low as she crawled to the gate and peered through. The other females, all sensing the danger as well, mimicked Sunray's actions.

Kane dropped, quietly dragged himself along the cool ground, and eased himself in beside her. "What is it?"

"Breathe and concentrate," she whispered, and gestured to the thick, clump of trees just beyond the security fence.

Kane inhaled and worked to sort through the medley of scents, not quite competent at deciphering all the different aromas just yet. But then one distinct smell caught his attention, and as his olfactory senses kicked in, his glance shot to Sunray, who looked at him with alarm.

At the exact same moment, they both exclaimed, "The Darkland cousins."

About the Author

A former government financial officer, **Cathryn Fox** graduated from university with a bachelor of business degree. Shortly into her career, Cathryn figured out that corporate life wasn't for her. Needing an outlet for her creative energy, she turned in her briefcase and calculator and began writing erotic romance full-time. Cathryn enjoys writing dark paranormals and humorous contemporaries. She lives in eastern Cananda with her husband, two kids, and chocolate Labrador retriever.

Turn the page for a sneak peek of the
next novel in the sizzling Eternal Pleasure series

Indulgent

BY CATHRYN FOX

Available from Heat in January 2011

Colorado: Fifteenth Century

Something was wrong. Terribly wrong. Even at six years old, Lily was old enough to realize that her entire coven was in danger, and it had something to do with her.

With her eyes stinging from the blinding smoke darkening the afternoon sky, Lily blinked rapidly and glanced up at her mother, who was hurrying her along the damp, weed-choked path and up the side of Brighton Mountain. Lily had never been up the mountain before; it was too dangerous. Her mother had told her so. But today her mother was weaving her around the tall trees and dashing with her to the top, to shield her from the raging fires below. Fires that were ignited by the group of angry masked men who'd invaded her colony.

Her mother squeezed Lily's hand hard, and Lily bit back a

tear. She did not want to upset her mother any more than she already was. Striving to be a big girl, she rushed her steps, working extra hard not to slip on the rain-soaked ground while she kept up with her mommy's fast pace, but the higher up the steep mountain they climbed, the harder and harder it became for Lily to draw in air.

Chalky white powder that resembled the winter's first snow fell from the treetops and sprinkled the muddy soil, but Lily pinched her lips tight, not daring to open her mouth to catch the flakes like she normally would, because it was summer and she was smart enough to know that it never snowed in summer. She guessed that whatever was in the sky had something to do with those scary men, and that made it dangerous.

As frightened screams pierced the air, she stole a quick glance behind her as she continued her upward trek. She squinted to see though the thin haze of smoke, then off in the distance spotted her aunt Nelly fall to the ground. Others scurried around her, their shrieks of fear going unanswered.

Lily began to sweat, and the stickiness made her light dress cling to her body. Scared and feeling helpless, she darted a glance around at the landscape below and counted the men gathered near the bonfire. She could hear them chanting, but from her distance she couldn't make out the words, nor could she identify their features, not with the dark hoods hiding their faces. One of the five men stepped forward, and when he threw something onto the blaze, flames shot to the sky, and spread out on the ground, chasing Lily and her mother up the mountain. Lily shivered despite the warmth in the air.

As her mother dragged her along, Lily twisted her head and turned her attention back to her aunt, who was on the ground, digging her nails into the grass as she tried to crawl away. A man dropped to his knees beside her, wrapped a rope around her wrists, and then roughly hauled her to her feet. Nelly released an anguished cry and Lily's whole body tightened in response.

Why was he hurting Aunt Nelly?

Lily let loose a thread of magic, then clutched her stomach, feeling her aunt's pain and fear as if they were her own. Being able to "feel" other people was a gift, her mother had told her, but right now it really didn't make Lily feel so special. It made her feel so very sick. As her mother watched her double over, she bent down with her, and placed both palms over Lily's stomach to soothe the ache, but the strange, strangled noise coming from her throat worried Lily terribly.

"Mommy?" Lily reached out to wipe away the tears running down her mother's mud-caked face. Her mother rapidly flashed dark lashes over her violet eyes, and Lily watched the way the black circles in the center grew larger, eating up almost all of the purple. "Are you hurt?"

Her mother shook her head, but Lily didn't believe her. Lily drew another small thread of magic, and touched her mother's mind, but what she found there made her teeth chatter. Panic seized her hard as she read her mother's chilling thoughts. Then

Lily's own eyes widened, and she suddenly had the strangest sensation that someone was sneaking up behind her.

"Come on, Lily. We need to move," her mother warned and caught hold of her hand again. She gave a quick tug to force her to focus on the winding path up ahead.

Lily tried to concentrate but her tummy hurt and she could no longer hold back the tears, not after seeing the moisture in her mommy's eyes. As her vision blurred, she blinked, confused about what was going on, why those men were building fires and hurting her family.

She pinched her burning nose and coughed, but the sound was drowned out by the screams below. Lily stopped running as dry, blistering heat rushed over her body, like her skin had just been lit on fire.

"No . . ." she cried out, and tried to turn around, to run back and help her coven.

"Lily," her mother urged.

Lily licked the salty tears from the corner of her mouth and cried, "But, Mommy . . ."

"No buts, Lily," her mother said in that same low voice she only ever used when she was angry. "Now be a big girl for me, and hurry along."

Mud clung to Lily's legs and branches snapped beneath her bare feet. The sharp twigs dug into her soles and lodged between her toes, but she ignored the discomfort. She sniffled softly and wondered what she'd done to make everyone so angry with her.

"I'm sorry, Mommy."

"Oh, Lily." Her mother dropped to her knees and pulled her into a warm embrace. Lily buried her face in her mother's dress and tried to breathe in her pretty perfume because it always made her feel cozy and safe, but her nose was too wet and runny from crying to be able to smell anything. "Lily, honey, I'm not angry with you. I just need you to hurry."

Lily wiped her cheeks with the back of her hand, and made a face. "Why are those men hurting everyone?"

When a deep male voice called out to them, the sound vibrating off the mountainside, Lily craned her neck to see, but her mother placed her hands on either side of Lily's head to stop her from turning.

Lily frowned. "Do they want to hurt me, too?"

Her mother didn't answer her. Instead, she inched back and brushed a soft kiss over Lily's forehead. Then her mommy blinked the water from her pretty purple eyes, and Lily could tell she was scared, but trying so hard to be brave for Lily's sake. Lily didn't like seeing her mommy so afraid. It frightened her.

"Oh, little one, you really are my special, gifted child, aren't you?"

Lily tried to grin; she liked when her mother called her that. But the smile fell from her mouth when off in the distance something exploded and her mother's face turned as white as the falling flakes.

Lily's mouth went dry and she shifted from one foot to the other as her heart crashed against her chest. "Mommy, I'm scared."

"I know, baby. I know. Come on."

A sweaty palm closed over Lily's hand, and they ran and ran until Lily couldn't run anymore. She took deep gasping breaths, but gagged on the yucky-tasting make-believe winter snowflakes.

"We're here," he mother said breathlessly, stopping to roll a heavy rock away from a small opening. She cast a quick glance past Lily's shoulder before crawling inside and dragging Lily in with her.

Not knowing where she was, Lily touched the cold rock walls with the tips of her fingers and snuggled in closer to her mother. It was hard to breathe in the dark cave, but Lily didn't want to complain.

Her mother unclasped her amulet and put it around Lily's neck. She found Lily's arm, then placed Lily's palm on the warm charm. "Lily," she whispered and closed both of her hands over Lily's to secure the amulet beneath. "Keep this, Lily. As long as you have this, I'll always be with you."

"Mommy . . ." she whined, fearful of what her mother was going to do next.

"I have to go. I have no choice," her mother explained, her voice soft and low, almost musical. "They can find you if I stay here. You'll be safer without me."

Lily choked on her tears. "No, Mommy. Don't go." Lily gripped her mommy's wet muddy dress as panic welled up inside her.

Her mother's fingers dug into Lily's shoulder and held her

tight, but her voice changed when she asked, "Lilith, sweetheart, do you remember what I taught you about blocking your thoughts?"

Lily nodded and wiped her runny nose, trying so hard to be a big girl like her mommy wanted.

"Good. I want you to do that for me. I want you to shield your mind, and no matter what you see or hear, stay in here. Okay?" She gave a wobbly smile, tapped Lily on the nose, and added, "No flying, little birdie."

Lily understood just how important it was for her to stay hidden. Her mommy had called her Lilith, and she only ever did that when she was serious.

"I love you, baby girl. Now be brave, and do what I told you to."

Lily made a fist around the amulet and squeezed until it hurt her hand. "I love you, too, Mommy."

"I have to go now, Lily. But we'll see each other again. I promise." Her mommy gave her one last look, slipped out of the small cave, and pushed the heavy rock back into place. Lily shuddered as blackness closed in on her, the only light coming from the few rays of sunlight that peered in from the small cracks between the big boulder and the edges of her tiny shelter.

Lily tucked her knees into her chest and rocked back and forth as she waited for her mommy to come back. But soon day turned to night, and as fear completely overtook her, she could feel the pull of her raven. A long time ago her mother had explained to her that she was a shifter—her mommy's special, gifted child. She also explained that her feathers could show when she dreamed, or when she experienced strong feelings, like now. But her mother also warned her to keep her raven grounded, and never to show her wings to anyone, especially to any of the Darkland clan.

Lily sucked in a breath. Could it be the Darkland men down there looking for her? Had they found out she was special? Would they hurt her mommy if they captured her and she didn't tell them where Lily was?

Her mommy said no flying, but as her bellyache got worse, Lily had a hard time fighting off the change. She didn't want to go against her mommy's rules—she really didn't—but the pull of the raven was too strong and Lily didn't think she could hold it back anymore. With both panic and desperation overcoming her, Lily closed her eyes and drew a deep soothing breath like her mommy had taught her. Her head flopped forward as she felt herself fall into a dreamlike state, her spirit leaving her mortal body, shifting into raven form and becoming solid. Her raven stretched her wings and momentarily floated over her slumped figure in the damp cave as her one being took two forms.

From her raven's eyes she memorized her surroundings, then exited her hiding place. Her raven took to the sky, mimicking the loud shrills on the ground below as she soared above the blazing fire. As her family ran about in the dark, outnumbered by the men hunting them for reasons Lily didn't understand, she dipped down low to observe the battle. When she caught her mother's scent with her heightened raven senses, her heart raced faster, and she followed the distinct aroma until she came upon her.

From her position near the ground, she caught her mother's eyes. She gave Lily a feeble smile before a man tied her to the post and set the muddy hem of her dress ablaze.

"Mommy . . . no . . . " she cried out, but the sound came out garbled in her raven's throat. In that instant, fear stole the breath from her lungs and her heart beat quicker than her wings. Shaky and light-headed, she began falling to the ground, her wings suddenly immobile, useless.

Somewhere behind her a man yelled, and tossed fire into the night sky at her. The burning piece of lumber skimmed her beak and snapped her awake. A moment later something exploded nearby and flames singed her feathers.

As pain erupted inside Lily's head—her mother's pain—and smoke choked her airway, her vision went fuzzy. Instinctively, her raven flew higher, to suck in a fresh breath before diving to the ground below. With fear and anger closing in on her, she aimed for the man who'd captured her mommy. The man swung a burning piece of wood at her, barely missing her wings. Fueled by rage, she dove again, and gripped his hood with her talons. She let loose a wail and ripped it clear off his head.

The man tipped his chin to see her and the dark eyes that stared back made her feel ill. She immediately recognized the man grinning up at her. He was the leader of the Darkland clan, their neighboring community.

"I'm coming for you, Lily," he announced. "You can run,

but you can't hide." She drew her magic and touched his thoughts, but when she did, he dropped to the ground, appearing disoriented. He held his head between his palms, and yelled out at her, his words jumbled, as if her brush had somehow dazed him.

Lily turned her attention back to her mother. As she hovered over her, her parting words erupted inside her head. *I have to go now, Lily. We'll see each other again. I promise.*

With terror striking from all angles, tears poured from her eyes and dripped over her mother's burning dress, but it wasn't near enough water to put out the flames. Lily tried to think, but was unable to gather her thoughts or do anything to help while in her primal form.

She had to get back to her body. It was the only way to save her mommy. Her raven flew back to the cave, and Lily awoke with a gasp. Climbing to her feet, she pushed on the rock with all her might, but she was too little, and the rock too heavy. Big hiccupping sobs echoed around her as she pounded on the boulder until her knuckles bled.

Hours later, exhausted and battered, she clasped her amulet and fell to the ground, where she stayed for a long time, until all the cries from her burned village subsided and the smoke cleared from the mountain.

Lily had no idea how long she hid in that cave, reciting her mother's parting words over and over again. She was hungry and thirsty, but none of that mattered.

Day turned to night, back to day again, and after what felt like a week to Lily, she heard movement outside the cave. Not knowing if it was one of the bad men, she covered her mouth to keep herself quiet. When the rock slid to the side, Lily shaded the blinding sunlight from her eyes to take in the silhouette of the woman before her.

"Mommy?" she asked, her heart racing with hope.

"Shush, little one. I won't hurt you," the woman responded, her gaze immediately going to Lily's amulet. Lily covered it with her hand and scurried backward, but the pretty violet eyes that met hers immediately put her at ease. The lady held her hand out to Lily, and when Lily tentatively placed her palm in it, the woman's eyes widened in delight. "Well, well," she said, "such a special, gifted child, a prized possession for sure." A look Lily didn't understand came over the woman's face when she added, "What ever will I do with you?"